OUR STREET AT
The Schoolmistress
MAGGIE SULLIVAN

T0037382

Maggie Sullivan loves to travel, is an avid reader – never going anywhere without a book – and her abiding love is watching football. She is also a freelance university lecturer and has a keen interest in drama and theatre. Maggie was born and brought up in Manchester, after living abroad for several years, she settled in London where she still lives.

Also by Maggie Sullivan

Christmas on Coronation Street
Mother's Day on Cornonation Street
Snow on the Cobbles
The Land Girls from Coronation Street
We'll Meet Again on Coronation Street

Our Street at War series
The Postmistress

· OUR STREET AT WAR ·

The
Schoolmistress

MAGGIE SULLIVAN

One More Chapter
a division of HarperCollins*Publishers*
The News Building
1 London Bridge Street
London SE1 9GF

www.harpercollins.co.uk

HarperCollins*Publishers*
1st Floor, Watermarque Building, Ringsend Road
Dublin 4, Ireland

This paperback edition 2022

1

First published in Great Britain in ebook format by
HarperCollins*Publishers* 2022

A catalogue record for this book
is available from the British Library

ISBN: 9780008419899

Set in Sabon LT Std by Palimpsest Book Production Limited,
Falkirk, Stirlingshire

Printed and Bound in the UK using 100%
Renewable Electricity at CPI Group (UK) Ltd

To Judy Wiener and Peter Austen

Greenhill, Lancashire

March 1940

Chapter 1

VIOLET

Violet Pegg stood in the middle of the school playground, poised with her teacher's whistle in hand, ready to break up any skirmishes and, unusually for her, wishing that playtime would soon be over. Normally, she went straight home after school to the little two-up-two-down cottage on the edge of town that she shared with her mother, Eileen. But today, she was thinking about her pen friend Daniel in Toronto, Canada, and the letter that she hoped would be waiting for her at the post office. She pulled the edges of her coat tightly together against the chill of the afternoon as it was colder than usual for a crisp March day. She was glad of the hand-knitted hat her mother had made for her, and insisted that she wore, as there was a hoary frost clinging to the edges of the paving stones. At least, she thought, as she pulled on a pair of matching gloves, there were no longer any signs of the ice storms that had bombarded the small northern town this past winter and it was good to see that the erstwhile frozen river and its tributary streams were flowing freely once more, gliding silently behind the rusted railings on the other side of the road.

She watched with interest as her charges raced around carefree, energetic and noisy, though the squeals were mostly of delight. She peered over the children's heads beyond the school railings to where Billy Pritchard's old cart horse was firmly tethered to a fence post, standing patiently in front of the flat-bedded milk cart it had been pulling throughout the day, steam rising from the grey blanket that covered the horse's back. Billy himself was doing his best to safely deliver the daily pints to every house along Greenhill's main street without slipping on the damp cobblestones. As he went to pick more bottles out of the crates, he waved to Violet from across the street.

'Afternoon, Miss Pegg!' he called as he stopped to stroke the nose of his faithful nag, 'I hope the children are behaving themselves?' The old carthorse seemed to smile as it tossed its head and gave an acknowledging whinny which made Violet laugh. 'It's business as usual, Mr Pritchard,' she called, waving back.

'I wish I could say the same,' he said with a shrug, 'but most of my young helpers have deserted me. Either they've gone to do what they like to call war work which pays a lot more than I can offer, or many of them who were over the age of eighteen have been called up into the armed forces.'

He looked so dejected as he said this that Violet felt sorry for him, but he managed a grin as he touched his cap. Untethering the horse and cart, he set off up the hill.

'Miss, Miss, can we go out and pat the horse before it goes?' Violet looked down as a small group of children surrounded her, with begging eyes.

'Not now, Frankie.' Violet looked at the ringleader and laughed at the thought of all the other children who would want to immediately follow suit. 'But if you ask Mr Pritchard nicely, maybe he'll let you after school.'

'Miss, he won't give me ball back.' A little girl now tugged at the hem of Violet's coat, her eyes tearing up. Violet's eyes looked from her to the boy who was standing defiantly beside her, the ball tucked under his arm.

'Oh, I think he will, if you ask him nicely, Alison,' Violet said. 'Won't you, Craig?' she then directed at the boy, giving him a disarming smile and watching as he reluctantly complied. 'But it's almost time to go in, so you'll have to put the ball away in any case.' As she spoke there was the clang of a hand bell and Mrs

Diamond the headmistress appeared at the arched entrance, signalling it was time for them all to go back to their classrooms.

'Can I come with you, Miss?' the same little voice asked her and Violet felt Alison's small, warm fingers slipping into hers. Violet never minded being on yard duty as she loved to watch the children play, the little ones in particular who were intent on learning the rules of evergreen games such as she'd once enjoyed like tag, two-ball and skipping. She loved their play almost as much as she loved teaching them and watching them develop in the classroom, and despite her mother's teasing that she would end up an old maid, she did not regret for a moment the time she had devoted to completing her teacher's training when all her friends were out earning money and having fun. But she was getting impatient now to have children of her own and she hoped it might not be too long before she would, even though she had no regular boyfriend at present. But she kept those thoughts to herself for whenever a boy's name was mentioned at home, her mother immediately interrogated the matter closely in case of a prospective husband and father.

Violet sighed then, thinking how close she had come to becoming a foster mother recently, a role she would have gladly embraced – but that was not what Eileen Pegg had in mind for her daughter and she had intervened when they had been asked to take in two traumatised children. Eva and her younger brother Jacob had fled from the mayhem in Europe, and their parents, desperate to save them from Hitler's threat, had managed to secure two places for them in the charge of a young charity worker, Czech-born Martin Vasicek, on one of the last evacuation Kindertransport trains to leave Czechoslovakia. Martin was only 21 years of age but he had worked for a refugee charity for some time, travelling back and forth to rescue children, and after he'd returned to England for the final time, he had canvassed the neighbourhood urgently seeking shelter for his charges. When he approached the Peggs, Violet was more than willing to offer them a home for as long as necessary, but to her dismay her mother had strongly opposed the idea, apologising to Martin that as there were already two of them in the small house, they didn't actually have any spare capacity.

'But they're refugees,' Violet had protested, 'I don't imagine they'll care how big the house is or where they'll sleep.'

'That's exactly my point,' Eileen had argued, a triumphant tone in her voice. 'You never know where they might have come from or where they might have been sleeping until now. We can't open our home to just anyone, Violet. They're not like us. I'm sure Martin understands.'

Violet was shocked, not wanting to meet Martin's gaze to see what he thought of her mother's refusal.

'They're no different from us, Mum.' Violet didn't want to back down. 'Except that it's worse for them, they're only children. Imagine if everyone thought like you, then no one would help anyone else.' Violet tried to reason, but Eileen refused to listen.

'Perhaps we can . . . com . . . com . . .?' Martin said hesitantly. Meet in the middle?' he explained in his carefully articulated English trying to hide his obvious exasperation.

'Compromise?' Violet suggested.

'Yes, yes,' Martin agreed eagerly. 'That is the word I want. Perhaps the children they stay here for very short time. I will find somewhere else. Very quickly. They go to top of the list.'

Unfortunately, they had stayed for a shorter time than anyone intended. For when Eileen had called old Dr Buckley who was standing in for his son – now on active duty – to check on young Eva's persistent cough, he had been concerned at first that they might have contracted TB.

'I warned you!' Eileen said, wagging her finger in Violet's face. 'But would you listen? I don't know what you were thinking of,' she had ended up shouting at her daughter.

'That's not very fair,' Violet said, on the verge of tears. 'It was hardly my fault. I understood they were all supposed to have been examined before they came. They must have picked it up somehow on the journey.'

'*Hmph!* So much for that! Thank goodness old Dr Buckley recognised it quickly or, we could have had an epidemic on our hands,' Eileen said. 'I told you, you never know what they might be bringing with them. And you a teacher! Think what you could have been passing onto your poor little mites at school.'

Violet had immediately informed Martin about the doctor's diagnosis and the brother and sister were removed instantly to a sanatorium where luckily for them they were found to be clear of anything more serious than a bronchitic chest infection. However, despite Violet's pleas Eileen refused to consider taking them back again and Martin had to look for new accommodation. Fortunately he was able to find a young couple who had no children and thought they might like to adopt the brother and sister.

Violet shook her head sadly as she thought of them now, two lost little souls, the casualties of war. She looked down at Alison still holding her hand, the little girl smiling up at her, then thought once more of Eva's and Jacob's terrified faces as the doors had closed on the ambulance and they had been driven away.

She squeezed Alison's hand and forced herself back into the present, watching as the children began to drift towards the school entrance. She looked across the playground as they dutifully lined up by the door marked Infants. It was a tranquil enough scene, but how long would it remain as calm and peaceful-looking as it seemed now?

It was hard to think of Greenhill at war. Violet had lived in the small market town for all of her 22 years, but who knew or could even guess at what it might look like in the future? What lay ahead for the children of today? Violet looked into the distance; on a clear day like today she could clearly see the old cotton mill that not long ago had re-opened as a munitions factory against the backdrop of the rugged moorland hills. Now the factory manufactured small-bore ammunition and essential components for handguns, as if determined to define its own place in history. But it did seem that the phoney war was over now and the threat of bombs and the resultant casualties was becoming more real every day. Would the fathers of these children be called up to serve their country as her father had been, leaving their families to grow up fatherless, as she had done when he had died tragically and needlessly at the end of the Great War? Violet shuddered as she recalled the conversation she had had with her mother only that morning about the very real shortages that were beginning to bite, shortages that would no doubt soon lead to an increase in rationing.

She drew in a deep breath. There would be time enough for that, she didn't want to think about such things right now. Today, she had other things on her mind, brighter, more exciting things, like how quickly she could get up to the post office at the top of the hill after school and whether or not the much hoped-for airmail letter would be waiting for her there. She rubbed her hands together in delight as they re-entered the school building, thinking about the slim blue envelope with the Canadian postmark from Daniel that might be waiting for her. It usually arrived towards the end of every month, and she liked to collect it from Vicky the postmistress at the post office on her way to school, who kept them especially for her. But today she had been delayed and, not wanting to be late for work, had decided to check at the end of the day instead. She set the children to tidying the classroom so that she would be able to get away on time.

As soon as school was over, Violet ran up Greenhill's main street, her head down against the wind that had sprung up, determined to get to there as quickly as possible. She almost bumped into Lawrence Boardman, the owner of the newsagent's next door on the shopping parade where her mother helped out part-time, although she wasn't working today. Always wanting to be one step ahead of his neighbours, Lawrence had been one of the first to volunteer for the newly formed Civil Defence Service and she briefly noticed as he gave her a mock salute, that he was proudly sporting his ARP warden's armband. Violet finally stopped, gasping from the unusual exercise, when she reached the shops that crowned the top of the hill, the short puffs of her breath that clouded the air registering the descending chill of the late afternoon.

'I've run all the way, I was worried you might be closing early the night before your wedding,' Violet said to the postmistress who was behind the counter as she pushed open the shop door, panting.

'Not quite this early, there's time to catch your breath,' Vicky said with a smile as she peered up at the large clock. Then she extracted an air letter from the rack of pigeon holes on the wall behind her. 'I think this might be what you're after,' she said producing the letter with a flourish.

Violet's eyes lit up as Vicky handed her the Canadian stamped envelope. She recognised the scribbled signature of Daniel Gabinsky that had been scrawled on the back alongside the familiar address in Toronto, Ontario. 'Yes, it is. Thank you, Vicky,' Violet said brightly. 'I was worried I wasn't going to make it in time.' She glanced at the envelope one more time before dropping it into her capacious handbag and hoped Vicky hadn't noticed that her gaze had been drawn to the corner where the envelope flap had been sealed and over written with the acronym SWALK. She felt a flutter in her chest like she had felt the first time Daniel had written it and she'd had to ask him what it meant; in his reply, he had told her the initials stood for 'Sealed With A Loving Kiss'. She closed her eyes for a moment trying to conjure up once more the grainy picture of the boy she had been writing to for so many years, the boy she had fallen in love with and secretly hoped to marry even though they had never met. He had sent her the picture several years ago and she still cherished it, but although he had asked her many times, she had never plucked up the courage to send him one in return.

'So long as I haven't kept you from closing up,' Violet said, 'But I won't keep you now, so thanks for this, Vicky.' Violet waved the letter. 'And I'll take the opportunity to wish you and the doctor all the very best for the big day in case I don't get a chance tomorrow when I'm sure you'll be too busy to talk to the likes of me.' She reached across the counter and squeezed Vicky's hand. 'Good luck,' she said, stepping back towards the door. 'You both deserve it and I hope the whole of the day goes well.' She ran from the shop, almost bumping into Lawrence Boardman again as she scrutinised once more Daniel's private message on the back of the envelope that she gripped tightly in her hand.

Chapter 2

VICKY

As soon as Victoria Parrott – known to her friends as Vicky, the postmistress in charge of Greenhill's only post office – had handed over the precious letter to Violet, she beamed, determined that it would be her last transaction of the day. She scurried about behind the counter, preparing to close up, when a familiar-looking shadow passed across the window, and she drew in her breath sharply as a feeling of excitement washed over her. She glanced up at the clock. Could it really be . . .? She almost hadn't recognised him in his smart uniform and she peered towards the window, hoping to catch a second glimpse.

A bell tinkled faintly from deep inside the living quarters and by this time Vicky had her gaze fixed firmly on the door even though it had not yet opened. She straightened up behind the counter, patted her dark curls into place and smiled broadly. It felt like such a long time since she had seen him; her breath was coming in short gasps.

It had felt strange when he had first gone away, and she'd no longer had to hand over correspondence to the local GP, Dr Roger Buckley at the start of each day. He had always been the first customer when she opened up the shop in the morning. But now here he was, on leave if only for a short time, and she was very excited knowing that this time she would see him on every one of the precious days he was home. Indeed, by this time tomorrow she would be Mrs Roger Buckley and they would be sharing their home, for wherever he was, they would be a married couple! She could hardly believe it. Then she drew in her breath sharply as another thought struck her; what if he hadn't managed to collect the special marriage licence he'd so triumphantly negotiated in order that they could be married before he finally went overseas? But she had no time to brood on this thought for it was interrupted by the sound of his voice.

'I was expecting to see Ruby, is she not in today?' were the first words Roger said as he stepped inside tentatively, glancing around the shop looking for Vicky's young assistant.

'Why? Would you rather see her than me?' Vicky said with a frown, halting in her tracks.

Roger grinned. 'Hardly, I was just checking but if she's already gone then I think I've timed it rather well,' he said and he looked relieved as he stretched out his arms. 'Come here, fiancée! I'm delighted she's not here, I want to make the most of our first special moment alone,' he said a mischievous grin on his face as he advanced towards her. 'It's been too long.'

Vicky stepped out from behind the counter with a diffident air and sidestepped his embrace. For a moment Roger looked astonished until he saw her slip the catch on the front door and turn the key, before she flipped the sign to say Closed. Then he wasted no time and before she could say anything further, he clasped her to him in a giant embrace and lifted her off her feet, leaving her gasping. Then he kissed her on both cheeks and her forehead before covering her lips with his for several wondrous moments.

'I didn't think you'd be working today,' Roger said when he finally came up for air. I was worried I might not see you before the actual day itself.' Vicky pulled her head back marvelling at how lucky she was to be wanted by such a good-looking man with his strong, smoothly shaven chin and perfectly chiselled nose, a man who drew admiring glances from almost all of the women in the neighbourhood.

'I'm working today, and for an hour or so in the

morning before my substitute takes over,' Vicky said, coming back to earth. 'I reckon it'll keep my mind occupied. But I sent Ruby home early today as she was getting too excited, and I don't want her to get over tired before tomorrow even begins. That wretched calliper on her leg weighs a ton and she'll need all her strength if she's to manage all the standing about.'

'There'll be a lot of that, indeed,' Roger said.

Ruby Bowdon from the greengrocer's shop on the parade had been his patient from a very early age when she had been struck down by an unfortunate bout of childhood polio. After her recovery the previous year, he had introduced her to Vicky when she had left school at the age of 14, suggesting that she might like to train as a post-office assistant. Fortunately, the young girl had proved to be an excellent worker despite her wasted leg and the introduction had worked out well. 'I told Ruby to come in a bit later tomorrow so that she can help with anything last minute here before we have to get dressed and set off. Her dress is here, I thought that would be easier as we'll both need time to get ready.

'I presume she's got a special bridesmaid's rig out?' Roger asked.

'Yes, of course, she's got a lovely dress, similar to Julie's. Don't tell me your daughter hasn't told you all about hers?'

'I've only seen Julie briefly and she kept saying it's a secret; she wants to surprise me on the day. I tried to tell her it's your day, not hers, but I suppose it's not every seven-year-old that gets to be bridesmaid at her father's wedding and I'd hate to spoil her fun.'

'Typical Julie!' Vicky laughed, thinking endearingly of her stepdaughter-to-be. 'But it's important she enjoys the day, too, as she's never been to any wedding before. I wouldn't begrudge her that. And once Ruby and I are dressed, your dad has arranged for a car to pick us all up here – that will include my dad – and they'll take us down to your house to collect Julie and your mum. Then we'll all go to the church together. I believe several of the neighbours have offered to provide transport and your dad will make sure we get to the church in good time. We're planning on walking back to your parents' house for the reception afterwards unless my dad's chest plays up and he needs a ride. At least I don't think it will rain. I believe so far we've been having record temperatures for the end of March.'

Roger laughed. He was still thinking about his little daughter and how excited she was, thrilled at the thought of finally having a new mother. He was lucky she had taken so quickly to Vicky and that the feelings were obviously mutual, too.

'There's quite an age difference between the brides-maids, isn't there? Is Ruby happy to be standing alongside someone as young as Julie?' Roger asked.

'Are you kidding?' Vicky's eyebrows shot up. 'Ruby's as excited as Julie and neither of them would give up on a chance to get dressed up as a bridesmaid no matter who they had to stand next to. Besides, as far as Ruby goes, you're her hero, didn't you know? She's always talking about how you saved her life.' Roger looked surprised and his cheeks reddened. 'When you rushed her off to hospital when she first got polio,' Vicky explained, 'not to mention when you put in a good word with me for her to come to work at the post office and saved her from having to work in her parents' greengrocery shop.'

Now Roger laughed. 'I suppose I did.'

'And Julie's no better,' Vicky said. 'She might only be seven, but at times she can seem older than Ruby,' she added with a grin, thinking of some of the almost adult-like conversations she had had with Julie recently.

'Anyway, it's hats off to your mum,' Vicky continued. 'My future mother-in-law can you believe? She's been an absolute brick. She's worked so hard to make it all work out for us. She wouldn't let me do anything towards the reception even though I did offer. She's responsible for the girls' outfits, having run up the most amazing dresses for the two of them. As you can imagine, Julie insisted on having something long, and Ruby was desperate to have something that would cover her calliper. I don't know where your mum found all that material.' She shook her head in wonder. 'I think she may have unpicked one or other of those precious ball gowns that she used to go dancing in.

But I know that both girls are delighted with the outcome. She's promised to help them both finish getting dressed and down to the church on time and then tell them where to stand and such like. Not that the service will be very long, thank goodness, the vicar has promised that, and I won't care what any of us do once the service is over and we get back to your house afterwards for the party. Though I imagine you'll have some thoughts.' She gave him a flirtatious smile.

'I'm sure I'll think of something,' Roger said, giving her another kiss and a squeeze. 'But you'll be Mrs Buckley by then so no one will be able to tell us what to do.' He kissed her on the nose this time and Vicky giggled. 'That tickles,' she said, making no attempt to move her face. Then she rested her cheek on his chest and sighed. She could hardly believe that she really was going to get married this time and that she would soon be like any other serviceman's wife, praying that her husband would come home safe and intact. Not like the last time she had been engaged . . . when she and her first fiancé Stan had never made it to the altar. He'd gone off to Spain to fight the fascists before they'd had a chance to get married and he'd not returned. She shuddered and instinctively Roger drew her closer.

'Penny for them,' he asked. 'Thinking about Stan?'

Vicky nodded and said a silent thank you for his

intuition. Her eyes felt moist as she remembered how Stan had left her pregnant, with a child that she had lost shortly after hearing about her fiancé's untimely death. Suddenly, she had to blink hard and she clung to Roger.

'Hey!' he said gently, pushing her away from him so that he could study her face. He teased her underneath her chin with his fingers, then soothingly stroked her cheek. 'Hey! He said again, 'this is not the time for tears. We're getting married, tomorrow, remember?

'I know,' she whispered, and this time she was thinking of the sadness that had blighted his own life when he'd lost his young wife, Anna, shortly after Julie was born. Vicky held onto him tightly, loving him all over again for his compassion and sensitivity, and thinking they both deserved a bit of happiness. 'I just can't really believe that it's going to happen, they're tears of joy really. Roger, I love you so much,' she whispered,

'I love you, too,' he whispered in return. 'And I'll be coming back. I promise you,' he added. 'Before you've even had time to miss me.'

They stood together in the middle of the empty shop, both silent for a moment. Then Roger said, his voice strong and almost jovial, 'Well, I'm very impressed by your organisational skills not to mention the delegating, but what about the bride's outfit?' he said. 'I know it would be bad luck if I were to actually see your dress beforehand so I won't even ask but surely you can tell me something about it at least?'

Vicky reddened and looked down at her hands where she was playing with the gold love knot ring that Roger had given her when he had asked her to marry him. She thought about the slender gold band engraved with orange blossoms he had promised to give her to go with it on their wedding day, though she'd not yet seen it.

'I'm not sure I should tell you anything,' she said coyly, 'particularly as I've actually changed my mind several times.'

'A bride's prerogative,' Roger said, 'but aren't you going to give me any clues? What if I don't recognise you coming down the aisle?'

Vicky laughed then she thought for a moment. 'I was going to wear my navy costume with the frilly blouse with the lace jabot held in place by my pearl brooch, I'll tell you that much,' she said, looking at him to gauge his reaction.

He was gazing at her questioningly, with love in his eyes, his smile so sincere that she could only smile back. 'All I'm going to say is that my dad has persuaded me to wear something of my mother's.'

'It will be the next best thing to having your mum with you,' Roger said solemnly, 'I'm sure you'll look gorgeous in whatever you choose.' He kissed the end of her nose once more. 'And you'll know for once your dad will be pleased with you if it was his suggestion.

How is he by the way?' Roger asked. 'Has his chest been playing him up?'

Vicky sighed and held up her hands, her index and middle fingers crossed on both. 'He's been doing well, but he was up all night, coughing,' she said. 'I seriously worried that he wouldn't be fit enough to get through the day tomorrow. But by this morning it had all calmed down. I think he's more nervous about the whole thing than I am.'

'What's he got to be nervous about?' Roger said.

'He doesn't. But I suppose it makes him think of my poor brother Henry and the wedding he'll never have.' Vicky paused, caught up with her memories. 'Dad had such high hopes for my younger brother before he got killed.'

'Well, at least your dad knows you'll not be going far when you leave home and of course you don't have to do that immediately. You can stay here as long as you need to while I'm away so his life won't be changing too quickly,' Roger said.

'No, but mine will very soon,' Vicky said with another sigh. 'One way or another. Just as soon as I get used to having you here I'll have to face things on my own again.' She ran her hand gently through her hair and stretched her lips into an ironic smile. 'I can't bear to think of you being sent far away again so soon . . .' She was whispering although there was no one else there but that didn't stop her voice from cracking.

'It's possible I might be going to warmer climes,' Roger said cheerily, forcing a chuckle. 'Maybe I'll be able to bottle some of the sunshine specially for you and send you some.'

'Don't even joke about it.' There was an edge to Vicky's voice now. 'I can't bear to think of you going abroad.'

'At least we'll be able to keep in touch. You understand I won't be able to tell you where I am, but you can write to me, you know. They may take a while to get there but letters do get forwarded. I won't be able to bear it if you don't,' he said as brightly as he could. 'But let's not get ahead of ourselves. I've not gone yet. Let's enjoy our wedding and make the most of the time we have got.'

'You're right,' Vicky said. 'I'm sorry, but I think I'm the one who's getting overexcited now. I honestly don't know whether I'm coming or going today.' This time she laughed.

'Do you realise that this is the last time I shall be seeing you as a single woman?' he said, a flirtatious look in his eye. 'The next time we spend any time together we shall be husband and wife.'

Now Vicky giggled. 'What a wonderful thought!' she said and smiled up at him.

'So, let me say farewell like they do in all the best films,' Roger said, pulling her towards him once more. 'I'll see you tomorrow in church, Mrs Buckley-to-be,' he said. 'And I will promise to love and honour you no matter what you are wearing.'

Vicky started to laugh but then he pressed his body firmly against hers and gently nudging her mouth, smothered the sound with his lips.

Chapter 3

TILLY

'What's she doing here?'

Tilly McFadden, caught unawares, cringed just like she always did at the sound of her father's voice and cowered into the corner of the room, not daring to catch her mother's eye. She'd had it in mind to leave the house before her father got back, but it was just so nice to be in Ma's kitchen once more, sitting on a decently cushioned chair and feeling the comfort of her mother's hand clasping hers, that she had lost track of time.

She knew from 17 miserable years' worth of experience that the longer the old man was out, the more dangerous he would be on his return. He was always particularly mean when he'd had a skinful. Tilly pulled the much darned and patched shawl that swaddled the tiny infant she was cradling in her arms even more tightly around him as if to cover his ears and shut out the words that she knew were about to explode from her father's mouth and that she didn't want little Eddie to hear. But as if he knew what was coming, Eddie's tiny face suddenly crumpled like a scrunched red ball and he let out a long pathetic wail. He almost seemed to stop breathing as he alternated between hiccoughs and sobs and Tilly held him closer to her, whispering soothingly to him as her father advanced menacingly towards her. She only just managed to sidestep out of his way in good time before his hand lashed out. Thankfully, he didn't make contact with the baby's face, the only flesh that was visible peeking out from underneath the blanket.

'I thought I'd thrown her out before I left for the King's Arms,' Jeremiah McFadden shouted, ignoring Tilly. 'And yet you let her sneak in behind my back, woman, the bloody moment I've gone?' he berated his wife. 'Are you going soft, woman? What were you thinking?'

'She didn't sneak in. I let her in,' Agnes McFadden said, trying to stand up to him as stoutly as she could. 'It's her home after all.'

'Not anymore, it ain't,' Jeremiah growled. 'I warned

her . . . What do you mean, letting her bring that . . .'
This time he waved his arm about ineffectually. 'That
. . . thing in here?'

'But she's fresh from birthing,' Agnes protested.
'Where else should she go? Give the lass a chance, she
needs feeding, not to mention the babby. It's hardly his
fault.'

'She can go wherever she's been till now, she'll not
find food at my table.' Jeremiah lurched, spun in a
circle and managed to fall into a chair before falling
on the floor. He belched loudly as his body seemed to
fold in half. 'When I told her not to come back here
ever again I meant it,' he shouted and this time he
banged his fist so hard on the table that Tilly jumped
and the thick white cups danced, spilling their content
onto the oilcloth cover.

'I don't care where the hell she goes so long as it's
nowhere near my house.' He was back to shouting.
'And you can remind the rest of the bairns they're to
have nowt to do with her either. I've told you before,
I've disowned her. She's no longer any lass of mine and
I warned her the minute she showed up here with that
. . . with that . . . bastard in her belly that I would not
let her set foot in here again.'

Tears trickled from the corner of Tilly's eyes even
though she had desperately tried to prevent them spilling
down her cheeks as she thought of the dreadful place
she had just left, where she had spent the last several

months awaiting the arrival of her baby. She clenched her teeth with resolve. Wherever she ended up, she had no intention of ever going back there. Not only had she and all the other unfortunate girls been treated like prisoners, forced by the caretaker nuns to undertake all manner of menial work, even towards the end when most of them could hardly move let alone get down on their knees to scrub the floors, but they also had their babies taken from them. Tilly had seen it happen to so many of the other girls who had been locked away with her in the Sanctuary for Troubled Women, as the home for unmarried mothers was called, that Tilly was more determined than ever it would not happen to her and her precious baby. She knew what she had to do. She confided in no one for fear of being chained to her bed or having Eddie snatched within hours of being born in order that he could be given away. It was whispered that the babies were sold, and may even have been sent overseas, so that their rightful mothers never saw them again, though Tilly didn't want to believe that. But the rumour mongering affected her sufficiently that it did make her harden her resolve and she became even more determined not to give them any opportunity to take her baby. Even before he was born, she plotted and planned how she would rescue him from the babies' nursery where all the babies were kept as soon as she was able to stand on her feet, and they would run away together.

Tilly had started to tell her mother about the conditions in that dreadful place, hoping her mother might be moved to help her but then her father arrived back sooner than expected and Tilly realised he would never relent and that she was fighting a lost cause.

Tilly was jigging the baby gently and speaking directly into his ear in as calm a voice as she could muster when she saw her father's face had turned almost as puce as Eddie's and she knew that if she didn't leave now they both might be in physical danger. Her mother made a gesture towards her, but Tilly sighed and pulled her old coat about her shoulders.

'It's no good Ma,' she said softly, 'I can see that now. I made a mistake even thinking things might have changed.' Out of the corner of her eye, she could see that Jeremiah was doing his best to stand up, and from the treacherous look on his face she knew she was lucky that all he could do was to keep falling back into the chair. 'Thanks for trying,' she whispered, 'but I can see it's a lost cause,' and before her father could reach out to touch her, she opened the front door and plunged out into the street.

Chapter 4

CLAIRE

Claire Gold was a newcomer to Greenhill after being evacuated from London and sent north by her parents less than a year ago. She had gone to live with her mother's sister Sylvia Barker, her husband Archie Barker and their daughter, Rosie, even though the families had not been in touch for years. Many children from the cities were evacuated to the country when the war began and while Claire at 22 years old was hardly a child, her parents thought that living in the middle of a large expanse of moorland would be safer for their precious daughter than being trapped in a place like London once the war took hold, and Claire had to concede that it was unlikely that the barren scrubland of the countryside was to become a target for German bombs. But for Claire that was no compensation. Greenhill might be a pretty place with its own meandering river and a picturesque backdrop of craggy hills, but it was a long bus ride from Manchester and any kind of social life. As far as she was concerned it was in the middle of nowhere.

But she didn't want to seem ungrateful and once the move had been agreed, she never complained to her parents in any of her weekly letters home, even though she knew no one. On the contrary, she avoided telling them of her homesickness and how much she missed them and all her friends at home. While her aunt Sylvia had welcomed her warmly and had done her best to help her settle down, it had taken her cousin Rosie some time to accept that Claire was there to stay. No matter how hard Claire tried, Greenhill never felt like home. This was perhaps not surprising as the two had to share not only Rosie's cramped bedroom but also her bed, and at first Rosie had taken every opportunity to make her resentment known. It wasn't until Claire helped to save Rosie from a doomed romance with a young lad from the munitions factory that her relationship with her cousin began to improve.

The most difficult aspect of living with the Barkers had been not to get caught up in their family arguments when disagreements between Sylvia and Archie had at one time been occurring with increasing frequency and ferocity. At first, Claire was concerned that she might be the root cause of these arguments and longed to tell her mother about her fears, but ultimately she knew better than to interfere in other people's business and kept her own counsel. But now that Archie had signed up to the navy and been posted away at sea, that was no longer an issue.

Claire had to admit her new life in Greenhill was far from miserable, for she found unexpected compensation in her new job and she was thrilled when her aunt entrusted her with a level of responsibility that no one had ever considered her capable of before.

Sylvia Barker owned the haberdashers' Knit and Sew on the shopping parade that crested the hill of the main street and she had tried for years, unsuccessfully, to encourage her daughter Rosie to go into the business with her. It was not surprising therefore that when Claire showed an immediate interest, initiating suggestions for improvements and even volunteering to undertake new projects, that a delighted Sylvia offered her a proper job.

'You've obviously got a flair for this kind of work,' Sylvia had told Claire when her niece showed considerable skills in both sewing and knitting.

'I do know the basics, thanks to my mum, of course, but I'm very keen to learn more,' Claire replied.

'Well, that makes a welcome change,' Sylvia said. 'As you know, my Rosie has never wanted anything to do with the shop. She's more interested in making the kind of money that only places like the munitions factory can afford to pay,' she said with disdain, 'which I can't hope to match, of course. But to my way of thinking I get more pleasure out of making clothes that are practical and needed by everyone, than I would making guns.'

Claire who had been worrying that she might prove to be a drain on the Barkers' resources as rationing began to bite, readily agreed to earn her keep by helping out in the shop.

Initially Claire was selling knitting wools, knitting needles and accessories as well as clothing patterns and materials new and second hand that her aunt had found at the local market and charity shops. But gradually she made all kinds of helpful suggestions that involved expanding the range of services the shop could offer. Claire took the government's slogan of 'make do and mend' very seriously and soon she was making up garments to order and offering clothing repairs, alterations and a re-make service for those who were not handy with a needle. To her aunt's obvious delight, Claire gradually took on more responsibility for the day-to-day running of the shop and it didn't take long for Claire to suggest that she might offer sessions to teach women how to mend, and make alterations for themselves.

'I could even teach them how to follow a pattern

and to make some simple things from scratch, and I'd be happy to give basic knitting and sewing lessons to anyone who's willing to learn,' Claire said with enthusiasm. 'If we don't charge them too much, they'll probably want to come back for more and that way everyone benefits.'

Claire was delighted with Sylvia's response to her suggestions and she worked harder than ever to make them a success.

Claire, Sylvia and Rosie were eating their evening meal together one night, as they usually did now that Archie was no longer at home. Suddenly, Rosie put down her knife and fork. 'I've something important to tell you,' she announced, much to Claire's consternation. 'I've decided to leave Greenhill.'

Claire stared at her cousin in astonishment while Sylvia stopped eating and looked like she had been hit with a brick.

Claire's immediate instinct was to apologise, feeling that she might be responsible for pushing her cousin out of the nest. 'I'm really sorry Rosie, I didn't mean to force you . . .' Claire began eventually, trying to pick her words carefully, but Rosie cut her short.

'No, Claire, there's no need for you to worry on that score. It has nothing to do with you being here, or because of the work you've been doing in the shop. I'm just ready for a fresh start, that's all, I'm sure you can understand that.'

Claire was aware of the pleading look in her cousin's eyes and sat back, more concerned now for Sylvia's response. Her aunt had laid down her knife and fork and looked like she was going to be ill.

'I can assure you, Claire, it's certainly not your fault,' Rosie continued, adding good-humouredly, 'if anything you've done me a favour,'

Claire frowned. 'In what way?

Rosie giggled. 'I'm sure you already know how relieved I am that I'll no longer have to concern myself with anything to do with *haberdashery*!' She said the word in a mocking tone and Sylvia looked as if she was about to cry.

'You don't have to worry Mum, I won't be going far, and I won't be signing up for any of the armed forces,' Rosie said, 'but I am fed up at the factory and I've handed in my notice.' She paused as if for dramatic effect and lowered her voice before announcing, 'I intend to go north to train as a nurse.' She made it sound like a proclamation and both Claire and Sylvia stared at her in surprise but before they could say anything Rosie said, 'If history is anything to go by and the war continues then there's bound to be a shortage of nurses at some stage,' Rosie said, 'It just so happens that there's a large hospital near Newcastle that's looking for trainees right now. I've written to them telling them my background and they're keen to take me on.' She hesitated for a moment before she added, 'Don't worry, I'll be back to visit.' Then she grinned. 'But in between whiles, Claire, you may as well make the most of having the whole bed to yourself.'

Chapter 5

TILLY

Tilly McFadden certainly had nothing to look forward to after she walked out of her father's home. She was determined to hold her head high and not to show her hurt, but that was harder now for she had nowhere to go other than the bench in Greenhill's church graveyard. It was chilly now and her body was stiff, her ears and face numb, her angry tears having dried on her cheeks. She felt frightened as she clutched her crying baby to her bosom in an effort to keep him warm. She had been in trouble before but had never sunk so low. She knew that she must find some food soon and even more urgently some shelter for them both so that she could try to feed the poor little mite who hadn't stopped crying since he had woken up. She was realising each day how little she knew about babies, and she wished for once that she had listened to the nuns, for now she was terrified lest he could starve.

She wondered whether she might be able to get into the church; perhaps somebody there could help her. When she went to test the doors, Tilly was delighted to find that they were not only open, but the church was warm and welcoming inside, and surprisingly, there were lots of pretty, fresh wildflower sprays at the end of each set of the front pews that still gave off their rich perfume. She was so hungry that she even thought about looking for any Easter eggs that might have been missed, but decided that was not a good idea. There was no one about and she slipped inside and sat down on one of the benches that was in the shadows at the back. The baby latched onto her breast almost immediately and his obvious hunger was almost too painful for her to bear. She was concentrating so hard on giving him what he needed she didn't hear the footsteps coming down the central aisle towards her.

'Good evening, miss, and welcome,' a friendly male voice said, and Tilly looked up in alarm. She hastily covered herself and tried to stand up, not sure what she should say for he was wearing a dog collar and was obviously a man of the church.

'Please don't be upset,' the man said, I'm Reverend

Laycock and this is my church.' He gave a little nod and smiled. 'I was just going back to my house for some tea and cake, it's the old rectory next door. You'd be very welcome to join me, in fact, I would be honoured if you would. You must be hungry,' he said.

When he said the word cake all Tilly could think of was strong, piping-hot tea and rich Jamaica ginger cake of the kind she used to enjoy as a child before food rationing – before her father had started drinking so heavily and when money was not so tight. Reverend Laycock didn't wait for her to answer but set off through the double doors beckoning her to join him.

Chapter 6

VIOLET

'Violet, is that you?' a voice called out followed by a prolonged throat clearing.

'Yes, of course it's me, Mum. Who else could it be?' Violet stepped out onto the tiny landing to listen. She heard a muffled noise, then a clatter, and then a thin strip of light appeared under the ill-fitting bedroom door.

'You're very late. Have you had a nice time at the wedding?'

'Yes, lovely, thanks.'

'Then why don't you come in and tell me all about it while it's still fresh. I'm up now in any case so you may as well.'

Violet was tired and had hoped to avoid this. That's why she was carrying her sling back shoes in her hand, so as not wake her mother as she climbed the stairs, but she guessed that Eileen had been lying awake waiting for her as she always did whenever Violet went out for the evening. At the age of 22, and already an experienced schoolteacher Violet felt she was quite grown up enough to go out without her mother worrying about her all the time. But Eileen had other ideas as a widow struggling to make ends meet and solely responsible for her daughter's safety. Violet sighed resignedly. She supposed she should be grateful that her mother cared so much. She twisted the doorknob and went inside, shivering as she stepped into the chilly room. Eileen Pegg was sitting up in bed, propped up on her pillow with a shawl pulled across her bony shoulders. She turned down the corner of the thin cotton sheet and smoothed a small patch of blanket that she patted with her hand. Violet reluctantly sat down.

Eileen's face was instantly animated as she tied two ends of the shawl into a loose knot. 'So, come on, tell me, who was there. What did Vicky look like? What did she wear?'

'You know Vicky, she's an extremely pretty girl and she looked as attractive and radiant as most brides do,' Violet said, hoping to steer her mother away from any more personal questions that might reflect her own single status which always seemed to be inevitable whenever she went to a wedding. 'And not only did she look excited and beautiful,' Violet added, 'but I'd say for once she looked happy as well. I think Roger is really good for her, it's only a shame he's got to go away so soon.'

'Did her father behave himself? Better than he behaved towards her last fiancé, I hope. Arthur Parrott can be quite a handful when he's a mind.'

Violet held up her hands to ward off her mother's barrage of questions. 'Nobody talked about the past, Mum. Besides, the circumstances were quite different this time,' she said. 'Vicky isn't pregnant and Mr Parrott thoroughly approves of Roger Buckley. As I've already told you, Vicky looked lovely, as only brides can. Mrs Buckley laid on a lovely spread given all the food shortages, everyone behaved themselves and it was a nice affair.'

'I'm glad. I only wanted to know.' Eileen sniffed.

'That's fine,' Violet said, 'but can you stop trying to sensationalise it? Nothing untoward happened and there really is nothing more to tell. Reverend Laycock went through all the required rituals with no major fuss, no last-minute objections.'

'Didn't he give a sermon?'

'Yes, of course, but it was very short and to the point, talking mainly about the happiness he wished for the young couple's future. He also didn't dwell on the past, that would hardly have been appropriate under the circumstances and would certainly have upset Julie, Roger's little girl.'

'Was she a bridesmaid?

Violet nodded.

'That must have been difficult.' Eileen sounded surprised.

'Not really. She and young Ruby Bowdon, who's been working at the post office as Vicky's assistant, were both bridesmaids and it actually worked out very well.'

'Is she fully recovered, that Ruby? Didn't she have a bad case of polio? That was terrible.' Eileen sparked to life once more with her questions.

'Yes, she did,' Violet said. 'But, thankfully, she's all right, now, although one of her legs is likely to remain weak and she'll probably always have to wear a calliper.'

'Oh dear, that is a shame for such a young girl. She used to be so lively. It must be hard on her family.' Eileen swiped her eyes with the back of her hand. 'It must have been quite a sad occasion then, what with Vicky's mother and her brother Henry no longer being with us, and the doctor's first wife.'

Violet felt exasperated by her mother. 'No, it wasn't sad at all! That's what I'm trying to tell you. I think the two of them have really found love again so there was a lot to celebrate,'

Violet knew her mother often laughed at her for being ever the optimist, even in difficult situations, but her words were genuinely heartfelt. 'They chose some nice hymns to sing in church and they'd asked Geoffrey, the vicar's son to accompany them on the organ. Apparently, it will be his last chance to play at a local function for some time. He's signed up for the army and he's on embarkation leave. He'll be gone by the time the next celebration in the church comes up.'

'That's a shame,' Eileen said with a sigh. 'I've always thought him such a nice young man. He's about your age, isn't he?'

Violet rolled her eyes, not willing to follow the conversation down the route it seemed to be heading. It was enough that she'd told her mother about her pen friend Daniel in Toronto and made the mistake of implying that there may be something between them. 'Geoff seems nice enough, but I don't really know him,' Violet said. 'And before you get any ideas, he's actually younger than me and he was years behind me at school. If anything, he'd be more suitable for Ruby! But his organ playing certainly brightened up the atmosphere in the church and encouraged everyone to join in the singing.'

'I'm sure it did,' Eileen said, though she suddenly sounded distant, like she was no longer paying attention. 'And if he goes away now that will be very hard on the vicar. He dotes on him, you know and I know just how he feels.'

Violet looked at her, hoping that her mood wasn't

going to plummet as it often did when they talked about the war, as it always reminded Eileen of her own husband and his untimely death. Violet had never known her father who had died before she was born, killed needlessly in a road accident. He had survived many months in the trenches and escaped with only minor war wounds but an oversized truck had smashed into his bike and wounded him fatally when he was on his way back to his base one night while he was waiting to be demobilised after the Great War. Violet couldn't really blame Eileen when one of her melancholy moods settled on her but she dreaded them because once they descended, they could take a long time to lift.

'It's awful how quickly families can be broken up.' Eileen was still gazing off into the distance. She sighed then and her whole body shuddered. 'I'm only glad I don't have any sons to send marching off to war.' She reached out and squeezed Violet's hand. 'And I'm thankful that you're not signed up for any of the armed forces. I couldn't bear to think you might be anywhere near the front line.'

Violet flashed a look at her mother who looked as if she was about to cry. 'You really won't ever have to worry about that, Mum.' Violet's voice was conciliatory. 'Firstly, they won't be sending women to the front and secondly my job's far too important for me to be sent anywhere,' she said with a laugh. 'In any case, no one spoke about the war today. We were all aware of counting our blessings and we were determined to make the most of what we did have to celebrate.'

'And what happened to the bride's flowers?' Eileen wanted to know. 'I presume she had some?'

Violet was pleased to have distracted her mother. 'She did. A small posy of fresh wildflowers, and after the service when we gathered on the church steps to give a final cheer for the bride and groom and Vicky threw it into the air, as you'd expect.'

Eileen's face visibly brightened as Violet said that. 'I hope you caught it,' she said eagerly.

'I'm afraid not, you know my luck. It was Ruby who managed to get hold of it.' Violet laughed though she couldn't help noticing that Eileen's face had clouded over. 'I was pleased for her,' Violet quickly added, 'not that I believe in any of that superstitious nonsense, but Ruby deserves a bit of luck, too, and it would be nice if she managed to find a nice boyfriend. Anyway, we then formed a sort of procession so that we could all walk together back from the church to the Buckleys' house where they'd finally decided to hold the reception. But that took much longer than planned because people kept stopping us to wish Vicky and Roger well. Vicky looked every inch the bride.'

'What did she wear?' Eileen asked. 'You haven't told me that yet.'

'Her father persuaded her to wear her mother's ivory

satin wedding dress. It fitted her perfectly and went well with the lacy headdress that had been her mother's, too. She really did look gorgeous.'

'But I thought you were to go to the post office afterwards for the party,' Eileen said.

'They had thought about it but the Buckleys' house is much nearer to the church and much nicer for a party.'

'What about the food? How was that?'

'Rationed of course, but Roger's mother somehow laid on a very tasty spread. I reckon Freda Buckley is a very resourceful woman.'

'As I remember, old Dr Buckley was pretty resourceful, too, in his younger days. You know that he ran the surgery before he passed it onto Roger?' Eileen said with a chuckle. 'He was always generous with those who couldn't afford to pay him much. I think him and his wife make a good pair.'

'They do. He was determined that everyone should have a good time. He rooted out some of his gramophone records – apparently, he has quite a collection – and he chose songs most people knew the words to. He played them on this rather grand radiogram that he has while we all joined in. Then little Julie insisted on dancing, and tried dragging the rest of us to dance with her. She's a real bundle of joy that one, she kept us quite entertained. You can tell that she's very fond of Vicky.'

'I'm glad,' Eileen said and she cast her eyes down. 'We both know that gathering together a ready-made family isn't always easy, but this sounds like it could be good for both of them.'

Violet's cheeks flamed thinking of her failed attempts to foster an instant family that her mother had put a stop to, and she didn't respond immediately. 'Julie's certainly far too young to be without a mother,' she said eventually, her voice soft and Eileen sighed.

'No young child should be without their parents,' she said, 'although sometimes of course, painful as it is, it isn't always possible to . . .' Her voice trailed off.

Violet stood up, stretched and yawned. 'Have you seen the time, Mum?' she said. 'I've got to be up for school in the morning, so I'd best be getting off to bed.'

Eileen glanced at the small clock by her bedside. 'Oh, yes, you'd better!' She threw off her shawl and tucked her pillow back under her head before leaning across to switch off the light.

'I'll say goodnight, Mum.'

'Night, night, love,' Eileen said. 'God bless, sweet dreams and see you in the morning,' she added automatically as Violet gave her a peck on the cheek. 'I'm glad you had a nice time. It's only a pity you didn't manage to catch Vicky's bouquet,' she said as Violet turned away. 'Maybe next time.'

Violet crossed the tiny landing to her own room shaking her head at the thought of her mother's long held superstitions. Then she gasped as she saw Daniel's letter staring up at her from her bedside table. She had intended to read it last night immediately after she'd collected it but there had been so much hustle and bustle sorting out her own wedding outfit that she'd quite forgotten about it. She gave a wry smile at the irony. Eileen was always so anxious for Violet to find a fiancé before she was left on the shelf, and here she was ignoring the only person she had ever seriously envisaged marrying.

She picked up the envelope and inspected it again, feeling the same flicker of excitement that she had felt when she had first collected it from the post office – but did she have the energy to give it the attention it deserved? Her thoughts were too jumbled and her eyes felt too scratchy to decipher his spidery script in the dim light that emanated from her bedside lamp. She undressed and changed into her cotton nightdress then pulled back the covers and slipped between the sheets. She let her lips make contact with the flimsy paper as she kissed the corner of the still sealed envelope knowing she would have to wait another day. She turned off the light and shut her eyes almost instantly, drifting off to sleep with her mind full of what she had to look forward to tomorrow.

Chapter 7

RUBY

Ruby Bowdon tossed and turned, not able to sleep for thinking of the wonderful time she had had at the wedding, reliving the details from the first magical moment when she had slipped into her long organza dress, to being driven home after all the laughter and the singing and dancing in old Dr Buckley's motorcar. She'd been allowed to stay up much later than usual and was disappointed to find her mother had been waiting up for her.

'Now, you get up them stairs and go straight to bed,' she scolded as soon as her daughter arrived home, like Ruby was a little girl. 'You're not the one who's going on honeymoon tomorrow,' Maria Bowdon reminded her. 'On the contrary, you're the one Vicky's relying on to keep things going at the post office,' she said, shooing Ruby up the stairs.

Ruby reluctantly stepped out of the dress that had made her feel like a princess for the day, and sighed, knowing that she would never wear it again. She had been far too busy and too excited the whole day to be able to eat much and she was hungry now but she slipped into bed realising that it was too late, now. Everyone else had gone to bed and she knew she wouldn't easily be able to slip downstairs again to see what might be in the larder without waking up the entire household.

Her two younger brothers had school the next morning and her father always rose early to get to the market in good time to buy the freshest fruit and vegetables. Ruby reached over to her bedside table and picked up the bride's posy she had been determined to catch when Vicky had thrown it, no doubt aiming at Violet Pegg. She put it to her nose once more, surprised that the lily of the valley still smelled so sweetly. It took her back to the beginning of the day when she had watched the doctor's eyes light up as he first saw his bride enter the church, just like they always did when he saw Vicky, and she knew it was time to stop dreaming. Ruby had been in love with the young doctor ever since she had first been ill but today in church was probably the first time that she had been able to accept that what she felt for Roger Buckley was nothing more than a schoolgirl crush, as everyone had always said. But that didn't stop her remembering with delight, the moment when the doctor had asked her to dance with him at the reception afterwards. It had not been easy watching her hero putting a ring on someone else's finger or start off the dancing with his new bride, for in her dreams that was always meant to be Ruby's role. But didn't they always say in films that if you really loved someone then you had to be prepared to let them go? It suddenly made her feel very grown up and she began to think that maybe she should find someone else to love, maybe someone more of her own age.

Stifling her hunger, Ruby tried to sort out the sudden rush of thoughts. She pulled the posy under the covers with her as she snuggled down between the sheets. Then she grinned. The doctor would always be her friend but now she had to get herself ready to fall in love with the real man of her dreams.

Chapter 8

CLAIRE

With Rosie's departure imminent, Claire realised for the first time how much she was going to miss her cousin and just how close the two of them had become. Her various activities in the shop kept her busy during the day but she was anxious to meet more people of her own age and she wondered if her aunt could help.

'I know I don't have much spare time,' she said to Sylvia not long after Rosie had dropped her bombshell, 'but I've been thinking about volunteering my services to the war effort in some way – in whatever time I do have.' She laughed awkwardly but Sylvia was listening.

'That sounds like an excellent idea,' Sylvia said. 'I must say I've been thinking that you need to get out a bit more and meet younger people.' She picked up the local newspaper that was on the table and turned to the classified ads. 'There are plenty of charities crying out for helpers, if you were interested? And there are always articles calling for more volunteers. I'm sure you would have lots to offer, what with you being an evacuee yourself,' Sylvia said.

Claire felt her cheeks heat up at the thought of having to share her own experiences. Would she really be able to talk about how miserable she had felt at first? Would she ever be able to tell anyone about the loneliness she had so often felt at leaving her family behind in London? 'I don't usually think of myself like that,' she said, 'but yes, I suppose I have been evacuated.'

'I bet you'd soon find a charity what would be eager to sign you up,' Sylvia said, 'and it would certainly give you the opportunity to meet new people. In fact, why don't you have a word with Rosie's old friend Violet Pegg? She teaches the infants at Greenhill County Primary School. If memory serves me right, I believe she had links with one of those European organisations that offers support to the children who came over to England on the Kindertransport. She wanted to foster a couple of the children as far as I know, though her mother wasn't keen.' She got up to riffle through a large stationery box that stood on the sideboard and triumphantly retrieved a letter written on a sheet of foolscap paper.

'Here we are,' she said, 'I think this was the group Vi was involved with, Rosie was, too, for a short time. And that's why they were writing to her.' She pointed to the notepaper heading. 'They were partly responsible for organising the Kindertransport trains out of Europe, although I understand they've stopped running them now. But if you see here it tells you that the committee is now called the Friends Committee for Refugees and Aliens. I believe they've played a key part in evacuating thousands of children to safety although sadly their parents are left behind facing imminent danger.' She scanned the letter. 'They're still supporting thousands of the children who fled on the Kindertransport and, would you believe it, they're hoping to set up a new local branch of the committee in Greenhill? Now that might be something for you to think about, Claire.'

Chapter 9

VIOLET

Violet had been so looking forward to reading Daniel's letter that when she finally picked it up from her bedside table she wasn't sure why she felt hesitant to open it. Despite the fact that they had been corresponding for so many years now, she still looked forward to his letters although the contents were more often predictable and not necessarily exciting. So, why did she expect this one to be somehow different now? Perhaps it was the use of the acronym SWALK that he'd now used for the second time which led her to think something was changing and she was suddenly filled with a strange mix of excitement and trepidation.

Was he suggesting the possibility that after all the years of writing, they might become more than mere friends? She hardly dared to guess. As far as she was concerned, she had been in love with him for years, although she had never told Daniel for she wasn't sure that he felt the same way. She had always been convinced that one day they would marry, something else she had never told him, but maybe he was now coming to that conclusion, too? Violet had been in love with the idea of having a boyfriend overseas ever since her first form teacher at the grammar school had asked for volunteers to correspond with some French-speaking children in Quebec, Canada. Violet had readily accepted the challenge and she had felt very excited at the prospect of writing to a boy of her own age when she had been given the name and address of Daniel Gabinsky in Montreal. To her it had all seemed very romantic although the aim was to give children on both sides of the Atlantic an opportunity to become fluent in another language. It had been fun at first, but it had soon proved to be more difficult than she had imagined, and she could only admire how quickly and effortlessly Daniel seemed to come to terms with English while she had such problems trying to master French. She had been considering giving up their correspondence when Daniel's family had moved from the province of Quebec to the essentially English-speaking city of Toronto in Ontario, and Daniel became so comfortable writing in

English that he suggested they should continue their correspondence in English only.

Over the years their friendship had developed and occasionally there had been a hesitant attempt at flirtation between them. That was when Daniel had first expressed a wish to meet. He had sent her a photograph and requested she send one of herself, but when she saw how tall and strikingly handsome he was, she felt too insecure to respond. She'd made endless excuses not to send him her picture in return.

Now, it was all Violet could do to stop her hand shaking as she took a sharp knife and slit around the edges of the envelope then smoothed the letter across the bedcover. His first words set her nerve ends jangling as she could see immediately what had changed. They looked as if he had dashed them off in his excitement and his spider-like scrawl had filled the page.

I am being posted to England!! We can meet up at last!!

These were the first words that jumped off the page at her. They were underscored and peppered with so many exclamation marks that in places they had perforated the thin page.

My squadron is being posted to a base somewhere in the north of England to a place called Hill Vale. I don't know if you know it but as far as I can tell it's quite close to a Greenhill which I presume is YOUR Greenhill?!

Violet gasped all the while nodding her head. As far as she knew there was only one Greenhill housing an RAF squadron nearby, and she had passed the base on the bus on the way back from Manchester. It was surrounded by barbed wire and KEEP OUT notices. She had even seen aircraft taking off and landing there on occasion.

Can you believe it, after all these years, we could actually be seeing each other in the flesh very soon?

He had signed it with the now commonplace three kisses.

Abruptly, Violet sat down on her narrow metal-framed bed in order to take in his words, the wire of the coiled springs pressing hard into the pale skin of her slim legs. She raked her fingers through the knot of shining auburn hair that was gathered at the nape of her neck, and she twisted it this way and that, wondering whether she should comb it forwards, letting it hang loose over her slender shoulders or completely sweep it back off her face in the style that she knew showed off to greater advantage her powder-blue eyes. She smiled as she considered the problem, for it did indeed look as if the light-hearted correspondence that she and Daniel had enjoyed for so many years was about to change – a strange sort of excitement coursed through her at the thought that they were actually going to meet.

She picked up the photo frame where she kept the

only photograph she had of Daniel and stared at it again. The picture must be well out of date by now. Would he still be as good-looking as he had appeared to be then, with his dark wavy hair and easy relaxed smile? She tried to consider it from all angles. What would he make of her?

As she got dressed, a new thought struck her and it felt as if butterflies were fluttering around in her stomach. She had always referred to Daniel as her boyfriend to her friends. Violet was comforted by the thought of having someone waiting in the wings. She had gone so far as to tell her mother that she liked him although she had never actually called him her boyfriend, but it hadn't mattered. He lived too far away for her mother to take him seriously as there had been little chance of them meeting. But now that Flying Officer Daniel Gabinsky would soon be part of the overseas fighting force that would be based at the nearby American airbase, it took on a new level of importance. She also wondered how Daniel would react if she introduced him as her boyfriend? Violet picked up the letter and as she gazed once more at the words that Daniel had written and couldn't help feeling a stab of disappointment. There would be nothing romantic about their first meeting, not like the one she had once dreamed of. Daniel would be coming with his squadron in order to join the battle in Europe and despite his enthusiasm, they might be lucky to meet up at all.

Chapter 10

CLAIRE

It was to be a time for change at every level, Claire thought with an ironic laugh. In Westminster, Winston Churchill was taking over from Neville Chamberlain as the coalition Prime Minister while in Greenhill, Claire was eager to follow up Sylvia's suggestion as soon as she could to become part of a charity committee. She had discovered that the first meeting of the new local offshoot committee for refugees and aliens was to be held in the church hall and she was keen to get started. She was surprised to find that it looked more like a shepherd's hut than a grand hall. From the outside it looked as if it was being propped up against the back wall of the church.

However, inside there were rows of chairs that had been carefully laid out to accommodate the surprisingly large number of people who were gathering, and the hall was filling up quickly. She thought she spotted Rosie's friend Violet with an older woman who looked to be her mother taking their places towards the back of the hall. She waved and tried to catch her eye but Violet didn't seem to notice and Claire didn't want to move and lose her place.

Several tables had been pushed together at the front for the organising panel of committee members and before long a young woman stood up behind the first table and wielded a gavel calling the meeting to order. She introduced herself as Enid, one of the organisers, and thanked everyone for coming.

'It's heart-warming to see so many of you willing to help people who, through no fault of their own, find they are in dire straits and have unexpectedly become refugees. Unfortunately, the numbers of refugees arriving in this country from the continent is growing every day,' she said. 'But as more and more people are being forced to flee their homelands and seek shelter elsewhere, the least we can do is to help them through their most traumatic times. For those of you who are not yet familiar with our work we are going to hear tonight about the plight of some of those unfortunate individuals first hand.'

She took a sip of water and turned to indicate a

number of people sitting beside her at the table, who all seemed to be riffling through papers preparing to speak. 'You will hear how you can help them and people like them and I hope by the end of the evening you will also be inspired to go and persuade others to join in our cause.'

A young boy and girl began the session. 'We committed no crime other than the fact that we are both Jewish and our families were hounded out of their businesses and homes in the small German town where we lived,' the boy began, then they took it in turns to tell the story of their rescue. They said they had been told they were being sent to safety in England on one of the early Kindertransport trains and at first Claire could see people sitting back in their chairs anticipating a warm-hearted tale with a happy ending. But as their tale unfolded, the mood shifted. A lump came into Claire's throat and the smiles turned to expressions of horror as the siblings described how their parents had been given less than an hour's notice to pack no more than one bag per child and to prepare the children as much as they could for a long journey. Their rescuers were urging them to hurry, in the end snapping their bags shut and almost pushing them out of their houses and onto the truck in order to keep one step ahead of the German soldiers who were rounding up the adults and were only minutes behind. When they described the moments when they were torn from the arms of their parents at the train station and bundled onto the train, it sounded more like a kidnap than a rescue and the speakers and their audience were all in tears thinking of the traumatic circumstances; the children had sat by the window, catatonic, unable even to wave goodbye as the train had slowly pulled out of the station and they hadn't seen their parents again.

There was a shocked silence as the two children returned to their seats. Then there were low mumblings interspersed with higher pitched scraps of conversation until finally there was a scraping of chair legs on flagstones and a tall, scrawny-looking young man stood up to speak next. He was tall and looked as if he had once had a large frame, but now he looked gaunt and pinched His fair hair looked as if it had been dyed, possibly to make him look more Slavic. Claire was struck by the dark circles that ringed his clear blue eyes giving him an almost haggard appearance. The notes he was carrying trembled slightly in his long fingers, but even before he began to speak he abandoned the papers on the table. He had told his story too many times to forget what he wanted to say. He gazed out at the audience for a moment and held them under scrutiny as though trying to memorise their faces but then his shoulders dropped. 'I would like to thank you all for coming here to join us this evening.' He spoke in a heavily marked eastern European accent, and as

Claire glanced about her, she noticed that Violet had sat forward suddenly in her seat, cupping her chin in her hands.

'My name is Martin Vasicek,' the young man said, 'and I shall be working on the new committee as I have been involved in this operation from the start, mostly in London. I try to help anyone who is in danger, because sadly I have learned that any one of us can become homeless and need help in a moment.' He snapped his fingers to signify the speed at which disaster could overtake the most ordinary of people.

'In the beginning, when it was not a proper war in Europe, I worked on the committee who developed the Kindertransport, the special trains that rescue the children. I bring many children here from my country,' Martin said. 'I persuade little ones when they cling to their parents and do not want to leave. "You come with me to England," I say. "You will be safe there. Mummy and Daddy will come, too," I tell them.'

He frowned as he paused. 'And I go back and collect more children and tell them the same story. But this time I find out it is not true. There is no train for grown-ups. And soon even the children's trains will stop. No more Kindertransport.'

Martin stopped for a moment. He made a cutting gesture with one hand across the palm of the other and seemed to be struggling as if he were having difficulty breathing. Then he said, 'But what will happen to the thousands of children we already bring to England? They are alone here, no? What can they do?'

Martin paused again and this time took a handkerchief from his pocket and wiped his eyes as he looked around the audience. 'They can do nothing without your help,' he said.

'These children need support so that they can learn how to live in England, learn to speak the language, learn how to be English, like you.' He smiled as he said that.

'The lucky ones may already have been chosen to go to live with new families where they will be cared for. Some of the older ones may go to work and live together in a hostel. But what about the others who have no new home? Will they ever see their parents again?'

He stopped talking as his voice choked. Claire couldn't stop looking at him as he continued to dab at his eyes. 'I left my family home to help children to escape, but now my parents have disappeared. And my girlfriend Katya – we are to be married. But where is she? I try to find information but nobody sees them. I try to go back, maybe she is at home, but the soldiers on the borders, they say, "*Stop!* Or we shoot. You go back to England."' He held up his hand as if stopping traffic. 'OK, so I am now in England, but with nothing.' He spread his palms helplessly once more. 'I leave everything behind when I come with children. I think it is only for short stay. They each have one small suitcase and I have nothing, but I cannot go home to look for Katya and my parents. All I can do now is to look after the children who are here and that is something we can all do. So, please, sign up to help in whatever way you can. That is what I ask of you all,' he said, his voice breaking.

'What do you say in English? While we are still alive we can continue to hope. But please remember, in order to carry on with our work we need money. No donation is too small, but most of all we need people and that means you,' he added, his eyes scanning the room. 'Please fill in your name and address on one of these forms, he pointed to the leaflets that he had piled onto the table. There was a momentary silence as Martin sat down and then a smattering of spontaneous applause but Claire was interested to see how many heads were nodding and to hear snippets of conversations of people who had been moved to consider offering their help even before the final speaker had spoken.

At the end of the meeting Claire turned towards the back of the room, keen to make her way over to talk to Violet before the crowd dispersed but by the time she reached her, Violet was already deep in conversation with Martin Vasicek. Claire was about to turn away when she heard Violet call her name.

'Did you sign on the dotted line and become a fully paid up member?' Violet asked.

'I certainly intend to see if there is something useful I can do,' Claire said. 'That is why I came. How about you?'

'I'm trying to persuade my mother to get involved, too,' Violet said, 'and Martin, here, is doing his best.'

Claire smiled and nodded towards Mrs Pegg. Then she turned to Martin to tell him how moved she had been by his story. 'It was truly inspiring,' she said, not able to keep the sadness out of her own voice. 'Even if I hadn't already wanted to join.'

'Thank you, that is very encouraging,' Martin said. 'I will look forward to seeing you again.'

'Me, too,' Claire said, and she waved to Violet and Mrs Pegg as they each peeled off in their different directions.

Chapter 11

VIOLET

Violet was pleased that her mother seemed to have been impressed by the presentations at the meeting and that she had begun to take an interest in the work of the committee even if she didn't immediately join her at any of the meetings that followed. But Violet's mind was also occupied with other things, not least the impending visit of Daniel Gabinsky. When she had responded to him briefly, she had tried to appear offhand and not reveal the strange mix of excitement and fear that overtook her whenever she thought about him coming to England; excitement that she was going to meet him at last, and fear that she had overemphasised his role and his importance in her life to those around her. She was grateful that the young children in her class were able to distract her, forcing her to concentrate on other things during the day at least, and for once she welcomed their constant demands.

She had almost given up hope of hearing from Daniel, convinced that he wasn't allowed to make contact with friends in England, when her mother handed her a letter one evening when she came home from school.

'This arrived for you this morning,' Eileen said waving a scrappy brown windowed envelope in front of her. 'I thought it might be important. I almost came down to school with it but I didn't think you'd like that.'

Violet drew in her breath, not surprised by her mother's curiosity. Brown envelopes were usually reserved for bills or official letters, something she wasn't expecting. She was amazed at Eileen's restraint but then tried not snatch it out of her mother's hand as she

quickly scanned the envelope and recognised the handwriting. She was relieved to find that it hadn't been adorned by any personal acronyms. She was aware that Eileen was scrutinising the envelope and kept peering over her shoulder, forcing Violet to twist her body away in order to read the contents. Fortunately, the note inside was brief and to the point, and he wasted no time apologising or even referring to the amount of time that had elapsed since his last letter.

Hi Vi! I'm here at last. He began the letter informally in what she had come to recognise as North American style.

I've a day's furlough on Saturday! Hoped you might be free? Would be great to finally see you. I can hitch a ride downtown so thought we could meet in Manchester. Easy enough for you to get to? Maybe meet at one of the department stores? Someone suggested Lewis's might be good. Presume you know it? Let me know what you think. Can't wait to meet you!! Drop me a note to above address. There might have been nothing personal on the envelope but he had added three kisses after his name, it was something she had come to expect but Violet still felt the blood rush to her cheeks and hoped her mother wouldn't notice.

Lewis's was one of the larger shops in the centre of town, and one of the busiest, and her first concern was that she might miss him in all the crowds on a Saturday. But at least it was central and easy to get to from Greenhill even if it did involve a bus followed by a tram. The tram would drop her off right outside the main entrance of the store on the corner of High Street where it became Fountain Street and intersected with the major thoroughfare of Market Street. She closed her eyes to picture the scene and could immediately smell the familiar perfumes and make-up that lined the front counters and wafted gently through the double sets of doors. She tried to picture herself strolling down the street on the arm of a young man in uniform; at least she assumed he'd come in his uniform.

'Is the letter from who I think it's from?' Eileen asked, suddenly bringing Violet back into the room.

'Yes,' Violet said, 'Daniel has arrived at last.' She smiled as she slipped the note back into the envelope without showing it to her mother. 'He wants to meet me in Manchester on Saturday would you believe, so that doesn't give me much time. I'd better get back to him right away and confirm that that's OK.'

She grabbed a pencil and a piece of note paper from the little pad they kept on the corner shelf and began to scribble an immediate response. She wanted to get the envelope into the post as quickly as possible.

Dear Daniel, she wrote.

It was very nice to hear from you. She held back from sounding too enthusiastic by adding 'at last'.

Lewis's in Manchester will be a very good place to meet. I can get there without too much bother and it sounds like you can, too.

Violet paused, surprised that she felt all of a flutter as she wrote the words: *I'm already looking forward to Saturday.*

She looked over what she had scribbled and took a deep breath as she prepared to slide the paper into the envelope. 'It looks as if I am actually going to see him at last,' she said out loud, forgetting she wasn't alone until she saw her mother draw her head up sharply.

'What's that you say?' Eileen said.

'What if we don't recognise each other?' Violet said. After all, it had been many years since she had received that grainy black-and-white photograph of a tall scraggy youth standing beside his sledge in the snow.

Eileen made a tut-tut sound. 'Why? How many other Canadian airmen will there be outside Lewis's?'

But Violet was more concerned that he wouldn't know her. The photograph had showed that he had dark wavy hair and a cheerful smile, and for the first time she wished that she had sent him a photograph of herself. Suddenly, she giggled. Perhaps she should have told him that she would be carrying a *Manchester Guardian* newspaper under her arm, or was that something that only happened in novels? Nevertheless, she hastily scribbled a postscript underneath her signature:

You'll know me because I'll have a red rose tucked into my hat band.

She was thinking about the silk rosebud the children had given her on Valentine's Day and that made her smile. Without further delay she put the paper back into the envelope and sealed it before Eileen could read it. Then she slid it together with Daniel's letter into her cardigan pocket.

'I'll post it when I go out later. Did you remember that we'd had a note from Martin about there being a meeting tonight?' Violet said. 'Do you plan on going, Mum?'

'Yes, I did remember but I think not tonight, love,' Eileen said, 'Maybe next time. But that shouldn't stop you going. Perhaps Claire from the wool shop might be there,' Eileen continued. 'You like her, don't you?'

'Yes, I do,' Violet said, 'It would be nice to see her again, it would be good to have a chat.' *It would be good to be able to share my thoughts about Daniel with someone other than my mother*, Violet thought as she dabbed some face powder on her flushed cheeks and added a slash of bright-red lipstick in preparation for her outing. 'Rumour has it that her cousin Rosie is going away so she might be glad of having something to fill her time,' Violet said.

Violet sat where she always liked to sit in the church hall, towards the back so that she could see people as they came in. She waved when she saw Claire, indicating the empty chair beside her.

'Had a good day?' Violet asked politely as Claire sat down and she was surprised when Claire nodded enthusiastically.

'Yes, I have, a few good days, as a matter of fact. Everyone seems to want to learn to knit. How about you? Keeping busy?'

'Thankfully, the kids keep me on my toes so I'm always busy.' Violet laughed. She was wondering if she should tell Claire something about Daniel when the decision was taken out of her hands for Claire then said, 'I understand you're expecting a visit from your Canadian boyfriend? A pilot, no less?'

Violet felt the blood rush to her cheeks, wondering if someone who'd seen her at the post office had perhaps spoken out of turn and wasn't sure how to respond. 'I don't know if he'd call himself my boyfriend,' she said as she gave a diffident laugh, 'but we have been pen friends for years.'

She thought Claire gave her an encouraging look so she went on, 'He's in the Canadian air force right now and his squadron has just been posted to England. They're based at the British air force base in Hill Vale.'

'Gosh, how exciting,' Claire said. 'I hope you don't think I was prying. Though I must admit I had heard some rumours, but I'd hate you to think that I was one to pass on gossip.'

Violet laughed again, though more heartily this time. 'It seems to me you can't help but pass on gossip in a place like Greenhill especially when you work in a shop, but I'm sure you're not one to start a rumour or even pass on anything malicious.' Now it was Claire's turn to blush and Violet felt guilty.

'Don't worry,' Violet said quickly, 'there are plenty in this neighbourhood who are only too happy to spread things about. Word gets round about all kinds of things, even when they're not true, so I'm not trying to blame you in any way. Besides, it won't be the first time I've been at the heart of their chatter. I've lived here long enough to know that folk round here love to try to match-make, so I've learned to grin and bear it.'

Claire sighed. 'I must confess I've heard stories about your pilot from so many different sources that I assumed it was something that everyone knew, that was the only reason I mentioned it. First when I was in the green-grocer's yesterday and then again from a completely different source at the post office this morning.' She wrinkled her brow and did manage to look contrite. ''

'Don't worry, I believe you,' Violet said with a smile, hating to see Claire's discomfort. 'And I'm sure things are different in London.'

Claire shrugged. 'I'm not so sure about that. Where I live in Cricklewood it's really no more than a village on the outskirts.'

'I suppose the bottom line is that you can't stop people being interested in everyone else's business. I imagine that habit goes back more centuries than we do.' Violet sighed. 'Most people mean well, or so I'm always being told.'

'I suppose in your case everyone is dying to set eyes on him,' Claire said.

At that Violet laughed out loud. 'And so am I!' she said. 'They probably don't realise that I've never met him.' She tried to keep her voice light but as she said the words Violet felt a sudden panic rise in her throat for she wanted to add the words that had been reverberating in her head ever since she had posted her reply to Daniel's note and arranged to meet him in town. *What if he doesn't like me?* 'As I've only posted my latest note to him on the way here I don't suppose anyone knows I'm going to meet him on Saturday in Manchester?' Violet tried to laugh it off as a joke.

'No, I must say I haven't heard anything about that,' Claire said with a smile, 'and I promise I won't tell a soul.'

Violet hesitated long enough to search Claire's face once more before she filled in the details of the arrangements she had made for the weekend.

'He won't have had time to get back to me again to confirm, I imagine it must be difficult for him to make phone calls or anything like that, but I'm assuming that that's that we will finally get together on Saturday.' She sighed and grinned at Claire. 'There!' Violet said, 'Well, you now know as much as I do.'

'Thanks,' Claire said. 'Promise not to tell.'

'I'll let you into another secret,' Violet blurted out without thinking.

She noticed the chairman had lifted his gavel and was about to strike it on the table calling for silence, but not before Claire whispered back, 'What's that? You must tell me now.'

Violet wished she could retract the words but it was too late. She hesitated then she said, 'I'm actually feeling so nervous right now that I'm not sure I can face meeting him on my own.' She was aware that Claire's eyes had widened and her jaw had dropped open although she didn't say anything. But the noise level in the room momentarily rose again as people rushed to settle and take their seats and that gave her the courage to add in a rush, 'How would you feel about coming with me?'

Chapter 12

SYLVIA

Sylvia Barker felt pleased that she had encouraged Claire to go to a meeting of the new committee, anxious to offer her every opportunity to go out and have some independent life of her own but she realised how quiet the house was without her. She hoped that she might be meeting Violet again, someone of her own age, but she didn't like to pry. It was not that Claire was noisy, she was always quietly respectful, going about her business without any fuss, but now that Rosie had moved away in order to train as a nurse, Sylvia noticed how much of a good companion Claire was proving to be.

Rosie had almost slipped away without anyone

noticing as she insisted that she didn't want any kind of a fuss over her departure. But Sylvia felt that she couldn't let such a momentous occasion pass without marking it in some way. 'It's not every day my only daughter leaves home,' Sylvia said firmly and she insisted on inviting several of the neighbours as well as Rosie's particular friends to an informal afternoon tea the day before she was set to leave.

'It's not the kind of farewell party I would normally have dreamed of giving for Rosie,' Sylvia announced with a shy laugh, when everyone filled the shop shortly after closing time. 'But we can raise a toast with a cup of tea and I'm grateful that I had enough bread to be able to make us a small sandwich each, even if the filling is a bit thinly spread.' Everyone smiled at that though no one checked the size of the fillings as a large board was passed around.

'And I don't like to mention the cake.' Sylvia gave a little cough. 'As I know it was very well intended . . .' She gave a wry smile as she pointed to a large china plate on the countertop that had once belonged to her mother, where a few surviving slices lay amid an abundance of crumbs.

'I'm really sorry, Rosie.' It was Claire who spoke up, 'That was to be my very humble contribution to the party, but I'm afraid I never have mastered the art of baking without real eggs, butter or sugar!'

Everyone laughed and commiserated as they tried to

scoop up a handful of well baked crumbs and they pronounced them delicious, under the circumstances.

Fortunately Claire's baking disaster ended up saving the day for when it was time for Sylvia to actually bid Rosie farewell, her tears were well diluted with laughter.

Tonight, Sylvia had promised that while Claire was out, she would help out with one of her special orders by running up the main seams of the skirt and nipping in the darts on the bodice. Sylvia stood for a moment after Claire had left, thinking about the task in hand before adjusting her chair and settling down to sew.

She concentrated hard as she carefully fed the material into the much loved Singer sewing machine she had allowed Claire to use recently. She didn't want to make any mistakes. The machine was one of the few pieces she had inherited from her mother that she treasured. She'd brought it with her from London when she had married Archie Barker and moved north. Her mother had been an excellent seamstress and had taught Sylvia and her sister Hannah, Claire's mother, well but she hadn't used it for a while. However, it didn't take her long to settle down and Sylvia was soon humming to herself as she rocked the treadle back and forth keeping the rhythm as steady as possible, one of the few pleasures she felt she had left in life.

Golly, but it feels good to be useful again, she thought, though she continued to proceed cautiously as she couldn't afford to damage the delicate fabric. Sylvia didn't do much sewing now that her niece had taken on so many more responsibilities in the shop and she hadn't realised how much she'd missed it.

After a while, the close needlework was too much for Sylvia's eyes to cope with as the light became poorer; They'd agreed to make economical use of the metered electricity by only buying small wattage light bulbs even though it made sewing difficult at night. And if Claire did make any comment about the economies, Sylvia merely laughed away her objections, not wanting to talk about how difficult things were becoming or to share how much she feared that as the war progressed they were bound to get much worse. Sylvia cut the thread neatly, close to the fabric, as she always did and immediately pinked the inside edges of the seams to prevent them fraying. Then she sat back and held the material up to the light to admire her work. That was when she finally smiled, pleased to see that she had not lost her touch.

It's the machine, she always said if anyone praised her sewing abilities. She had been so proud and pleased when her mother gave it to her for her 21st birthday. It was so precious that Archie had built a special cabinet around it so that it looked like any other piece of furniture in the living room behind the shop when it wasn't in use. She folded the body of the machine back into the cabinet covering it with the hinged lid gently patting the main door as it clicked shut. *I certainly couldn't afford to buy such a wonderful piece of equipment now*, she thought. *And I won't sell this one, Not that I intend to get rid of this one, even though it is quite valuable and I could probably earn some much needed cash.* But Sylvia knew she could never bring herself to sell it no matter how difficult her circumstances. She gave an ironic laugh, tickled at the thought that even if she couldn't afford to keep it, neither could she afford to sell it. The fact that her daughter showed no interest in it as a family heirloom was one of her great regrets and she sometimes wished that Claire was her daughter.

Sylvia shook her head and sighed, cross with herself for entertaining such thoughts, hiding behind the excuse that she couldn't think straight at this time of night. If she was honest, she hadn't really been able to think straight since Archie had signed up for the navy and been shipped overseas for as far as she was concerned her troubles had begun when his wages from the shoe company that he represented had stopped coming in, and she had to rely solely on the income from the shop. She had been led to believe that she might expect some kind of small wage from the navy but so far that didn't seem to have materialised. She had cut back on her spending although fortunately there was little enough tempting to buy in any of the shops now that rationing was really biting.

Sylvia couldn't help reflecting how strange life could

be sometimes. Rosie had left home, Archie had gone to sea, and she had been left behind in Greenhill where her once successful business was now struggling to make ends meet. This was not the life that she had dreamed of and she was more grateful than she had realised that she at least had Claire.

Sylvia recalled Claire's arrival in the small northern village, thinking how brave it had been of her sister Hannah to approach her on Claire's behalf after all those years of silence. *Broigus* was the word they had used in Sylvia's house when she was growing up to describe such a silence; it was the Yiddish word her parents had used to describe any of the family's fallings out, although she could no longer remember what the particular *broigus* with her own sister had been about. She had always thought of it like a disease, that would eat away at you and it did seem to affect most families that she knew of. It felt strange now when Sylvia thought back to her Jewish upbringing and the fact that her own daughter hadn't known anything about it, not even the fact that mother and daughter were Jewish until Claire had talked about it. Sylvia had hidden her own Jewish identity for so many years that most of the rituals and practices were long since forgotten. Every now and then, Claire, who had been brought up in a Jewish household, would mention something that jogged Sylvia's memory.

Sylvia looked up at the mantelpiece clock. Hopefully,

it wouldn't be long before Claire came home, though Sylvia tried not to fuss over her as if she was a small child. She tucked the sewing cabinet back into the corner and picked up an old copy of the *Women's Weekly* magazine that was passed around the neighbourhood each week. She liked to re-read the stories, catch up with the serials and double check the knitting patterns to make sure there was nothing she had missed that might be useful to show customers. She went over to the couch, determined to put her feet up for half an hour, and sat down to ponder her position. She had written to Archie asking why she hadn't received any money although true to form he hadn't responded. But it didn't seem right that he couldn't be forced to pay some portion of his salary to his wife. Perhaps there was some naval personnel department she could approach who might be able to shed some light on his missing salary or perhaps she should start with the enrolment centre where Archie had originally signed up.

Chapter 13

CLAIRE

Claire sat next to Violet on the bus journey into Manchester on Saturday morning wondering why she had agreed to come. Neither of them spoke for the first half of the journey until Claire finally broke the silence.

'Are you really sure you want to go ahead with this?' she said eventually, regretting her decision to play gooseberry. 'You know it's not too late to change your mind and send me packing. I could have a nosey around the shops and go home on the next bus. I honestly wouldn't mind.'

'Thanks, that's a kind thought and thank you for

asking but I'm sure,' Violet said. 'You have no idea how much more relaxed I feel, having you with me.'

'I'm sure you'll be fine once the first awkward moment is over,' Claire said, still wondering if she was doing the right thing. 'After all, you've been writing to him for all these years and you told me you feel as if he's not a stranger.'

'I know,' Violet said, 'and I can't explain it.

Claire turned her face to the window and stared out at the green fields of the freshly budding countryside. Then she looked directly back at Violet. 'There's still time to change your mind, you know?' she said.

'I know, but I won't, I feel much better having a friend with me.' Violet sounded more certain now. 'Oh, but I see you've got a rosebud pinned onto your beret.'

'Why? Is that a problem? It comes with the hat, I'm afraid,' Claire said.

'It's just that I told him he would know me by the rosebud in my hat band,' Violet explained, 'but I can't see him getting us muddled up, can you?' She laughed. 'Could you imagine if he ended up kissing the wrong person?' At that they both burst into a fit of giggles.

It took a moment for Claire to realise that the bus conductor was calling, 'Terminus! Terminus! Everybody off the bus! And don't forget your bags.'

As the passengers disembarked, Claire joined the queue in the aisle waiting to alight. She hadn't been into Manchester very often and didn't really know her way around so she was pleased to find they could pick up the tram to Lewis's in the bus station and they didn't have far to walk from the tram stop to the store itself. Claire tried to relax and enjoy the outing.

'I suppose people are glad to get out for an hour or two to catch a breath of fresh air while it's still light so that they can get home again in good time before blackout,' Claire said brightly as they joined the slow-moving crocodile piling onto the tram before it began its crawl up the main thoroughfare. 'I'm surprised how many people are about given that there's not much to buy in the shops and nothing to tempt them into the cafés.'

She looked out of the tram window as they passed the many shops, most with the now common sticky tape in criss-cross patterns lining to window to protect shoppers from shattered glass in the event of a bomb. 'It's not as though there's much to look at in the window displays. I'm glad I only work in a little local haber-dashery shop where we don't need to buy much stock, although it can be tough even to keep a shop like that going.'

'I bet Sylvia Barker's glad she's got you,' Violet said, and Claire reddened. 'You can teach them how to make all their own stuff,' Violet added with a grin.

'The irony is that I would love to be able to buy a few new clothes off the peg now and then,' Claire said.

'I don't have much time to sew things for myself and I get tired of always wearing the same thing.'

Shortly, they approached Lewis's and they both jumped off the tram. There weren't many cars on the road since petrol had become rationed, but pedestrians were bunching together on all sides of the pavement so that even the small number of cars that were trying to nudge their way through were causing congestion at the major road junctions. Claire realised too late that there was a policeman on traffic duty trying to send the cars in one direction and the pedestrians in the other; for a moment there was chaos as cars inched forwards while the people on the pavement who were getting off the tram jostled those already waiting to cross.

In the mêlée, Claire felt her beret being knocked sideways so that it was stuck at a jaunty angle feeling like it was about to fall off. She put her hand up to her head but couldn't prevent it from slipping onto the pavement where it was in danger of being trampled.

'Oh, goodness, my hat!' Claire cried out, dashing forward to try to catch it, unaware that Violet was no longer beside her; she couldn't see the hat as she was almost forced to cross the road, but she paused in front of the department store entrance as the crowd seemed to melt away.

'I believe this might be yours,' a deep American-sounding voice said, and Claire spun around to find herself looking up into the face of an extremely handsome young man with a shock of dark wavy hair, a smooth lean chin and dark, velvety eyes. He seemed to be at least six feet tall and looked extremely smart in a blue dress services uniform that was different from any uniform she had seen before.

He was holding her beret out towards her, his long fingers playing with the rosebud that was pinned to one side. He looked directly at her, smiling as he looked her up and down. When their gaze finally locked Claire caught her breath. She was thinking that this was exactly the kind of man she had always dreamed of, the kind of man who could sweep her off her feet, but was suddenly alarmed to find that it was literally so, for without warning he had bent down and lifted her off the ground. Claire squealed as she felt his strong arms tuck around hers, then she gasped as she felt her feet dangling and twirling beneath her like she was a rag doll at a funfair, almost knocking over several people who had stopped by the main entrance and were battling to open the doors.

His eyes looked into hers and he held her gaze for several moments before putting her down. 'A rosebud?' he said, and he tilted his head to one side as his fingers caressed the artificial flower pinned to her hat. 'That can only mean one thing,' he said, and his face wreathed into smiles. 'You must be Violet!'

Claire didn't immediately process the full meaning

of his words; she was still trying to catch her breath and control the flutter of feelings he had sparked, so she coughed in an attempt to cover up her momentary inability to speak,

He took a step back to look at her, holding her at arm's length 'You know, you really didn't need to provide proof of identity. I'd have known you anywhere' he said with a grin. 'You're even lovelier than you sounded in your letters.'

Then he enfolded the astonished Claire in his arms once more while she felt like she was hardly able to breathe. She wasn't aware at first of where they were standing until several people in the crowd pushed them aside, complaining about the need to keep the entranceway clear to the store.

'Here, let me look at you again.' Daniel ignored the crowd and he shook his head. 'I really can't believe it, Violet! After all these years!' He continued to gaze at Claire with such an adoring look that momentarily she was reluctant to let him go until she became aware of Violet standing open-mouthed beside her.

'What's going on?' Violet said, an unmistakable tremor in her voice. 'Daniel?

'You've got it wrong, I'm not Violet,' Claire said, clearing her throat. 'My name is Claire. This is Violet.'

He nodded and this time Claire saw a change in the expression on his face and knew that he understood.

'I'm so sorry, please forgive me,' Daniel stuttered,

looking back at Claire. 'It was the rosebud in your hat, I just assumed . . .' he said.

'That's all right,' Claire said. She tried to sound casual although she actually felt embarrassed, and she didn't know what to say. Then she noticed that Violet was hanging back, staring at Daniel in dismay, her eyes brimming with tears.

Chapter 14

VIOLET

Violet had spotted the tall man with dark wavy hair, dressed in what looked like an air-force uniform as soon as they alighted from the tram, and guessed immediately who he must be. He looked even more handsome than she had dared to hope, and she could feel her excitement bubbling, as she savoured the fantasy of their first moment together.

Violet had been surprised when Claire had darted forward to try to catch her hat, which seemed to take her straight into the arms of Daniel, of whom there could be no mistake. She was even more astonished when she saw him suddenly lift Claire up, gazing into her eyes as he swung her off the ground. Violet stared at them in dismay, horrified that Claire had stolen her big moment. Now they were stood awkwardly together and all she wanted to do was to run away. But before she could move Daniel was reaching out to her with his arm outstretched.

'Violet?' he said, 'I can only apologise for my mistake. But Claire quickly set me straight, so no harm done.' He grinned as he picked up Violet's hand which was still by her side and pumped it vigorously. 'Gosh,' he said, 'I'm so pleased to meet you at last and apologies again for the error. And apologies to you, too, miss.' Daniel said, his eyes fixed on Claire this time, 'I do hope you'll excuse my over-enthusiasm. We Canadians pride ourselves on being nothing if not friendly.'

Claire laughed when he said this, particularly when he accompanied his words with a salute. But Violet's stomach was churning over in humiliation and jealousy, and she couldn't find it funny, stepping aside as he tried to give her a hug. All she wanted to do right now was to make an excuse and disappear. Claire had spoiled everything. She thought about going back home on the next bus, but before she had a chance to say anything Daniel spoke up, apparently determined that they should carry out their original plan.

'All's well that ends well. Isn't that how your William Shakespeare would have put it?' Daniel said. 'I reckon that means we should go into the store and find the café like we planned so that this can end well. I don't know about you, but I could certainly do with a drink. Claire are you free to join us?' When Claire nodded, he ploughed on, 'Violet, why don't you lead the way and allow me to buy both of you ladies a nice cup of coffee, or tea if you prefer.' He spoke quickly, hinting at his own awkwardness. 'Things should get a whole lot easier now that we know who everyone is,' he added with a chuckle.

Violet hesitated, her gay mood having been shattered, but then Daniel nudged her forward saying, 'Come on Violet, you lead the way.' Violet managed to swallow her feelings and headed for the escalators, at a pace, ahead of the other two.

She regretted her actions as soon as the steps began to rise and realised how close she was once more to tears. She half turned to see that they were only several steps behind and she wished she could pass off the incident in the entrance as if it wasn't important, as Daniel seemed to be doing – but from where she had been standing it hadn't looked quite as simple as he had made it sound. She could never eradicate from her mind the spark that had flashed between him and Claire.

Knowing she was brooding but helpless to stop herself, she looked up sharply when she heard Daniel say, 'At least it's not raining today' as he stepped off the escalator and followed her into the café. 'I believe you Brits love to talk about the weather, particularly about the amount of rain you guys have here in Manchester.'

'That's a myth.' Violet was surprised to hear Claire respond sounding surprisingly passionate in defence of her adopted home and Violet watched angrily as Daniel's lips twitched into a smile. Violet has no idea how she was going to get through a cup of tea with the other two.

Chapter 15

CLAIRE

Claire sat on the bus home wishing she could be anywhere but sitting next to Violet, although she was glad finally to be on the way back to Greenhill. It had been one of the most rotten days she could remember since leaving the comfort of her parents' home in London. She wished that she had left Daniel and Violet in town together before they had all gone for tea, as her instinct had told her to do.

Daniel had done his best to be sociable in the café and to keep them all entertained, mostly with air force anecdotes, but after their initial introduction all Claire had been able to think about was how she would have liked to be with him alone and to have the opportunity to get to know him on her own. It made her feel terribly guilty, and she just wished she had never agreed to come in the first place.

Claire had been aware of waves of tension coming her way from Violet immediately after they had met Daniel, and before they sat down in the café she had excused herself to visit the powder room so that she could have a few private moments to gather her thoughts.

When she returned to the table Claire was aware that Violet stopped talking as Daniel jumped up to politely hold out her chair. The conversation had picked up again, mainly thanks to Daniel but the atmosphere between them remained strained. It hadn't helped that despite the china and the fancy silverware, the tea in the café had been so weak it was more like hot water and the so-called fairy cakes had crumbled into sawdust with each bite. It had been a relief when Daniel had finally pushed his chair back and said that regrettably he would have to go. He insisted on taking care of the bill and then he looked at his wristwatch as the wait-ress took away the money in order to bring his change.

'Well!' he said. 'Great as it's been to meet you two ladies, I'm afraid I'll have to call it a day. If I can find my way back to the cathedral where they dropped us off this morning, I should be in good time to hitch a ride on the truck back to base with the rest of the squad. How will you be getting back? Can I see you to your bus?'

'No need, thanks,' Violet responded tersely. 'We can get the tram to the bus station by ourselves, it's not far and we can pick up our bus from there.'

'If you're sure?' Daniel seemed hesitant, as he looked directly at Claire.

'Yes, that will be fine, thanks all the same,' Claire said, anxious to leave. 'I presume you know which direction you'll find the cathedral?'

'If I don't then I have no business being a pilot!' Daniel's face broke into a grin. Claire couldn't help but grin back, relieved to share a lighter moment, then she watched Violet stiffen as Daniel gravely shook hands with them both and wished them well for the rest of the day.

Now, as the driver pulled out of the bus station and headed out of town, Claire heaved a sigh of relief. Not that it helped much, for her mind was still in great turmoil following the events of the day and no matter how hard she tried she still didn't know what to make of it all.

She didn't really understand why Violet couldn't have gone to meet Daniel on her own and she was cross with herself for agreeing to go with her. Playing gooseberry never did work in Claire's experience though it was too late to be thinking about that now.

Claire sneaked a glance at her friend, upset that the

day had gone so badly wrong. Indeed, she could no longer be sure that they were still even friends. They had barely spoken since meeting Daniel except when they had first sat down on the bus and Violet had sharply accused her of making sheep's eyes at him in order to steer him away. Now Violet was looking hard and stony-faced, her jaw set, her eyes angry as if that was something she would never be able to forgive. Claire had never seen Violet in such a mood; she was usually so sweet-natured and gentle. How on earth had things got so out of hand? Claire stared in front of her, and as the red brick of the houses gradually gave way to trees and green fields she was aware of her vision blurring.

She could hardly be blamed for Daniel's mistake or the effusiveness of his greeting. Although the memory of it still made her tingle from head to foot as she relived the scenario in her head. Though she couldn't deny that she had been bowled over at first sight of him and it did look as if he felt the same way about her. Claire had not set out to attract Daniel, not when she knew how much Violet had been looking forward to seeing him.

Claire stole another glance at Violet whose jaw was stiff, her eyes staring straight ahead. Just then Violet turned towards her and snapped, 'I hope you're happy?'

Claire shot a glance at her abruptly. 'What do you mean?'

'Well, things didn't exactly go to my plan, did they? So I hope at least one of us is happy.'

Claire looked at her, unsure how to respond.

'I asked for your company,' Violet said, 'not for you to step into my shoes and take over my life. I didn't know you were so jealous of what I had.'

'You think it was my intention to steal Daniel from you?' Claire was stung. 'Well, that's something, given that you weren't committed to each other in the first place. You might have called him your boyfriend, but Daniel didn't seem to think you were his girlfriend?' Claire regretted the words as soon as she'd said them, and she wasn't surprised when Violet glared at her and didn't reply.

Claire took a deep breath. 'I can see how it might have looked from where you were standing,' she conceded, her voice not as harsh, 'but I honestly wasn't.'

'Are you trying to tell me you didn't take a fancy to him as soon as you saw him? You were all over him!' Violet's tone was acid.

Claire's cheeks flamed and she hesitated before answering. She could hardly deny the chemistry that had sparked between her and Daniel, however unexpectedly it had hit her. And how could she forget the feeling of being enveloped in his arms, or the brush of his lips on hers? She had never felt anything like that before. In fact, her breathing was fluttering unsteadily just thinking about it.

Claire frowned. 'He made an honest mistake, that's all,' she said. 'It doesn't mean he thinks any the less of you.' But she had to look away.

'Oh, don't be so naïve, or maybe men always look at you like that,' Violet scoffed.

Claire bit her lip. She hated to admit it, but Violet was right, and Daniel trying to pretend that it didn't matter had probably only made things worse. She opened her mouth to speak but she could see from the look on Violet's face that there was no point in trying to convince her right now. By the time they parted company by the parade of shops in Greenhill, Claire was relieved to disappear inside her aunt's haberdashery shop with a brief wave, slamming the door firmly shut behind her.

Chapter 16

VICKY

Vicky Buckley was still trying to get used to her new name and was about to deny that the letters were hers when her assistant Ruby thrust the bundle towards her. But she laughed instead when she realised what she had done. 'You'd think I'd have got used to being called Mrs Buckley by now, wouldn't you?' she said. 'Roger writes so often.'

'And Buckley's such a lovely name,' Ruby said.

'A whole lot better than Parrott!' Vicky added.

'You've certainly had enough letters from Dr Buckley,' Ruby ventured with a giggle.

Vicky giggled, too. 'I'm only just getting used to hearing little Julie calling me "Mummy",' she admitted. 'You've no idea how odd that sounded at first. These things take time.'

'How does it make you feel when you hear that?' Ruby asked. 'She certainly does it very naturally now.'

'Funnily enough, I like it and I don't mind as much as I thought I might. I've always been very wary of her thinking I'm trying to replace her own mother and I think she understands that, so coming from her, it sounds sort of cute.'

Vicky was aware that Ruby was still scrutinising her. 'So, are you going to accept that this bunch of air letters are yours, or do I have to send them back address unknown?' asked Ruby.

Vicky was concerned that a level of impatience had crept into Ruby's voice but she laughed and held out her hands. 'Cheeky monkey! Hand them over before I make you go and wash the floors all over again for being rude!'

Ruby limped across the room to where Vicky was preparing to pull down the blinds that covered all the windows but before she could lock the front door it was suddenly pushed open almost knocking her over. The bell tinkled to announce what she hoped would be the final customer of the day. There was a gust of wind as a young woman stepped inside, and she held on tightly to the well-wrapped bundle she was cradling as she kicked the door shut behind her. The swaddling in her arms looked so heavy that at first it didn't seem like there could be a baby inside. Nothing could be seen of its face, but little blue bobbles stuck out at the edges of the pale blue and white blanket giving the only indication that there might be human life inside.

The girl entered the shop, striding up to the counter without invitation or acknowledgement that the door was about to be locked and the business shut up for the day. Then she saw Vicky and spun on her heels to face her.

'Are you Vicky?' she said.

'That's what folk round here call me,' Vicky said. 'But you're not from round here?'

The girl shook her head.

'Then who are you? And how can I help you?'

The girl lifted her head and, making direct contact with Vicky's eyes, announced loftily, 'I'm Mathilda McFadden, known to my friends as Tilly.' She struck a defiant pose as if challenging Vicky to face her full on. When Vicky smiled but failed to look impressed the girl visibly deflated. She went to sit on the chair on the customers' side of the counter, dumping the bundle onto the countertop with such force that the baby suddenly stirred and began to wail.

'Can I get yer anything?' Ruby asked politely, leaning over to peer at the howling infant.

'Cuppa tea might be nice,' Tilly said. 'I've got to feed him soon.'

'How about you fetch a glass of water for the lady,' Vicky said to Ruby, 'and then I suggest you go home.'

'Will do, Mrs Buckley.' Ruby perked up and almost ran behind the counter and into the kitchen.

'Now, then, Mrs . . .?' Vicky said. Then, turning to Tilly, she glanced at her empty ring finger. 'Mrs McFadden, was it?' she said deliberately.

'I didn't say but it's *Miss*, actually,' Tilly said, adding under her breath, 'As if you didn't know.' Vicky raised her eyebrows.

'Well, *Miss* McFadden, although I can assure you that your marital status makes no difference to me, happy to serve you either way. The only thing that does bother me, I'm afraid, is the fact that we are just about to close.' Ruby had returned with a glass of cold water and the young woman looked at Ruby as if she expected her to refute Vicky's assertion but Vicky acted as if she hadn't noticed.

'So, is it a telegram you're after? Or some stamps, maybe?' Vicky said in what she hoped sounded like a reasonable voice. 'I'd be happy to serve you with whatever you require before we total up for the night. So if you'd just let me know . . .'

'I don't want nothing, thanks,' Tilly said, 'and you needn't keep the shop open specially for me, cos it's me as has summat for you.' She picked up the still crying child and thrust it towards Vicky. 'I've brought your new nephew to see you.'

Vicky frowned, not understanding, then opened her eyes wide as the penny dropped. She had always had her suspicions about her brother and what he got up to.

'That's right,' Tilly said a look of triumph crossing her face. 'This is your Henry's brat. Poor fatherless sod that he is.' She thrust the bundle up towards Vicky, who peered inside the blanket, pulling the edges away from the baby's face.

Then Vicky had to sit down as she felt the blood drain away from her own face. 'I can see that. Does he have a name?' Her voice was almost a whisper.

'It's Eddie,' Tilly said. 'He's called Eddie. That was Henry's choice before he snuffed it, not mine, though I decided to go along with it.'

'Henry knew about him?' Vicky felt she hardly dared to ask.

'Oh, he knew about him, all right, in theory at least; not that he knew it was definitely a him. He chose the name a long while back, one that could go either way. "Eddie if it's a boy, Edie if it's a girl," he said before he left. "And don't worry, I'll be back before it has to go to school," were his final words to me. Not much of a romantic wasn't your brother.' The look Tilly shot over to Vicky was steely and challenging, causing Vicky's eyes to tear before looking away. She turned to Ruby and gave a slight nod of her head in the direction of the door that led into the living quarters. It took a moment but then Ruby caught on. 'I . . . I think I'll be off if it's all the same to you, *Mrs Buckley*?' she said with special emphasis.

'Yes, that's fine, Ruby, love,' Vicky responded immediately. 'Bright and early tomorrow though so we can get the ordering done.

'I won't be late, don't worry,' Ruby said. She offered a weak smile to Tilly. 'Bye, then, I'll see you tomorrow,' she said to Vicky, then she hobbled over and was out of the door as quickly as she could drag her callipered leg.

'Why have you come to us? Did Henry say what he wanted to happen about the baby? Only he never even let on to us that there was one in the offing and he never said owt about you.' Vicky confronted Tilly as soon as they were alone hoping that the direct challenge would show her up to be not quite as sure of herself as she tried to pretend.

Vicky did wonder what if Tilly had made up the whole story in order to extort money from her and her father. If so, it was up to her to call Tilly's bluff. Vicky looked across to the young girl who still had an air of defiance about her, though her eyes were darting around the room as if she realised that her future could well be hanging by a slender thread.

'Are you calling me a liar? I wouldn't have come

round here begging if I didn't have to. He seemed to think he'd be back home by the time the kid would be off to school. But he won't be, will he?'

Vicky could now see the girl was tearful and sounded sincere. Her mind was working overtime trying to assess the genuineness of Tilly's case. She didn't remember Henry talking about having a girlfriend. But then if she was honest, Henry had never spoken much about his personal life either to her or to her father. Not that Arthur Parrott would have ever chastised Henry for his behaviour, no matter how carefree or reckless. He'd be only too thrilled at the thought of being a grand-father to Henry's child. In his eyes his son had never been able to put a foot wrong.

'How do I know you are telling me the truth?' Vicky asked the girl.

'What are you trying to imply? That I'm *that* sort of girl? How dare you!' Tilly shouted and she picked up the bundle and thrust it into Vicky's arms as if there really was nothing inside. Vicky jumped back and almost dropped it. 'Here, have a closer look and dare to tell me you don't think he's your flesh and blood who deserves to be recognised,' Tilly snapped. She was bordering on the hysterical and Vicky was suddenly afraid that she might be teetering on the edge.

'I'm not implying anything,' Vicky said quietly. She eyed her a bit more closely, and could see that her clothes had a careworn appearance and she looked dog tired. She knew it was best to defuse the situation and calm things down but she didn't want the girl to take anything for granted. Besides, it was just the sort of thing her late brother would do. Irresponsible and careless, even to the last.

'I didn't mean it to come out as badly as it sounded.' Her voice was kinder now. 'You must see that it's a lot for me to take in. You march in here, claiming to be family, without any form of proof and you act like the poor mite is somehow my responsibility. Forgive me if I'm just a tad sceptical.'

Tilly looked away then and Vicky continued while she felt she still had the upper hand. 'Even if he is my nephew,' she said. 'What do you expect me or my father to do about it?'

Tilly leaned forward so that she was almost in Vicky's face. 'I expect you to give us a roof over our heads at the very least,' she spoke slowly and clearly now. 'And as I assume you'll not want the neighbours to know all your business, I *don't* expect you to leave us out there to starve or to sleep on the streets.' She flung her arm out dramatically indicating the pavement outside beyond the window.

'Hang on a minute!' Vicky said. 'You're the one who got yourself into this mess, so isn't it your responsibility to get yourself out of it? You can't come in here shouting the odds like it's all of a sudden our fault—' Vicky stopped abruptly, remembering her own situation all those years ago. Hadn't she ranted at her father for threatening to throw her and her baby out on the streets, expecting her to take full responsibility for the situation she and Stan had created even though she was only a young girl?

'I didn't say it was your *fault*,' Tilly shot back. 'If it was up to anyone, it's your brother that we've all got to thank for creating this situation in the first place, but as that's not possible perhaps you can tell me what I am supposed to do? How can I get out of this mess as you put it when the father of my child got drafted and killed before we'd had a chance to get wed and make it legal?'

Tilly's voice cracked as she said that and as she looked down at her baby, for the first time her eyes filled with compassion. 'What are we supposed to do when the silly sod went and got himself killed?' she said, her voice finally breaking. 'Leaving me with a bun in the oven!' Now she began to sob. 'I've got to look after him all on my own from now on, is that it? Without a job, without anywhere to live? You tell me how I'm supposed to manage that, Miss Clever Clogs.'

Vicky could feel a lump rising in her throat as she recognised the very words that she had thrown back at her father when he had refused to help her all those years ago. She was ashamed at herself for being harsh now and for a moment she was overcome.

'Where have you been living until now?' Vicky asked, eventually. She noticed the baby had gone quiet since she'd been holding him and she didn't want to disturb him again.

'I've been stopping at the rectory,' Tilly said. 'I tell you, if it hadn't been for the kindness of the vicar at the church here, I wouldn't have eaten or had a bed to sleep in this last while. Them bloody nuns didn't want to know. All they wanted to do was to pass my little Eddie onto a new family and I was having none of that, I can tell you The vicar said I could stop on there if I had nowhere else to go, but I reckoned that wasn't right, not when Eddie's got his own family right here in Greenhill. And I didn't want us to outstay our welcome at the church. I reckon he's got enough of his own problems what with his son going off to the war.'

Tilly put her hand up to Eddie's face and stroked his cheek with a crooked finger.

'And Henry told you to come here and cry to us if you were ever in trouble, is that it?' Vicky looked resigned. 'That's so typical of my brother.'

'No, he didn't, as a matter of fact even though he knew I was expecting. I never got the chance to write to him after I'd had the baby. Not that it would have made much difference, according to you,' Tilly said with a sigh.

'Henry never was one for taking responsibility for

any serious things, though you must have known that,' Vicky said. 'From what you say you'd known him a while.'

'Aye, I'm afraid I did. Long enough to know that he never looked beyond the next five minutes of pleasure,' Tilly said bitterly as she sat down again, 'I'm not sure what he'd have made of this little lot.' She jerked her thumb towards Eddie who was still lying quietly in Vicky's arms. 'Though he did sometimes talk about us getting married and having a family,' she added hastily. 'I'm not making that up.' She sounded dejected at having missed her chance to pin him down.

'I never said you were making anything up,' Vicky said. 'Though I bet he probably mentioned the idea of marriage once or twice in passing while you dreamed about it most of the time?' She sighed. 'Most of us do, particularly once the drums of war started beating and we had to watch our loved ones marching off to fight, not knowing when we'll see them again.'

Tilly shrugged 'He didn't really like talking about the future and he certainly refused to admit that he might not come back.'

'I know what you mean, but he wouldn't have been the only one to stick his head in the sand so that he couldn't see the road ahead.' Vicky looked away into the distance, feeling the moisture accumulating in the corners of her eyes as she relived scenes from her own youth. The time when she had been the poor girl left behind with a bun in the oven, as Tilly had so graphically described it, while her intended had marched off so optimistically to fight in the Spanish Civil War.

Stan had been killed before he'd had time to make an honest woman of her, even though they were engaged and he had pledged himself to her. Hadn't she cried then that her plight was not her fault and begged her father not to throw her out onto the street? She had been left in no doubt then that he would have carried out his threat, only nature intervened and Vickie had miscarried the baby.

'How old are you, Tilly?' Vicky switched the emphasis. 'I must admit you don't look old enough to have all this piled on your shoulders.'

Tilly lifted her head and but rather than looking cowed gave Vicky a long defiant look. 'I'm seventeen,' she said proudly, and Vicky wanted to weep.

Suddenly, there was a loud bang on the door that separated the post office from the living quarters and Tilly and Vicky both jumped. The baby let out a long, loud, startled cry quickly followed by heart wrenching snuffled sobs as he struggled to catch his breath.

'I'm coming, Dad!' Vicky called through the closed door, also giving three short raps in case he hadn't heard her. 'I'll just finish locking up.'

Tilly stood up but she made no attempt to take Eddie

from Vicky or to move away from the counter. Instead she planted her feet firmly apart and folded her arms, a look of grim determination on her face.

'Tilly, I'm afraid you'll have to go for now,' Vicky said as gently as she could, while she attempted to place Eddie back in his mother's reluctant arms. 'As you can gather this has all come as rather a shock to me, and it certainly will be to my dad who's supposed to take things easy.' She indicated Eddie whose cries had reduced to whimpers that sounded more like irregular hiccups. 'You'll appreciate that there's nothing I can do right now, because, as I say, it's not only up to me, I do have to consider others, like my father.'

'And what about your husband?' Tilly demanded. 'A doctor, eh? What will he have to say when you tell him? From what I hear he won't stand by and watch us being thrown out on the street.' She stood her ground looking defiant and immovable once more and this time her jaw was set, too. She made no attempt to remove little Eddie from Vicky's arms.

'My husband is away in the army like most of the men round here,' Vickie said, determined to keep her voice strong, 'so, I'm left to make the decisions. I can't promise you anything, like I say, but you'll have to leave it with me, for now. Let me talk to my dad and I'll see what I can do.'

'Don't you try fobbing me off,' Tilly began. 'I know

your kind.' She wagged her finger in Vickie's face so that she had to take a step back. But there was fear in Tilly's voice and a scared look in her eyes.

'Believe me, I wouldn't dream of fobbing you off,' Vickie said, and she couldn't help a sigh escaping. 'I know what it's like, but I do have to handle my dad carefully if I want him to agree. I'm afraid you'll have to trust me, but I promise to do the best I can for you and the little one, and I'll not let you starve or be put out on the street.'

Tilly looked at her warily. 'I'll be back this time tomorrow,' Tilly threatened. 'I'll not put out that nice vicar one day longer than necessary.'

'That's fine.' Vickie nodded her agreement though she had no idea whether she could achieve what she needed to in that short time, or what she was actually going to say to her father. All she could think of was that she wished Roger would magically appear so that he could be with her when she confronted Arthur Parrott; but she knew that he was too far away for that to even be a possibility.

Besides, she knew what Roger would have had to say on the subject. Wasn't he the only one who had befriended her when Stan and the baby had died? And she also knew that he wouldn't have had to think twice about his course of action. She imagined his calm way of talking, in what she called his voice of reason, and when she went over the quandary in her head one more time, she could hear him making his suggestions and knew very soon how she might reach a suitable solution. Somewhat reluctantly she handed little Eddie back to his mother.

'I'll see you tomorrow,' Tilly said. Her attempts at sounding threatening were no longer effective but it was as though she had to have the last word before Vicky closed and locked the door firmly behind her.

'She said what!' Arthur Parrott exclaimed when Vicky started to explain why she had been so late locking up the post office. His voice was incredulous. 'What kind of a cock and bull story was that?' he demanded. 'You didn't believe her that our Henry could have done such a thing?'

'I don't know.' Vicky shrugged. 'I . . . I'm not sure.' She seemed uncertain at first, but when she was satisfied that her father's voice sounded steady enough she said more boldly, 'Why not? He was no different from any of the other young lads in this neighbourhood, sowing his oats, and it's certainly possible if you look at the timing.'

Her father looked shocked for a moment and she was worried that she might have gone too far, but then Arthur frowned as he asked calmly, 'Did he ever say anything to you about having a girlfriend?'

'No, never, but then Henry never discussed his personal life with me any more than he did with you.

At least . . . I presuming you didn't know about this Tilly?'

Arthur looked thoughtful and didn't bother responding. 'I want to see this child,' he announced instead. 'I need to see him. If he's a grandson of mine, I'll know.'

Vicky wanted to laugh though she did her best to keep a straight face. 'Oh, yes, and how exactly will you know?' she said.

She was trying to keep the scorn from her voice, and she took courage when Arthur didn't reply immediately. But she was feeling hopeful. All she had to do was to convince her stubborn father.

'I know people like to talk about their babies having the family chin or their mother's eyes,' Vicky said, rolling her eyes heavenwards, 'You might say he's got a bit of a Parrott look about the mouth but there's nothing that would be recognisable.' Now it was Vicky's turn to sound sceptical. 'I was much more concerned with her story about being put out onto the street by the nuns and her own family, as that's something that I do find to be very believable.'

She lowered her eyelids as she shot a glance in Arthur's direction, wondering if he would recognise her own story in there and his part in it.

'Her father has put her out on the street, you say?' There was a flicker of interest in Arthur's eyes.

'Yes,' Vicky said, and she plucked up the courage to

stare directly at her father now as she explained the situation about the vicar and Tilly seeking temporary refuge at the rectory. She found his gaze disconcerting but to her surprise Arthur was the one to look away first, though his face showed no signs of any memory of having made a similar threat himself to his own daughter.

'It's not as though we could offer her a bed here,' Vicky ventured to suggest after a slight pause, and was surprised that it didn't provoke the kind of immediate angry response it might once have done. Instead, he spoke slowly and carefully as though weighing and measuring his words.

'Let's assume this child is one of us: my grandson, Henry's son, your nephew.' He said the words as though they all meant something different, and he was evaluating their weight and meaning. 'Then supposing that he is, what would be the very least that we could do for him, that we would *want* to do for him?' Vicky noted that it was the child that he was discussing, not the mother. 'Well, the point is that we do have a bed here in this house . . . if you were to go to claim your rightful place in your marital home like Roger's asked you to do time and again.'

Arthur was in full flow now and was looking very pleased with himself. 'I'm sure the Buckleys would be delighted to have you move into that big house with them now. They're expecting it, they said as much to me on the day of your wedding. There'll be plenty of room and not only will they be pleased but little Julie will be delighted to have you all to herself for a bit. If you did that then this Tilly creature could sleep in your room with whatever his name is.' He waved his hands in the air as if they were prompting his struggling memory.

'Eddie,' Vicky whispered almost imperceptibly as she stared at her father. At first she wanted to laugh for it was exactly what she had decided in her head that Roger would have suggested. She also knew that her father was right, Roger really wanted her to stay with his parents for the duration of the war while his father was taking over the doctor's practice. She was the one who had refused, arguing that she should stay at the post office to look out for her own father who hadn't been enjoying the best of health. She never would have imagined hearing him coming up with such suggestions on his own. In fact, she had never before heard him talking so reasonably or rationally about such an emotive subject, the kind of topic that usually made him rail and remonstrate in anger.

Vicky suppressed a smile, for she knew that such a sensible and practical solution would have her husband's backing. It reminded Vicky of when Roger had persuaded her to offer a job training to be her assistant in the post office to Ruby, the young disabled lass he'd been treating, whose future had at one point looked extremely precarious. He was the one who had believed in Ruby's ability to make her mark in the world after her remarkable recovery from polio and in the end he had insisted on Vicky giving her the opportunity to do so. Vicky had no doubt that he would want to help someone like Tilly, and he would expect his wife to do the same. She was delighted to think that her father would be coming on board, too.

Chapter 17

CLAIRE

Claire was upset to think that she hadn't seen her friend since their visit to Manchester and she wondered if Violet might be avoiding her. So when she heard the shop bell tinkle unusually early one morning at Knit and Sew, her aunt's shop on the parade, she thought it might be Violet collecting some balls of knitting wool for her mother on her way to school.

Violet often collected the wool she'd asked Claire to put by for Eileen first thing in the morning before she started work and Claire came out eagerly from their living quarters, bright words of greeting already on her lips. But it wasn't Violet, and Claire stopped suddenly as she stepped into the shop to see Daniel, the last person she would have expected. She watched him glance around the shop for a moment and she felt her legs quivering as she came forward with a smile.

'Hello again, how can I help you?' she asked, trying her best to keep her voice steady, and Daniel grinned.

'I'm afraid I won't be buying anything today,' he said. 'I hope that's OK, only you did say you lived here as well as worked here, and as we didn't get much of a chance to talk the other day, I thought it would be all right to visit.'

Claire felt her heart quickening. Why had Daniel come to visit her? 'That's fine, really,' Claire assured him. 'I'm in charge here so, my aunt is hardly going to tell me off for having a visitor. I'd invite you through except that I can't leave the shop, I'm sure you understand.'

'That's OK,' Daniel said. He stared at her intently for a moment before he looked away, playing with some keys in his pocket. 'The thing is that . . .' He hesitated and looked almost awkward. 'I wanted to tell you how much I enjoyed meeting you the other day. We've not really had an opportunity to get to know each other since.'

Claire looked up in astonishment to find him gazing at her and she felt the bloom on her cheeks spread.

'What I really wanted was to ask you to come out with me this evening.' Daniel shrugged. 'I thought we should try a bit harder to do that, while we've still got the chance.'

Claire stared up at him, her heart now pounding as he added, 'Who knows how many times we'll be able to do this?' For a moment, Claire wondered if he intended including Violet in the invitation and she frowned, her mouth open, about to speak, but Daniel went on.

'We've been warned that we can expect to be tied up in the coming weeks with no leave, no passes, probably not even a chance to get off the base,' Daniel said, 'so, I thought I'd try for the two of us to get together at least one more time before we all get confined to barracks.'

Claire smiled now. 'I'm flattered,' she said, knowing the word didn't begin to do justice to the tingling excitement she felt. Then she sighed resignedly. 'I suppose that's war for you. You don't know what's going to happen from one minute to the next.' She tried to make it sound light though she couldn't keep the disappointment out of her voice at the thought that their rendezvous might not happen.

Daniel put his finger to his lips and dropped his voice to a whisper. 'Well, they certainly won't let us in on any of their secrets. You know what they say, Loose Talk Costs Lives. We're the last to know what's going on. We don't get told and we don't ask. We never know where we're going to be, or what we might be doing, but we have to be on alert and ready to scramble at a moment's notice, so I don't know when I'll get the chance to see you again after tonight, so do say you'll come.'

Claire smiled and nodded her head vigorously. Then she whispered, 'Of course I'll come.' She was gratified when he beamed back at her. 'We've got to take our chances whenever we find them,' he said, then he came across to the counter where Claire was standing and without warning he picked up her hands in his and put them to his lips.

Claire was startled by the sudden gesture but she made no attempt to remove them, thrilled by the immediate spark she felt as he continued to stare down at her. It was as if her entire body was being fired into life just as it had when they had locked their gaze outside Lewis's. She was relieved that no customers had entered the shop. She could feel herself leaning in towards him, but then, just as suddenly he pulled back. Standing upright once more, his hand reached out to touch the small gold pendant necklace that she always wore around her neck.

'That's unusual,' he said, tracing the etched pattern with his finger. 'I noticed you had it on the first time we met, do you always wear it?'

Claire's hand flew to her neck. She was thrown by his sudden change of track as he leaned across the counter to get a closer look. She felt the warmth of his breath on her cheek as he peered closely at it and had to take a deep breath to steady herself.

'Does that say what I think it says?' Daniel asked, flipping the pendant over. Claire stepped back, a teasing look on her face. 'That depends what you think it says,' she said.

Daniel looked at her directly. 'I *know* that it says *mazel*, which is the Hebrew word for luck.'

He looked directly at her and this time Claire couldn't avoid meeting his gaze.

'And how do you know that?' she asked, facing him squarely.

'Because I learned to read Hebrew at Sunday classes after my twelfth birthday when I was training for my bar mitzvah,' he said.

Claire gasped. 'You're Jewish?' she said. 'I had no idea.' And for some inexplicable reason she burst into tears.

'Yes, I'm Jewish,' Daniel said. 'Do I take it from your reaction that you are, too?'

Claire nodded and made no attempt to stop him when he brushed away the tears from her cheek with his finger.

'Do you have any family caught up in the mess in Europe?' Claire asked. 'Is that why you came over here to join in the fight?'

'No, at least none that I know of. My family originally fled the pogroms in Russia at the turn of the century and managed to escape as far as Canada. I think they were headed for New York, though they somehow lost their way after the ship they were on sailed up the St Lawrence Seaway to Montreal instead of into New York Harbour.'

Claire laughed, glad to break the tension.

'But as far as I know I think they all moved on. No one was left in eastern Europe, thank goodness,' Daniel said. 'How about you? Do you have anyone stuck in Europe?'

'No, I'm also relieved to say that my family saw the writing on the wall and came to England many years ago and my grandfather fought in the Great War. The map of Europe looks completely different now, but wherever they were from originally, they never went back. They became English and have lived here through several generations now,' Claire said.

They both stood back from the counter, neither speaking for several moments, then Claire said softly, 'The strange thing is that before the war started, I used to be afraid to admit that I was Jewish. But since the war I wear this all the time.' She fingered her necklace once more. 'I wear it proudly as well.'

'Do your friends and neighbours around here know?' Daniel asked.

'I don't know,' Claire said. 'My cousin Rosie, Aunty Sylvia's daughter, didn't even know she and her mother were Jewish until I came here, and she found it difficult to deal with at first, but she got over it. We didn't exactly make a public announcement about it, so I don't know who in the neighbourhood knows about it now and who doesn't. And if anyone has any anti-Semitic leanings at least they've never called us names to our faces. My uncle isn't Jewish, but my aunt and cousin have never complained of anyone saying nasty things about Jews, although until the refugees started arriving from abroad and the evacuees came in from the cities, I'm sure they were the only Jewish family in the area.'

'It was like that when we used to live in a small village in the countryside in Quebec,' Daniel said. 'We were the only Jewish family and me and my brother often got called names. But that all changed when we moved to the city and even with a name like Gabinsky we managed to blend in.'

Claire nodded agreement. 'It's different where I live in London,' she said. 'It's not like here. There are lots of other Jewish families in our area, even in our street and there are Jewish kosher food shops and services and several synagogues in the general neighbourhood. But it's funny how things around here have changed since the war started and my cousin and I have both said that we feel a great pride in our heritage now. We've decided that we should be prepared to stand up and be counted and to do whatever we can to help those that have been directly caught up in the struggle. It seems like the least we can do.'

Claire had hardly finished speaking when she jumped as there was a sharp tapping on the front window and the shop door was pushed open roughly, setting the bell jangling more violently than usual. A young man in a matching uniform to Daniel stepped into the shop. 'Sorry, Gabs,' he said, in what sounded to Claire's untrained ear like an American accent. 'But if we don't leave now . . .' He held his hands out, palms up. 'We can't afford to hang about.'

'Just coming, Duval.' Daniel grinned as his colleague seemed to be giving Claire an appraising glance, raising his eyebrows in approval.

'I'll be waiting outside,' Duval said with a wink.

As the door closed, Daniel looked across at Claire and stretched out his hand towards her. 'I feel like we've only just got started.' Daniel sighed. 'But if all goes well, I'll see you later. I'll try and stop by soon after you close, but don't worry if I'm late. I'll try and get word to you if I can't come at all. You got a telephone here? Quick, give me the number.' He looked on impatiently as Claire wrote it down.

He grabbed hold of her hand and squeezed it tight. 'I'd better go,' he said, releasing her just as abruptly, and without another word he turned and left, setting the bell jangling once more.

Claire remained behind the counter staring at the door as he left and wondering what had just happened. She felt as if she had been caught up in a whirlwind and, still reeling, she put her hand to the pendant at her throat tracing once more the outline of the Hebrew word with her finger. Had Daniel really been here? Or had she dreamt it? And would she really see him again tonight? She gave a contented sigh for she could still feel the warmth of his hand on her neck.

Chapter 18

CLAIRE

Daniel arrived surprisingly promptly and when he suggested they walk into town to get a breath of fresh air before settling into a pub, Claire was excited by the idea of taking his arm. She was glad that she had changed out of her working clothes into her favourite pleated skirt and ribbed twinset that she had knitted herself. She felt that the way the jumper and cardigan widened out to cover the fashionable shoulder pads, and then narrowed into the nipped-in waist, complemented the best features of her figure. This outfit always made her feel very elegant. Claire was not familiar with the different local pubs but she needn't have worried for Daniel already seemed to know where to go. He laughed when Claire commented on his local knowledge.

'The watering holes are always the first thing the guys in my squadron check out in any new posting, as you might imagine, though I haven't been to this particular one myself before,' Daniel said, as he guided her to a fancy-looking hostelry overlooking the river. 'Apparently, it's what we Canadians think of as a "typically English pub".'

The Carpenter's Arms was one of the better known old coaching inns in Greenhill even if Claire had never actually ventured into it.

'Then allow me to introduce you to it now. This do you?' Daniel asked as he held open the heavily panelled wooden door.

'Why not?' Claire said looking round the cosy-looking room and feeling a surprising coyness. 'All we want is a quiet place to talk, isn't it?'

Daniel gave her a look that brought a blush to her cheeks, and a tingling to her limbs.

'It's a shame that we don't have any pubs in Canada,' he said. 'We only have bars but they are nothing like this. I'm really enjoying having beer on tap.' He rubbed his hands together.

Claire followed him to the counter where several men in various uniforms were already drinking.

'Anything you can recommend?' Daniel asked her.

Claire laughed. 'I'm afraid I know nothing about local brews. I don't even know what *I* should be drinking.'

'Warm beer if your country's reputation is anything to go by,' Daniel said with a grin. 'Although maybe women don't drink beer. I tell you what, why don't you go and grab that table over there, while I get the drinks. Then I can surprise you.'

Claire was impressed by the steadiness of Daniel's hands as she watched him carry their drinks to the table, but when he sat down she unexpectedly felt shy, not sure of what she should say. However, she needn't have worried for Daniel quickly reached across the table, almost immediately taking her hands into his.

'Well!' he said. 'We've a lot of catching up to do, don't we? Amazing as it seems, I hardly know anything about you.' His smile made her feel as if she was melting and she had to look away. 'How about we pretend that this is the first time we've met,' he said.

Claire scanned his face and was pleased to see that his eyes were laughing. She refused to let any thoughts of Violet spoil the excitement of the evening and she took a long sip of her drink in the hope that whatever alcohol was in the tall glass he had presented her with would help her to overcome her sudden rush of nerves.

There were so many things that she wanted to know but she wasn't sure whether she could ask. How long would he be staying in England? What were her chances of seeing him again? Would he be flying overseas and perhaps become involved in the evacuation of the British Expeditionary Forces from Dunkirk? She had read of so many selfless and courageous acts but maybe that was only for those in charge of ships and boats? Fortunately, Daniel seemed to be unaware of her scrutiny as she sat and gazed at him, the questions flying around silently in her head. And all she wanted to do was to pray that what already felt like a magical evening would last forever.

Chapter 19

RUBY

Ruby was perhaps the most surprised by Tilly's arrival at the post office. When she came into work one morning and heard a baby's cries, she hurried behind the scenes to check that everything was all right.

'Everything's fine,' Vicky said. She introduced Ruby to Tilly and Eddie and gave a brief explanation of Eddie being Henry's son without going into details about Tilly and Henry not actually being married. She made it sound as though she was delighted about the situation, though in Ruby's eyes Vicky looked tired and flustered and not her usual placid self. It was obvious that someone had slept on the living room couch the previous night and she wondered if it was possible that it was the postmistress who had been the one to draw the short straw. 'I was going to move into the annex at the Buckleys' house soon in any case, so it makes sense for me to go and get it ready for us to settle in to when the doctor comes home,' Vicky said as if to justify the unexpected upheaval. 'I shall just be moving out of here a little earlier than originally planned.'

'Why? Is the doctor coming back already?' Ruby couldn't hide her eagerness. But then her face fell as a thought struck her. 'He hasn't been wounded, has he?'

'Oh, no, of course not,' Vicky said immediately. 'But I'm afraid it will probably be some time before he's able to come home, and I know he's happy for me to go on ahead and prepare things rather than waiting until the last minute.' She was clearly doing her best to explain but Ruby still felt bemused.

'When I heard about Tilly being in a pickle it seemed like the perfect opportunity,' Vicky said dismissively although Ruby could only stare at her in amazement as she explained the sudden change in domestic arrangements.

It seemed strange hearing the baby's cries throughout the course of the day, and Ruby was glad that she was not expected to attend to him. It was bad enough having to help with her younger brothers at home. She was happy instead to take on extra post-office duties while she watched Vicky jumping to attention each time the child murmured, running back and forth, anxious that the baby shouldn't disturb her father. Tilly had gone out early saying she was going to look for a job and while Ruby was curious as to where she might be looking so early in the morning, she didn't like to ask, and Vicky didn't seem to mind having to look after the baby.

It was a busy morning in the post office and Ruby was glad when it was dinnertime and she could lock the front door and pull down the blinds. But rather than sitting in the kitchen at the back with Vicky in order to eat the sandwich her mother had made for her, she decided to go out for a walk so that she wouldn't have to listen to any more of the baby crying.

It was refreshing to get out into the sunshine and Ruby took a deep breath as she stood on the pavement outside the post office, trying to decide which way she should go. She had never been much of a churchgoer, despite her parents' urgings, but she did like to walk in the peace and quiet of the cemetery and the gardens surrounding the local church, and that was where she decided to head today. The gardens were always well tended, and despite their age the gravestones were as well cared for as they could be. She enjoyed the seasonal changes reflected in the flowering borders and in the occasional bouquets left to remember those who had passed away.

Indeed, very few people visited the grounds at all

except to use it as a cut-through to the park and to Ruby it was generally a place where she could enjoy nature and guarantee not to be disturbed. That was why she was surprised as she approached to see a young man sitting on the solitary bench where she usually sat. He was with a dog, a beautiful black and white collie, who rested patiently by his side. She always thought of it as her bench although it had actually been gifted by one of the church members in honour of their ancestors many years ago. It was weatherworn and splintered and looked as though it had barely survived the freezing weather and the ice storms that had plagued the whole country, and even frozen the River Thames in London, during the previous months. The metal plaque was usually just about discernible, but not today, for the young man's back was covering it entirely. Ruby slowed her walking trying to minimise her limp, something she usually tried to do when she knew other people were watching her, and as she approached she could see him put his hand to his brow to block out the glare of the sun. She blushed as she realised he was tracking her progress for she recognised his face, having seen him only recently when he played the organ at Vicky's wedding; it was Geoffrey Laycock, the vicar's son.

'Well, if it isn't Ruby from the greengrocer's, or should I say the post office, now?' he said with a grin. 'This is the last place I would have expected to see you,' he said, eyebrows raised. 'What brings you here?' He slid along the bench and indicated she should join him. 'This is Pepe by the way,' he said as the dog sniffed Ruby with obvious approval and licked her hand in a welcoming gesture.

Ruby laughed and tickled the dog's ears. 'I fancied a walk,' she said, 'and I like it here, it's always very peaceful.' She covered her awkwardness by offering him a sandwich which he politely refused, although Pepe looked at her wistfully.

'I'm sorry to intrude on your solitude and I wouldn't dream of taking away a worker's dinner break,' he said with a laugh. 'Besides I shan't be staying long, my dinner and my long-suffering father await.' He indicated the rectory. 'This is my last day at home before I have to join my unit and I'm sure you can imagine that my poor old dad is not too happy about it.'

'Oh, are you in the army, then? I didn't know,' Ruby said.

'I am indeed,' Geoffrey said proudly. 'Thought I should sign up and do my bit, though dad desperately tried to stop me, as you can imagine.'

'Where are you going to be shipped to?' Ruby asked.

'I've no idea about that.' Geoffrey tapped the side of his nose. 'Nobody is supposed to know such things. All I do know is that it will be my last chance for a while to wear civvies.' He indicated his smart-looking

151

grey flannel trousers and Viyella shirt with a rueful smile.

Ruby took a bite of her sandwich. 'Aren't you scared?' she asked. 'About going to war, I mean.'

'No time for that,' Geoffrey said heartily. 'Someone's got to show that Hitler fella what we're made of.'

Ruby stared up at him as he stood up and saluted with a resolute expression fixed on his face, looking every inch the soldier.

'Well, it's been nice to see you again,' Ruby said, suddenly realising the time, 'but I'd better be getting back. There's a lot going on at the post office. Maybe I'll see you when you're home on leave?'

Geoffrey winked. 'Happen we might, Ruby.'

Unsure what to do, she leaned over to shake his hand, which he returned with a smile making his eyes crinkle appealingly, and Ruby tried her best to stride away confidently hoping he didn't notice her limp too much.

Chapter 20

VIOLET

Violet was certain she recognised Daniel's handwriting on the letter that she'd picked up from the post office, but it felt strange seeing it scrawled across a plain white envelope instead of being on the usual blue air letter. Vicky hadn't been there when she'd called in to collect it and Violet hadn't quite understood Ruby's explanation about the arrival of Henry's baby; she hadn't even realised that Henry had been married. But the young assistant had at least put the letter to one side for Violet and seemed to be carrying out all her duties with great efficiency so she really didn't mind Vicky's absence. Violet looked down at the envelope as she walked home briskly and for a second or two felt the old familiar fluttering in her chest. It was the same frisson of excitement that she'd always felt on receiving a letter from Daniel, but this time the moment didn't last, as their situation had changed and the letter had clearly not come from abroad.

As far as she knew, Daniel was right now only a stone's throw away from Greenhill and yet he hadn't been in touch, not since the unfortunate trip to Manchester – though she blamed Claire for that. She turned the envelope over but there was no return address given on the back. Overcome by a feeling of foreboding, she slipped into the house and ran up the stairs to her bedroom as quickly as she could, not answering when her mother called out to her. She sat down on the bed as she usually did to read Daniel's letters and ripped the envelope open, anxious to read what was inside.

She was upset to find it was only a single page and that was not even a full one. It was a scrap torn from a notebook and it contained a few spidery words that looked like they had been scribbled in haste:

Hope you're well. Sorry have been too busy to see you.

The next sentence had been blacked out.

You can imagine! I'll be in touch again when I can. All the best, Daniel.

She stopped and she stared down, wondering what

he could have put that had required censorship. It had hardly been worth the effort of sending. Was *busy* an excuse? Or was that what all servicemen had been told to say so as not to give anything away about their position or pending operations? Were he and his squadron confined to base or out on flying missions somewhere? Maybe that was what had been blacked out. She sighed. She would never know. *No one* was supposed to know and she had heard that they had all been instructed not to talk about such things; *careless talk costs lives*, wasn't that the phrase? That didn't stop her from being desperately disappointed. Not only did she have no idea where he was, but she didn't know when she could expect to see him again. She looked one more time at the note before screwing it into a tight ball and aiming it angrily at the fireplace. She wondered if he had written a similar note to Claire.

There was to be a meeting of the refugee committee tonight that Violet had thought of attending. Perhaps Claire would be there, and she could ask her? Violet frowned, knowing that was unlikely. She had been trying to avoid speaking to Claire since they had come back from Manchester; she had no real wish to start now. She still felt angry with Claire for what she saw as enticing Daniel away. But she had no time to think about Claire right now as she had to get ready for the meeting. She intended taking her mother with her tonight in the hope that she might persuade her to re-consider her decision not to foster any more refugee children.

Violet and Eileen arrived late at the meeting that evening and as Violet cast a glance about her, she saw Claire sitting on the back row, and there were no empty seats nearby. The room was quite full, but she managed to spot two spaces on one of the side benches towards the front, and she encouraged her mother to slide in quickly as she could see the meeting was about to start.

'You've missed nothing, Violet,' the young man already sitting on the bench whispered in precise but heavily accented English and Violet looked up to see the tall, skinny frame of Martin Vasicek. He was smiling shyly but looked away when she smiled back, and she saw a flush of embarrassment on his pale cheeks that went up as far as the dark roots of his blond hair. It highlighted the dark circles round his pale blue eyes that told of sleepless nights. She had worked with Martin before when they'd been desperate to find places for the children arriving out of war-torn Europe on the Kindertransport, and she remembered how shy he had always seemed then. Even now, he seemed to be avoiding looking at her as he leaned forward, carefully studying a copy of the agenda. Finally, he removed a thick folder from his battered leather briefcase and, as the redness in his cheeks gradually subsided, he addressed her directly.

'I believe these are the children we'll be discussing,'

Martin said. 'I think there are still one or two that have not yet been placed. You might want to have a look at the reports,' he said, flicking through the folder. 'In case you can offer any help.'

'Thanks, I will,' Violet said. 'And I'll show them to my mother, if that's OK, she's the one who needs convincing that help is still needed, not me.'

'Do you think you might be able to try again to take a child into your home, Mrs Pegg?' Martin said eagerly.

'You never know,' Violet said, trying to ignore the fact that her mother had visibly stiffened at the question. 'Eh, Mum? What do you say? Shall we put our name on the list?'

'We'll have to see,' was all Eileen said.

'Maybe something short-term?' Violet suggested. 'I think Martin can understand why you might not want to make a long-term commitment, not after what happened last time,' Violet said, 'but we won't write it off completely.'

'I do understand,' Martin said, 'but maybe I put your name on the list for further discussion?' Martin looked at Eileen and for once his normally crinkled brow was lifted by his smile. 'In the meantime,' Martin went on, finally turning to face Violet, 'we need to help the children to learn some English as quickly as possible. Maybe that is something we can talk about, Violet. You have much teaching experience. It would be wonderful if you could help.'

Chapter 21

CLAIRE

Claire wondered if Daniel had visited Violet as well as coming to the shop, to warn her not to expect to see him for a while; had they been out together? She had no way of knowing what might have happened between them and she didn't think it was her place to ask Daniel. She could only cling onto her own treasured memories of their lovely night out at the Carpenter's Arms and hope that there might be time for them to spend at least one more evening together. Whatever happened in the future she would always cherish the precious moments that she and Daniel had been able to snatch even though his time at the airbase was likely to be limited. She was upset that Violet had made no attempt to contact her after that dreadful meeting in Lewis's although she did understand why. If anything, Claire felt guilty about what had happened between her and Daniel, even if it wasn't her fault, but she hated the thought that Violet was physically avoiding her. When she had seen her at the last meeting she had looked the other way. Claire felt so uncomfortable about the whole wretched business she could only suppose that Violet must feel the same. Claire's solution would have been for them to talk things through together so that the two of them could sort any differences rather than continuing to avoid each other in a way that only drove them further apart. But it didn't look as though that would be possible unless Violet could be encouraged to speak to her the next time they met. But she was upset to find that Violet wasn't there when she first arrived and when Violet did eventually arrive late, with her mother, she still managed to avoid talking to Claire during the course of the meeting.

Claire was disappointed when she saw Violet leave with Martin Vasicek at the end of the evening without making any attempt to speak to her. Claire was aware that there was still so much work to be done, but she realised that she had no wish to continue being ignored. As a result, she had reluctantly decided that there were other ways in which she might offer to help the war effort and she had resigned from the committee.

Instead she joined the local branch of a recently formed hospital support group who offered help to families suffering from any kind of illness, injury or disability and she was soon swamped with enough extra tasks to fit around her regular work in the shop that there was no time left for worrying about her spat with Violet.

'You might want to leave one or two of the shorter visits to the younger members,' the supervisor said as she looked down her list. 'There's a big one that will be coming up shortly, in your neighbourhood I believe. This one's a young soldier who's suffered a most appalling accident at his first training camp and he's only seventeen.'

Claire involuntarily shivered.

'Apparently, he's awaiting some kind of major surgery after which he'll be sent home to recuperate.' She looked down at her notes. 'Oh, goodness! I hadn't realised, you might even know him,' she exclaimed as she read the remaining details. 'It's the vicar's son, Geoffrey.'

Chapter 22

Vicky

Vicky furrowed her brow as she took the large book of various stamps from the safe where the post office stored all of its valuable items. She had already had a testing morning before she'd even started work, having been called on to intervene before an argument got out of hand between her father and Tilly.

'Why can't she stop the poor mite crying like that, she's taking too long to give him his breakfast?' Her father, sitting in his old woollen dressing gown and his pyjamas by the fire, had pointed towards Tilly as she warmed up a tin of Carnation infant milk on the small stove in the kitchen. Tilly was struggling to balance a grizzling Eddie on her hip at the same time.

'Here, let me hold him while you do that.' Vicky had said. Eddie wailed a little in protest but gave her a little smile as Vicky won him around by kissing his flushed cheek and making a funny face at him.

'I'm doing my best, can't you see that?' Tilly pushed her untidy hair out of her eyes. 'Not my fault we got up late, Eddie's teething and he's been running me ragged in the night trying to settle him down.'

'Don't we know it,' Vicky's father interjected. 'Can't understand know why you can't settle him properly, like. Instead of keeping all folks up half the night.'

'Now, Dad,' Vicky said, 'all little ones have teething problems.'

That moment, Tilly let out a cry. 'Oh, hell! That's blown it, I've burned the bottom of the pan!'

This led to more grumbling from Arthur while Tilly tried to rescue the milk before it was completely ruined, like the pan.

Vicky shook her head now as she laid out the stamps on the counter; her plan wasn't working out at all. She had been paving the way before she had left to prepare her father for her move into the annexe at the Buckley family home, but she was exhausted and could feel instinctively that her father was not happy with the arrangements regarding Tilly, even though he had been the one to suggest them. It was obvious that he hadn't thought through the domino effects of Vicky moving out and Tilly and Eddie moving in, and that he had underestimated the general upheaval such changes might cause. Surprisingly he had said nothing directly against Tilly or the baby; he proudly boasted about his grandson to anyone who would listen and he spent the afternoons playing with Eddie, so enabling Vicky to get on with her work. But there were obvious tensions in the air and Vicky could see Arthur's temper shortening day by day so that he often looked angry while Tilly was looking more and more distressed.

Unfortunately, Vicky realised she was guilty of the same thing as her father. She had encouraged him to think that her long-term plans to move in with the Buckleys would work if she instigated them now, without thinking through some of the potential consequences of her not being on hand all the time. Now she had left, she wasn't always there when Arthur needed her and she couldn't help Tilly look after Eddie even with Ruby offering to take on extra work in the post office. She recognised that no matter what they each said about everything being well, Vicky would have to take action soon if she was to avoid Tilly and her father being at each other's throats.

Not that it was all Vicky's fault either, for she could see that Tilly also had expected too much; she hadn't known how much time and effort a young baby demanded, and Eddie was sapping her energy. She hadn't reckoned with being tied to the house for so much of the time, and not being able to go out in the evenings and Vicky watched her getting more miserable.

Vicky didn't know a lot about babies. She had often wondered what kind of a mother she would have been had her own child lived but as far as she could see Eddie was a good baby and despite all the problems, he had brought a new spirit and life force into the house. She had grown very fond of him, but things couldn't go on as they were. Vicky knew she hadn't yet found the solution to the family's complex situation. Their current arrangements were not the answer she had hoped they would be, but she didn't know what else she could do.

Chapter 23

SYLVIA

Sylvia stood looking at the meagre takings in the till and shook her head. She knew Claire was doing her best but unless things improved soon, she wasn't sure how much longer they could manage. She could only hope one or other of what Claire liked to call 'her little projects' would pick up soon so that she could stop worrying; some of them at least had shown much promise and the local women had already begun to take up Claire's offer of making some smart clothes for them. Those who had sampled Claire's work were very impressed by her ability to make alterations to their existing wardrobes and they also liked how quickly she could run up something new and fashionable for them despite the shortages of new materials. There had also been much interest in the classes Claire was offering to women who wished to improve their own sewing skills and although the take-up had been slow at first, Sylvia could only hope that the business would pick up before too long.

'Is everything all right, Auntie Sylv?' Sylvia hadn't noticed Claire was still in the shop until she stepped out from behind the changing room screen.

Sylvia forced her lips into a smile. 'Of course, love. Everything's fine,'

'I'll give you a penny for them, then,' Claire said with a grin. 'You would tell me if something was wrong, wouldn't you?'

'I was just thinking that I really need to go out into Manchester tomorrow, if you think you can manage the whole day without me,' Sylvia said, recovering quickly. 'I have some chores in town.'

'Of course, that's fine,' Claire said. 'I think the shop and I will still be here when you get back.'

'You're a good girl,' Sylvia said, suddenly leaning forward and kissing Claire on the forehead. 'Your mum's done me the best turn ever. I don't know what I've done to deserve you, or how she manages without you.' She disappeared out into the living quarters before the gathering tears spilled down her cheeks.

* * *

Sylvia was surprised how quickly she was able to find the right department in the naval offices that were located behind the town hall in the centre of Manchester and she soon found out exactly where she should begin her enquiries in order to pinpoint the source of her husband Archie's salary. An older-looking gentleman wearing smart dark trousers with a knife-edge crease and a crisp, white shirt with a fine striped tie ushered her into his office and indicated a chair on the opposite side of his grand-looking desk.

'Now, then, Mrs Barker, is it? How can I help?' he asked. His voice was clear and sharp, his vowels well clipped and Sylvia could imagine him issuing orders and being instantly obeyed.

Sylvia nodded. She was impressed by his efficiency as it seemed to take no time at all for him to locate the appropriate file from the pile on his desk when she gave Archie's name.

'Here we are,' he said, 'Seaman Archibald Barker. 'And you're Mrs Barker, I take it?' He beamed at her over the top of the folder and Sylvia nodded.

'So, what seems to be the problem, Mrs Barker?' the officer asked.

'I haven't been receiving any of Archie's cheques,' she said. 'I understood there should have been one at the end of each month since he signed up.'

The officer looked puzzled. 'There should indeed. I wonder what could have happened to them? We've had no other complaints,' he said, 'and according to the file there doesn't seem to be a problem at this end either. The cheques have been despatched every month regular as clockwork from this department. Now let me see.' He flicked through several more sheets in the file. 'They've been sent to you at 59 Mount Road, Matlock in Derbyshire. That is the correct address I take it? If so, you might want to contact the post office; it's possible that's where the trouble lies.'

Matlock? Derbyshire? As he said that Sylvia stopped smiling and she had to look away. She felt winded, as if she had been thumped in the ribs and couldn't catch her breath. She was sure that all the blood must have drained from her face. 'Matlock, you say?' There was a lump in her throat and she felt barely able to speak.

The officer nodded. 'That's where we were instructed to send them to, yes.'

'I see. Archie . . . Mr Barker . . . didn't make that clear to me.'

The officer looked puzzled. 'That's not actually our home address,' Sylvia explained. 'It's . . . it's where my husband works,' she said, trying to think quickly over the thoughts that were flashing into her head and to cover up her obvious confusion in front of the officer.

'*A-ha!* Then I can see where the misunderstanding must have arisen,' the officer said, shutting the file abruptly. 'Why don't you check with them at his workplace? The cheques must be accumulating there and

I'm sure they'll be able to clear things up for you in no time.' He smiled at her.

'Yes, yes, thank you,' Sylvia said, anxious to depart. 'That's exactly what I'll do. I'll go now and I'll make enquiries there. I'm sure they'll be able to shed some light.' Her mind was whirling as she struggled to stand up.

'It sounds like mystery solved,' the officer said. 'But do let us know if there is anything further we can do to help.'

Sylvia wasn't sure how she managed to get out of the chair and across the floor without collapsing. It wasn't until she reached the door that she realised the officer had stretched out his hand to shake hers, but she didn't bother turning back. 'Sorry,' she mumbled, 'but I'd better go there as soon as possible. I do need to sort it out. I might even be able to get a train from Mayfield Station this afternoon if I hurry. Thanks for your help.' And she ran from the office and fled the building as quickly as she could.

Everything seemed to pass in a blur, and Sylvia barely registered her journey to the train station, or any of the scenery that flickered past her through the train window.

When Sylvia alighted from the train at Matlock, she looked around the pretty country station wondering whether she really should have come. What did she hope to achieve? Maybe Mount Road really was where

171

the headquarters of his offices were based, as they were certainly in Matlock. Or might the address be for something else entirely? She was gripped by fear. She should never have come. What situation might she be heading into? And would she be strong enough to face it head on?

All I want to do is to claim what's rightfully mine, she told herself as she left the station to follow the porter's directions to Mount Road. *What's wrong with that? What if . . .? What if . . .?*' She continued to wonder, not wanting to believe her own thoughts.

I'll make short work of her, that's what, if it's some fancy woman Archie's been keeping stashed away. She finally forced herself to think the dreaded words.

Could there really be someone pretending to be Mrs Barker living off her money? Sylvia was incensed and felt anger bubbling up inside her. Then she gave a bitter little laugh to herself. Well, if that was the case then she'd soon put a stop to it. Her eyes narrowed and she clenched her fists as she came upon the street sign and she took a deep breath before turning into Mount Road.

It wasn't a long walk from the station, and it seemed to be filled with railway cottages: terraced rows of tiny two-up-two-down houses separated into narrow cuttings. Each had a path separating it from a pocket handkerchief-sized garden at the front and a walled off yard that she knew must contain a privy at the back. The houses at this end of Mount Road started at number one and Sylvia kept her head down as she set off along the cobbled street to walk the gauntlet to number fifty-nine. She did her best to ignore the scruffily dressed children who stopped their games to stare at her like they had never seen a smartly dressed woman in a tailored skirt and smart court shoes in their street before. The women sat on their well-worn doorsteps, scrutinising her face, but Sylvia had no time to stop and talk to anyone.

Sylvia slowed as she approached the house she was looking for, disconcerted by the sight of the cracked glass panel and the chipped paint of the front door. She drew her in breath sharply. Was this really where Archie sought refuge on the occasions when he didn't come home? She thought of her own neatly kept home with its sparkling windows and well-swept front , then she rapped firmly with the blackened brass knocker before she lost courage.

She was not sure what to expect and when the door was cautiously opened. She was surprised to see a small, pretty young woman standing in the doorway that led into a tiny hall at the foot of a steep flight of stairs. Her long, curly hair was tied back with a red ribbon revealing, on closer scrutiny, a rather tired and careworn face – a face that possibly looked older than she was in years. But her eyes were bright and were immediately on alert when she saw Sylvia. Sylvia stared back at her, suddenly realising she didn't know what to say. All her fight and bluster disappeared and the opening speech that she had been preparing no longer seemed appropriate.

'Yes?' the woman said, warily. 'Can I help you?'

Sylvia opened her mouth but no sound came out. She cleared her throat. 'I'm looking for someone who goes by the name of Mrs Barker,' she managed eventually, trying to pick her words carefully. She was aware that the woman was looking her up and down and she was wishing that she hadn't worn her best outfit or her smart heels.

'And who would you be then?' was the woman's only reply.

Sylvia took a deep breath. 'Perhaps I could come inside?' she said. 'I think you and I have some important matters to discuss that would be best kept private. Unless you don't mind talking about your personal business in front of the whole street.' She nodded her head towards the women ogling them from further up the street.

The younger woman in the doorway frowned, looking puzzled, but then hesitantly opened the front door wide.

'You'd best come in then, though I'm not sure what you think we've got to say that's so private. You can't keep secrets in a street like this for longer than it takes to sneeze.' She gave a coarse laugh and led the way into a small living room. It was shabby but it looked

174

clean and well cared for; the cushions on the almost threadbare couch were plumped up and the floor looked freshly swept. A young boy of about five years of age and a girl no more than seven were sitting at the rough wood table, eating what looked like a thick porridge from large bowls. They glanced up when Sylvia entered but then carried on eating.

Ignoring them, the young woman stopped and turned to face Sylvia. She stood arms akimbo, challenging, threatening almost and Sylvia involuntarily took a step back, feeling she was at a disadvantage. She stood awkwardly in the middle of the room as she was not invited to sit down.

'*So!* I'm Mrs Leanne Barker,' the young woman said. 'Now are you going to tell me who you are and what the hell you want.'

'I'm Mrs Barker, too. Mrs Sylvia Barker,' Sylvia said. She was determined not to raise her voice and paused for a moment to let the words sink in. When there was no response she went on, 'I run a haberdashery shop in Greenhill, on the other side of Manchester.'

'So we've got the same name?' Leanne said, dismissively, 'You want to make something of it? Barker is hardly an uncommon name round these parts, or where you come from. You sound like you're a long way from home. What really brings you down Derbyshire way?'

'Missing money, that's what brings me down here,' Sylvia said.

'What? And you think I've got it?' Leanne gave a cackling laugh. 'Look around you, lady,' she taunted. 'I guarantee you won't find much of that here. Not with two kids in tow.'

'I believe that you've been receiving what by rights is my Archie's money,' Sylvia said sharply, 'and it's got to stop.'

'How do you mean, your Archie? What have you got to do with him? Archie Barker is my husband and I'm entitled to whatever pittance the navy doles out to him.'

'Pardon me, but I think you'll find that that can't be so. Archie Barker is my husband,' Sylvia said.

The two women squared up to each other, glaring. Then Leanne shook her head and turned towards the children at the table. 'Jamie! Sally!' she said, forcefully. 'Get up to your room.'

'But we've not finished us tea,' Jamie protested while Sally began to wail.

'Never mind that, you can take it with you for once. Just go! Go on, scram! This lady and me have things to discuss that's not for young ears.'

At that, Jamie's face sparked interest and he looked as if he might ignore his mother's command, until Leanne shouted, 'Go! Now! and he and his sister slipped off their chairs and ran out to the hallway and up the stairs.

After they had gone, Leanne turned to Sylvia her

arms folded tightly across her chest and took several steps towards her.

'Now, Mrs Lah-de-dah, perhaps you'll tell me what right you have coming here like this and . . .' Leanne began.

'I've every right,' Sylvia interrupted calmly.

'Why? You have no connection to my husband.'

'Oh, yes, I have. I'm married to him, and have been for twenty-odd years. Strong enough connection for you?'

Leanne laughed. 'Don't be so daft woman. He's married to me.'

'You'd better stop saying that,' Sylvia said. 'It could get you into a lot of trouble. You can't have got married to him. Not legally at any rate. Cos he was already married – to me.'

'Talk sense,' Leanne said confidently, 'You've seen our kids. Jamie's five and Sal's seven and they're living proof that Archie's my husband.' She pointed upstairs. 'I'll grant you that Archie had moved in long since before we actually got wed, but when I fell with Sal we got married almost immediately in the registry office in Matlock before she was born.'

'I'm afraid I'm not the one who's being daft. That doesn't prove anything,' Sylvia said patiently, and she lowered her tone. 'Archie and me have a twenty-one-year-old daughter, Rosie, and we got married in London well over a year before she was born.' Sylvia dived into her handbag and brought out a photo of Rosie. 'Here,' she said, 'that's our daughter, if you don't believe me.'

Leanne snatched the photograph from her hand and Sylvia watched as she sank into a chair. 'I don't know if you realise it, but you can be sent to prison for bigamy,' Sylvia said, 'and be warned I shall be informing the police.'

Leanne's demeanour suddenly changed, though she continued to stare at the photograph. 'But I swear I didn't know,' she whispered, sounding like she still didn't believe it. Sylvia had the satisfaction of watching the colour drain from Leanne's face.

'Maybe not, but Archie knew he wasn't in a position to get married. So, try telling that to a judge,' Sylvia said. 'Now you can see that the money that you've been getting from the navy is rightfully mine, and I can force you to pay it all back.' She said this without confidence for she didn't know if it was true, but she was pleased to see the fear in Leanne's eyes.

'Oh, but . . . I can't . . . You can see for yourself . . .' Leanne looked around the room desperately her face registering her despair.

'I'm not saying I will force you but what I am saying is that you had better start making new arrangements for you and the children because I can tell you that from now on, I intend to have whatever he earns from the navy, as is my right.' Sylvia hoped her uncertainly didn't show on her face, as she wondered if she would have the nerve to carry out her threat.

'Oh, but, please . . .' Leanne began. Sylvia stopped her short, realising she was running out of steam to continue the argument. Her face softened as she said, 'One piece of advice. There's no point in relying on Archie when you're working out your future plans. You can see what a terrible liar he is. And I don't know if he's ever shown you, but he's got a terrible temper, too.'

Sylvia took back the photograph and rose from the chair at the table where she had been sitting, aware that Leanne was looking warily at her now. 'I would suggest you sort things out for you and your kids alone,' Sylvia said, 'like I've had to do for me and my daughter.' She pushed past Leanne as she said this and headed for the door.

But then she stopped and said, 'Oh, and in case you've got any fancy ideas, I must warn you that I have no intention of making things easy for Archie. I shan't be giving him a divorce.' She was too upset to continue and didn't wait to see the impact of her words as she slammed out of the house. She practically ran all the way to the station, past the gawping faces on the street, as fast as her shoes would allow.

She was relieved that her breathing was almost back to normal, although her legs were still shaking from the effort when the train to Manchester finally arrived. She was grateful that she managed to find a seat. She sank back onto the stubble of the once plush upholstery and let out a deep breath. It wasn't until then that she realised that her whole body was trembling as she relived the scene that had left her in a state of shock.

She didn't normally get involved in such arguments, except of course in her battles with Archie, which unfortunately he would always win, and she would usually end up with at least one black eye. She had been left with a couple of more permanent scars that she managed to keep hidden underneath the thickness of her hair. She couldn't stop the wry smile that twitched at her lips as she thought about the irony of the situation. Her mother had tried her hardest to prevent her marrying Archie and marrying out of the Jewish faith. How she wished now that she had listened.

Sylvia closed her eyes and didn't open them again until she heard the indefinable muffled tones of the station loud speaker system announcing their arrival at Manchester's Mayfield station.

Chapter 24

Vicky

Vicky was still upset to think that all was not well behind the scenes at the post office. She knew she wouldn't be able to move back there once she had moved officially into the Buckleys' house and before she left, she made a huge effort to try to smooth things out.

'How are you and Eddie settling in?' she ventured to ask Tilly one morning when Arthur had been even more snappy than usual and had refused to join Tilly for breakfast. The young girl was coming downstairs having put the baby down for his morning nap and she seemed to be caught off guard.

'Fine,' Tilly said almost too quickly, but her face looked anxious and pinched. 'Why? Has someone been telling tales out of school?' Her answer sounded irritable and short-tempered and she refused to look at Vicky.

'If you mean has my father been complaining about you or the baby then the answer is no,' Vicky said. 'He might never admit it, but I think it's done him a lot of good having you both here, don't you?'

Tilly shrugged. 'I didn't know how he was before,' she said grumpily, and she shrugged her shoulders non-comitally. At that moment, there was a loud wail from the bedroom upstairs where Eddie was supposed to be sleeping and Vicky was shocked at the immediate change that came over Tilly's face. She clenched her jaw so hard that her cheeks were shot with pink and Vicky could see her wring her hands anxiously.

'So, what is the problem then?' Vicky was doing her best not to lose patience as she indicated that perhaps they should continue their discussion in the kitchen.

'Who says there's a problem?' Tilly retorted, choosing to ignore Eddie's cries.

'No one has to *say* anything,' Vicky said. 'You don't have to spell it out, Tilly. It's out there in plain sight for anyone to see.'

Tilly looked so startled that Vicky softened her tone. 'I know it can't be easy. The fact of the matter is that it's very hard bringing up a baby on your own,' Vicky said, 'I understand that but . . . is there something else you're not telling me?'

Tilly continued to glare at her but, at that moment, the baby let out another loud wail, as if sensing the situation, and Tilly crumpled like she had been shot. She slumped down into a chair with her head in her hands and began to sob, drowning out even the baby's escalating cries.

Vicky put her hand gently on Tilly's shoulder then sat down beside the young girl. When Ruby arrived to hang up her coat before starting work, Vicky signalled to her that she should leave them alone.

Unaware of Ruby's presence, Tilly began to sob again. 'I don't know what's the matter,' she cried. 'I'm not on the street, and you've been incredibly kind and generous, you and your dad, so I know I should be happy, but I'm not.' The sobs gave way to elongated wails, several decibels louder and even more disturbing than the baby's heart-rending cries but Vicky kept quiet and let her speak.

'The problem is,' Tilly said after a short while, her words punctuated by hiccupping sobs, 'I want to be going out to work like everyone else of my age. I want to be earning money and then going out to have some fun . . .' Her voice trailed off and Vicky stared at her. 'I know I'm not being fair because it's all my own fault,' Tilly said eventually, 'but when he cries like that all I want to do is to run away!' She practically screamed out the last then broke down into sobs again. 'I'm not cut out to be a mother!' she wailed. 'I don't know anything about babies.'

At that Vicky couldn't prevent a sad smile tugging at the corners of her mouth. 'I don't think anyone is, Tilly,' she said kindly. 'It's one of the hardest jobs in the world, because it generally means having to make some kind of sacrifice, and not everyone's ready for that.'

'I love Eddie,' Tilly cried, 'I don't want you to think badly of me. It's just that . . .'

'I know you love him,' Vicky said, 'and I think you make a very good mother.' She let out a loud sigh. 'But maybe you weren't really ready for a baby yet. You still have a lot of growing up to do yourself. Perhaps the responsibilities of motherhood came too soon.'

Tilly calmed for a few moments and taking the handkerchief Vicky offered mopped up the streams of tears that were still coursing down her cheeks. 'I need to go and try to calm him,' she said softly 'and you need to get back to the post office. I can't be spoiling your whole day.'

'You let me worry about that,' Vicky said, a determined look on her face. 'Ruby is perfectly capable of coming to ask if she needs help. She doesn't always need me fussing around her. But first I have something I want to say to you.'

Tilly looked up at Vicky, her eyes full of sadness.

'You want us to go, don't you, Eddie and me?' she said. 'I'm very sorry, but I do understand.'

'*No!*' Vicky said firmly. 'That's not what I want. I was going to say that we seem to be stuck in the middle of a very awkward situation right now. Everyone's nerves are jangled and tempers are getting frayed.'

Tilly nodded and gave a wry smile. 'I know mine certainly is,' she said.

'I think we need to take a long hard look at the situation and see if we can come up with something better,' Vicky said. 'We don't want to be rushing into anything but I'm sure there's must be something else that we can do.'

Tilly's head jerked up. 'You've already given me more than I deserve,' she said sheepishly.

'You let me be the judge of that,' Vicky said. 'Let me go away and think about it for a bit and I'll get back to you.' She patted Tilly's hand. 'Now, you go and sort Eddie out and I need to open the post office.

Chapter 25

CLAIRE

It was unusual for the shop telephone to ring. Sylvia had insisted that a business was not a business unless it had a telephone but the smart black Bakelite instrument that sat next to the till on the counter rang so seldom that when Claire heard the bell while her aunt was still out, she panicked, her first thought being that Sylvia might be in trouble.

Claire tried to sound business-like as she answered but she caught her breath when she recognised Daniel's voice at the other end of the line.

'Claire, is that you?' he began. 'I can't speak for long. All I want to know is whether I could see you tonight?'

Claire gasped. 'Tonight? Yes, of course,' she said without hesitation. 'My aunt is out but I can leave her a note. Where are you?' She glanced up at the wall clock. It was almost closing time and she had been on her own for the entire day. She deserved to have a bit of fun and it would be wonderful to see Daniel again. 'I could come and meet you somewhere as soon as I've closed up.' She knew she sounded very eager now. Too eager? She realised she didn't care.

'I've got a few hours off so I thought we might go to the movies,' Daniel said. 'I see that James Stewart film *Mr Smith Goes to Washington* is on right now.' He spoke quickly. 'I might be able to get hold of a vehicle so I could stop by to collect you, say at seven o'clock?'

Claire could feel her heart racing. The residents of Greenhill were close enough to the airbase to have heard that things were hotting up in the neighbourhood of Hill Vale, with planes constantly flying in and out of the base heading south, and she had given up hope of hearing from Daniel again. She was thrilled down to her toes that she was actually going to see him.

'Make sure you're ready,' he said.

'I'll be ready and waiting,' she replied, 'but what—' But he had already hung up.

Daniel's transport was not the staff car he had been hoping to borrow and instead he hauled Claire up into the back of a truck that was already half filled with

188

RAF personnel. His strong arms helped her clamber over the base board as the others made room for her to sit beside them on one of the long wooden benches.

'A few of us have got a couple of hours off tonight,' Daniel explained, 'so, we thought we'd make the most of the available transport. It could prove to be quite handy.'

'Particularly if you can't get into the movie,' someone joked, and Claire felt her cheeks redden as the others sniggered.

'Take no notice, some people have a one-track mind,' Daniel said. He put his arm protectively round her shoulders and it stayed there until the truck dropped them off.

A small queue had formed by the time they reached the cinema and Daniel insisted that they stood in the line for the more expensive seats.

'We may as well do it in style,' he said when she protested. 'We don't know if or when we'll be able to do this again,' and he pulled her to him, planting a light kiss on her forehead.

They sat on the back row and Claire didn't object when Daniel put his arm round her once again as soon as the lights dimmed. She could feel her blood begin to pump wildly when he rubbed his hand gently against her cheek and she hoped he wouldn't notice in the darkness of the auditorium the pinkness that she felt sure was rising from her neck to the roots of her hair.

The Pathé news pictures of the devastation in Europe, and the realisation that Italy had declared war on Britain and France recently, made them both sit up straight and take notice reminding Claire about the vulnerability of her own family in London. But when main feature film began Claire snuggled her face against Daniel's chest in relief.

They remained comfortably locked together like that, Claire only barely aware of the action, until the music indicated that the film was coming to an end. Claire wanted to pinch herself. She couldn't believe she really was with Daniel and that this was actually happening; when Daniel leaned into her face and pressed his lips against hers, she responded immediately. She didn't want to seem too eager, but it was hard to hold back and she couldn't help letting out a contented sigh when they finally pulled apart as the lights came slowly up and the credits rolled. Daniel cupped her chin in the palm of his hand and gave her a peck on each cheek as they stood to attention while the national anthem was played. It took Claire a few moments after the familiar tune ended to come back to earth.

The cinema had been packed and it took some time for the crowd to slowly filter through into the foyer which had been carefully blacked out. 'Are you OK?' Daniel asked.

Claire nodded. 'At least they ran the whole picture

without the sirens going off,' she said as they felt their way out from the back row. 'The last time I went to the cinema I was with Violet, and we only got to see half of the film before the alarms went off and we had to scramble down to the shelters.'

'I missed having chocolates and ice cream in the interval,' Daniel said with a grin. 'I didn't realise how much they were part of any movie outing until I came here and was hit with sugar rationing. But apart from that how did you enjoy it?' Daniel asked. He tilted her face towards him with his finger and brushed his lips across hers once more. He looked so serious that Claire wanted to laugh, and she longed to tell him about the feelings he had stirred.

'I enjoyed it very much, thank you.' she said softly, and she smiled up at him, wondering if she dared to return the light touch of his kiss. But it was then that her heart almost stopped as she saw Violet. She instantly caught her breath and sprang back. Violet, closely followed by Martin Vasicck, was heading in the opposite direction down the second aisle towards the exit that led directly onto the street. Claire stopped abruptly, realising by the stunned look on Violet's face not only that she had seen her but that she was still angry and upset. She felt a lump form in her throat, knowing that tonight could most likely be the death knell for their friendship. Claire suddenly felt overwhelmed and she coughed violently.

'What's up?' Daniel asked, stopping behind her. 'Are you all right?'

'I'll be fine,' Claire said, 'so long as we keep heading for the foyer.' She told him what she had seen.

Daniel shrugged. 'I suppose it's inevitable in a town this size and we weren't exactly trying to hide, were we?' he said. 'We've done nothing to be ashamed of.'

'No, of course not, I know that.' Claire said, but she knew she wouldn't be able to explain to Daniel the complexity of her feelings about the situation, or the knot in her stomach that had lodged itself there.

Chapter 26

CLAIRE

It was more difficult than the last time for Claire to say goodbye to Daniel after he had walked her back home and she stood with him for a moment in the rapidly descending twilight outside the shop, not far from where he would wait for the truck to pick him up. Each time they parted she feared it might be the last.

'Let's try and look on the bright side,' Daniel said. 'Tonight was a bonus and there could well be others. It's hard to know which way this wretched war is going.'

Claire was aware that he was behind her when she

let herself in through the back door. He stepped inside as she checked that the blackout curtains were in place before she switched on the light.

'There's no need to wait about in here any longer, I'll be fine now, thanks,' she assured him as he hovered uncertainly by the door. 'I'm sure my aunt must be home by now, so you needn't hang around. I'd hate you to miss your ride back to base. Thanks again for a lovely evening,' she added with a shy smile.

Daniel put his hands on her shoulders and, pulling her close, kissed her long and hard. Her knees began to shake before he pulled away, then with a final wave he slipped outside into the twilight. She turned the light off and watched as he disappeared into the growing darkness then she stood in the silent room and shivered. She glanced up at the clock, then realised that Sylvia was still not home as she also noticed the empty peg in the hallway where her aunt normally hung her coat. Claire suddenly felt very alone. *This war business is doing strange things to people, including me!*

Worrying about Sylvia made her realise how much she missed her friendship with Violet. She had no one of her own age to share any of her excitement about Daniel and no one that she could really talk to concerning her anxiety about her aunt. Sylvia had been acting furtively of late, like today when she had disappeared after breakfast without a word of explanation and had been gone for the whole day. In the past they had shared confidences but recently Sylvia seemed not to be paying attention to anything Claire said. Claire had done her best to encourage her aunt to talk, but when she had asked Sylvia if things were all right, Sylvia had switched on a smile and insisted that everything was fine. Yes, Claire decided, it would be good to be able to share her concerns with Violet and to come clean about Daniel. It was time to end the stupid feud between them and she made up her mind that the next day, once the shop was closed, she would take the initiative and break the deadlock between them; she would go down to the house and call on Violet herself.

She was so deeply engrossed in her thoughts that when she heard the bell ring on the kitchen door she imagined for one moment that it was Violet beating her to it and coming to make peace. Then she thought it must be Sylvia who had forgotten her keys and she remembered to turn off the tell-tale light before she opened the door a crack. She was so shocked to see two uniformed police officers that she didn't immediately register who they were. Then she felt a chill run down her spine as she automatically glanced up again at the clock. Sylvia had never been out this late before; something must be wrong. But she forced a broad smile.

'Yes? How can I help you?' Claire asked, her voice quavering as her shop training came to the fore. Even before they replied she was aware of her stomach lurching like it used to do in her school days when she had been forced to tumble over a wooden vaulting horse, or complete a mid-air somersault while precariously hanging onto a climbing rope. 'Does a Miss Claire Gold reside here?' the older of the two officers asked, his voice sounding unnaturally deep pitched as he peered down at his notebook.

Claire caught her breath, doing her best to continue to smile.

'Yes, that's me,' she said, 'I'm Claire Gold. But, what . . .?' She looked at him directly then instinctively glanced towards the stairs as fear clutched at her chest.

'Can we come in? Is there somewhere private where it might be possible for us to p'raps sit down and have a word?' the younger officer intervened.

Claire felt as if she had stopped breathing, but she opened the door wider and put the lights on again once the two officers were safely inside. Her knees were about to give way and she sat down at the kitchen table, indicating they should join her. She tried her best to keep her voice steady as she asked again how she could help them. The older officer withdrew his notepad and pencil from his jacket pocket.

'Are you on your own, Miss Gold?' he asked.

Now Claire's eyebrows shot up in alarm. 'Yes, I imagine I am. For the time being. I live with my aunt, she's been out and I don't think she's back yet. Has something happened?' She felt like a rabbit trapped in the headlights of a car. 'I'm expecting her back at any moment as it happens. It's her shop. I only help her out. I have done ever since I came to live with her last year. I come from London, you know, where some terrible things have been happening. My parents thought I'd be safer here . . .' She felt she had to keep talking, the words gushing out as if to prevent the policeman from saying something in between that she sensed she didn't want to hear. 'Tell me what's wrong. Something must have happened. Please, you must tell me,' Claire begged.

'You came to live here from London?' the policeman asked. 'May I ask where in London you came from?'

Claire was taken aback by the question, and lost focus for a moment as she stared past the policeman without really seeing him. 'Where?' she repeated, not fully processing the question. 'What is this about? Why are you here?'

The younger policeman was flicking through his notepad, refusing to look at Claire, but the older one leaned forward. Suddenly, his face seemed to disappear into a mist and Claire was unable to focus as she heard him say, 'I'm afraid there's been a terrible accident in North London.'

Claire gasped and continued to stare. 'Where in North London?' she asked. 'It's a big place.'

The younger officer looked down at his notepad. 'In

a place called Cricklewood,' he said. Claire gasped again and the room began to spin. She caught the words 'gas leak', 'cigarettes' and 'explosion' before she closed her eyes, and she thought she recognised the words 'casualties' and 'Mr and Mrs Gold', but the next thing she knew she was sitting on the floor sipping cold water from a cup and the older policeman was bending over her.

'We really are most terribly sorry that we have to bring you such shocking news,' the officer said as he helped Claire back onto the chair. 'Is there anyone here in Greenhill that we can contact to come and be with you until your aunt gets back?'

Claire thought she heard the sound of a key in the kitchen door but she felt too disorientated to be sure, and it was only when she thought she recognised the voice that said, 'Claire! Claire love! What's going on?' It was her aunt who was now speaking directly to the officers. 'What are you doing here?' she asked.

'And you are?' The younger one had his notebook and pen poised.

'I'm Sylvia Barker, Miss Gold's aunt. I own this shop and this house,' she said, 'What on earth is going on?'

Sylvia came to stand behind her. When she felt the touch of her aunt's hands on her shoulders, Claire covered them with her own and gazed ahead of her not knowing what to do, but feeling suddenly less alone.

'*Now!*' Sylvia said firmly, looking at each of the two officers in turn. 'Perhaps you could tell us again exactly what has happened . . .' Sylvia slipped into a seat at the table and grasping hold of Claire's hands, gently pulled her niece down beside her, holding on tightly as the policeman told the story once more of the gas explosion tragedy that had unfolded in North London earlier that afternoon, that would change Claire's life forever.

Chapter 27

RUBY

Ruby knocked rather nervously on the front door of the vicar's house, which stood next to the church. She knew that she wasn't the person he would be expecting and wondered if she was doing the right thing. It should have been Claire coming to visit Geoffrey today but Ruby had offered to take her place when the news about Claire's tragic loss and her immediate departure to London with her aunt had spread as far as the post office.

Ruby had never been to the house before and she gazed up at the wisteria that cascaded down the walls and tumbled into the shrubs as if each of the separate branches were competing in a race to smother the window frames. She would have liked to peer inside but the interior was too dark to see anything useful and she would feel foolish if she were caught. Ruby thought she heard Pepe barking briefly in response to her rap, somewhere deep within the house, but after a moment all went quiet again. Nothing stirred inside or out and she wondered if she should knock again. She was preparing to turn tail and limp back up the path when the door opened and she was surprised to see the vicar himself standing in the entrance. Ruby was overcome with shyness and she stood on the path that was smothered in moss and unidentifiable leaves blushing profusely.

'My name is . . .' she began.

'Ruby Bowdon, if I'm not mistaken,' the vicar said with a smile, and Ruby felt a blush rise on her cheeks.

'I saw you at the wedding recently though I remember you from Sunday school,' Reverend Laycock said. 'Do come in and tell me what I can do for you.' He held the door open for her to enter before leading the way inside the darkly wallpapered hallway and into the more cheerfully lit kitchen where a jolly-looking woman was busy drying dishes and setting them out on a tray. He introduced her as Mrs James the housekeeper.

'I . . . I hope I'm not intruding . . .' Ruby said.

'Not at all, my dear,' the vicar responded.

'I've actually come to see Geoff. I can't tell you how sorry I was to hear . . .' Ruby started to say although she realised as she spoke that she didn't know the full extent of Geoff's injuries and she felt her cheeks burn. 'I thought he might like some company,' she said, doing her best to sound cheerful.

The rather sad smile the vicar had been attempting crumpled almost as suddenly as it appeared and it was all Ruby could do not leave immediately. She stood twisting her fingers awkwardly.

'Claire Gold was originally down to come to visit . . . but . . .' Ruby said and Reverend Laycock nodded. 'Ah, yes,' he said, 'I did hear that she has been caught up in a terrible tragedy of her own.'

'She and her aunt have had to go back to London.' Ruby gave a self-conscious smile, relieved that she didn't have to provide any further details.

The vicar flashed a fleeting smile in return.

'It really is very kind of you to take her place,' he said solemnly, looking so sad for a moment that Ruby had to put her hand to her mouth to stop her lips quivering.

'I wasn't sure if Geoff was up to having visitors?' she said. 'Or whether I'd be in the way.'

'You're not in the way at all, my dear,' the vicar said. 'It's extremely kind of you to call.' He smiled at Ruby again. 'In these troubled times we all have to help each other,' he said. You can certainly come in and talk to

Geoffrey but the truth is that he won't actually be seeing anyone for a while. I don't know if you've been told the extent of the damage from the accident that he was involved in at the training camp, but for the time being at least, Geoffrey has gone blind.'

Ruby gasped, tears immediately filling her own eyes and she had to look away. She noticed Mrs James did the same.

'Oh . . . my . . . my . . . g–goodness! I hadn't realised it was that serious,' Ruby stammered. 'How did it happen?'

'I don't know if we'll ever know the full truth as to what happened, but his commanding officer wrote to me and explained that some live ammunition detonated in close proximity,' the vicar said. 'The army are just treating it as an accident, but the result was . . . well . . . why don't you come and see for yourself? After all, isn't that why you've come?'

Ruby followed him into the back sitting room that led off the long corridor from the hallway and was immediately struck by the darkness of the furniture and the fresh smell of lavender polish. The room itself was only in half light as the curtains had been drawn partway across the leaded windows and he indicated that she should sit in one of the two overstuffed leather armchairs that stood on either side of the empty fireplace. Ruby shivered. It might be summertime but there was still a decided chill in the room. There was enough light however for Ruby to be able to make out the figure of a young man reclining on a well-worn couch and he had been covered with a brightly coloured throw. To her relief she couldn't see much of him as his eyes and the top half of his head were covered by a thick wrapping of bandage that looked as though it had been freshly bound.

'Geoffrey!' the vicar said rather more loudly than was necessary. 'Are you awake?'

'Mm.' There was a deep throated rumble by way of a response as the figure stirred and Ruby could see his head tilt slightly in the direction of the sound.

'I've got Ruby here with me. You remember Ruby Bowdon from the greengrocer's shop?'

'I might be blind, Dad, but I've not lost my marbles,' Geoff said sarcastically and Ruby saw the vicar wince.

'I was very sorry to hear about your accident,' Ruby said quickly, speaking directly to Geoffrey.

'Amazing how bad news spreads like wildfire in a town the size of Greenhill,' Geoffrey said crustily.

'That's true,' Ruby said, trying not to be intimidated by the gruffness of his manner. 'I remember when I was in hospital after I got polio, I couldn't believe how quickly everyone knew. But I do remember feeling bored and that was why I wondered if you might like some company?' she said.

Geoff didn't reply immediately.

'But I can go if you'd rather. I won't be one bit

offended if you can't be mithered,' Ruby said, and she turned as if ready to leave.'

'No, please don't rush off.' It was the vicar who responded. 'Let me at least offer you a cup of coffee. You could see that Mrs James was already preparing it though I'm afraid it's only that Camp coffee essence; but I'm sure she can rustle up the odd cube of sugar or a biscuit or something to disguise the taste. We might not have much to offer but the cupboard's not completely bare.'

'No, thanks, you don't have to worry about me, I'm fine,' Ruby said, though she did sit down.

'What about you, Geoffrey?' the vicar said. 'Mrs James is always happy to oblige. Do you fancy another cuppa?' He turned to Ruby, palms spread, 'I do my best though I'm not a match for Mrs James, when it comes to refreshments, I'm afraid. I'm always amazed at what you women can make out of the most meagre of ingredients. I'll leave you both to it.'

As the vicar left, Geoffrey shifted his position slightly on the couch and the large black and white collie dog that had been lying on the floor beside the couch stirred. He uncurled his body and stretched out on the rug making an appreciative noise in his throat before trotting across to sniff happily around Ruby.

'Hello, boy!' She cupped his head in her hands. 'You remember me, do you?' She patted his head and entwined her fingers in the animal's wiry fur, smoothing the white patches on his nose and head that were illuminated as they caught an odd ray of direct sunlight.

'Is he bothering you?' Geoff sounded anxious.

'Not at all, he's just come to say hello, haven't you Pepe?' and Ruby gazed into the dog's large soulful eyes.

'I take it he's not an official guide dog?' she said. 'Though maybe he could be trained?'

'He's not an official anything,' Geoff said. 'He's just Pepe, but I bet he could be as good as any guide dog given half the chance.' Geoff reached out to where the dog had been lying and Pepe trotted back towards his master's outstretched hand. Geoff smoothed the rough fur on the dog's back and Pepe promptly rolled over, his feet in the air. He barked with obvious delight as Geoff tickled his tummy, his bright pink tongue flicking out occasionally to lick Geoff's hand. Then without warning he jumped onto the couch and he gave a series of loud barks before nuzzling his nose underneath the throw and resting his head on Geoff's chest.

Ruby laughed. 'He certainly knows where to go for his cuddles,' she said, and she went over to try to catch hold of Pepe's thudding tail that was beating time like an overworked metronome.

'Do you want a drink, Pepe?' Geoff asked. 'I bet if you ask Ruby nicely she'll go with you to the kitchen to get one.' At the sound of Geoff's voice Pepe rolled onto the floor, then he stood up and shook his whole body like he was emerging from a bath. He stretched out his front paws and arched his back before trotting silently alongside Ruby to the kitchen.

'My goodness, he was thirsty,' Ruby said when she returned. 'And Mrs James has made you some coffee. I'll put it down on the side table, shall I?'

Geoff grunted but made no move to retrieve it and Ruby wondered if she should offer to put it directly into his hands. But she remembered how she had not wanted to be treated like a chronic invalid when she had first come home from hospital, and she did nothing. She merely watched as Pepe instinctively took up his position by the couch once more and let Geoff's hand rest lightly on his head.

The room was silent for several minutes until Ruby said, 'I shall have to go shortly, I have to get back to work.' And she wanted to believe that a look of disappointment crossed Geoff's face. 'But I can come again, if you'd like me to,' she added. 'Maybe when you're ready to go out we can let Pepe take us for a walk,' and that time she was definitely rewarded by a grin. Pepe also responded to the sound of his name and nuzzled up to Ruby once more with obvious approval. Ruby took his face in her hands and stroked his cheeks with her thumbs. 'Why don't you see if you can persuade Geoff to get out of bed the next time I come to visit so that the three of us can go out, eh?' She spoke directly to the dog this time and Pepe lifted one of his front paws and patted her leg.

Chapter 28

VIOLET

Violet couldn't believe she was holding a blue air letter in her hand once more as she was walking home. It was the school holidays in August now and she was rejoicing in the fact of not having to go to work. She hadn't heard from Daniel since he had sent her the scrap of paper warning that he was too busy to see her. And then there had been the night she had seen him at the Greenhill cinema together with Claire. She wondered what could be in the letter that Ruby had just given to her in the post office and, for a moment, it felt like old times. The difference was that she didn't recognise the handwriting and when she turned it over, she was surprised at first to see the sender was called Gabinsky. But it had been posted in Toronto, Canada, not sent from an airbase in England and the initial of the sender was L and not D. Violet shuddered, overcome by a sudden ominous fear. She still had some feelings for Danny and for once she didn't wait until she got home but she tore the flaps open without delay.

Dear Violet, she read, *my mother asked me to write to you as we know you have been writing to Danny for many years. Mum thought you might appreciate having some information about Danny's whereabouts although I'm afraid there's not much to tell and what there is, isn't very promising.*

Violet's hand froze and she felt the flimsy blue paper scrunch in the tightness of her grip as she turned it over to see who had written it. The last line ended with the single word *sincerely* and it had been signed by *Louis Gabinsky* followed in brackets by *(Danny's younger brother).* The words in between began to swim as her vision blurred and she had to blink hard before she could go any further.

It seemed that Daniel had indeed been busy, involved in what was being dubbed as the Battle of Britain. The Royal Air Force, with help from many overseas pilots like Daniel, had been bravely defending the skies of Britain, mainly in the south, from German attempts to invade the country and bring it to its knees. It seemed that the whole country had been mobilised, even in

Greenhill there was no escaping the terrible moment that they were facing.

The family had been informed that Daniel's plane had been shot down. Violet gasped when she read that, dreading what might be coming next. The words *No survivors found* looked shockingly stark on the page and Violet drew in her breath sharply. It was several moments before she could go on but she caught the phrase *missing in action* and she was forced to stop walking and find a piece of low wall where she could sit down.

The powers that be tell us that there is always the possibility that he might have escaped to safety or been taken prisoner but so far there's been no evidence. The following few lines were so badly creased that they seemed to have disintegrated into unreadable scribble then it went on, *Danny was always the linchpin of our family, and none of us can believe it. We thought you should know.* It was signed *Louis*.

Violet sat on the wall for some time. *Missing in action* didn't seem completely final and gave a glimmer of hope. But *no survivors found* sounded pretty definite and sent shivers down Violet's spine. She felt as if the fates had been against them all along, and that they never had been destined to be together but what she regretted most of all was that she would now never have the chance of getting to know Daniel properly in person. She thought of the only time she had spent time with him and the dreadful way the day had ended, the bad feeling that had been sparked between her and Claire, leaving her hating Claire for stealing her boyfriend and not seeing each other for months. All that bickering seemed foolish and petty now, and she even wondered whether he had ever truly been her boyfriend. She had never had the chance to find out exactly what Daniel thought. But all that seemed irrelevant now. It was sad but as she tried to conjure up a picture of his face she had to accept that she would never be able to get to know him now.

Violet had no idea how long she sat on the wall but she was becoming aware that the cold of the bricks was beginning to strike through her thin skirt and she thought she had better go home. She realised that she hadn't moved far from the post office and was almost sitting outside of the haberdashers and she wondered if she should call into the shop and patch up her quarrel with Claire right now. She doubted that Claire would have heard the awful news about Daniel and although it seemed like a dreadful circumstance in which to offer an olive branch, it was surely better than making no attempt at an offering at all. Violet thought with shame now of the futile anger she had been harbouring against Claire and the more she thought about it the more it seemed like wasted energy; hatred was such a useless emotion. It was sad that it had taken such an awful happening to finally make her see sense and she hoped that it would at least be able to bring them back together and that Claire would be able to see sense, too. Violet stood up and looked behind her at the frontage of Knit and Sew, wondering if she might catch a glimpse of Claire and wave to her through the window. But it seemed like it was too late. Surprisingly the shop seemed to be in darkness with its blinds already drawn. There did seem to be a note pinned to the door but it was too dark for Violet to read it properly, something about the family going away. She would have to leave their reconciliation for another day.

When Violet woke up, she lay in bed for several minutes clutching the blanket to her chest and then started a fit of coughing that made her sit up sharply, feeling as if it was never going to stop. All she could think about was Daniel and that made her want to cry. She was glad it was the holidays and that she didn't have to get up for school for she wasn't sure that she could get out of bed. When she did eventually emerge in response to her mother's call for breakfast, she slumped down on the couch without even acknowledging Eileen's shocked look of concern. Violet sat there for several minutes and then started coughing again, this time not holding back when tears streamed down her face.

'What's up with you, then?' Mrs Pegg asked as Violet continued to cough.

Violet didn't look directly at her. 'I've not been feeling

great for the last day or so,' she managed to say eventually.

Mrs Pegg's eyebrows were raised. 'You didn't say anything?'

'I didn't want you to worry.' The coughing stopped and Violet did her best to take in deep if still wheezy-sounding breaths.

'I must say you don't look too clever,' her mother added, unnecessarily.

'Thanks very much!' Violet said with heavy sarcasm. 'I might be coming down with something.'

'There's been a lot of flu going around.' Eileen said. She put her hand to Violet's forehead. 'You do feel hot. You might need some M&B mixture and some aspirin to bring your temperature down.'

'I've also had a bit of a shock,' Violet said, and she told her mother about Louis Gabinsky's letter.

'Oh, my goodness!' Mrs Pegg was distraught. 'And here was me thinking maybe you were feeling off it because of the upsetting news about Claire and her family.'

Violet's eyes suddenly opened wide. 'What do you mean? What news?' she demanded and she told her mother about going to the shop. 'There was a closed sign on the door but I couldn't read it,' she said.

'No doubt it would have said something about Claire and her aunt closing the shop to go off to London,' Mrs Pegg said, warming to the theme. 'At first I thought it was a rumour but after a while I found out it was true.' Eileen explained what she had heard about the explosion in London, of someone smoking when there had been reports of a gas leak and several houses being damaged by an almighty blast that had rocked the whole street.

'Why didn't you tell me about this before now? Was anyone hurt?' Violet asked, not wanting to hear the answer.

Violet could see her mother's lip going and Eileen's voice broke as she said with a theatrical sob, 'Don't go on, I didn't think you wanted to know, you've been very funny every time her name is mentioned, going off in a huff usually. Oh, it's so awful, Vi. Both of Claire's parents were killed,'

Violet's hand flew to her mouth as she tried to cover her horrified expression and she groaned, '*Oh, no!* Poor Claire,' but she could feel her own tears already spilling down her cheeks as she continued to stare at her mother.

'Thankfully, her aunt was with Claire when she got the news, and they both went off on a train to London right away to sort out whatever needs to be done,' Eileen said. 'Apparently, Jewish people don't waste time with their funerals; the burials needed to be dealt with quickly and then they have a week's mourning period afterwards.'

Eileen reached out and put her hand on Violet's arm and they sat in silence for several minutes. Then Mrs Pegg stood up abruptly.

'Well, this isn't going to help anybody, least of all you,' she said. 'Why don't you get on upstairs and back to bed and I'll bring you a hot drink? No point putting out good food, it'll only go to waste if you're not up to eating it.'

Violet nodded and got up slowly from the couch. 'It seems like there's no end to the kinds of tragedy that war can bring.'

'I know, I was thinking about the vicar's son,' Eileen said. 'That was bad enough, but now this . . .' She spread her hands palms up in frustration.

'The only good news around here is about Vicky's sister-in-law and nephew turning up out of the blue, so that old Mr Parrott now has a grandson,' Violet said, 'though I'm sure that must be another story. You know how he always doted on his wonderful son Henry.

Violet turned to trudge back up the stairs, her thoughts now not only full of sadness for Daniel but for Claire, too, although there wasn't much she could do to help either of them at this moment. It wasn't cold but she couldn't help shivering as she got undressed and climbed into bed as quickly as she could, only wishing she had acted sooner to make things up with her friend.

Chapter 29

SYLVIA

Sylvia had served the last customer of the day at Knit and Sew and she was more than ready to close up. It had been an unusually busy day but at least she hadn't been interrupted by endless air raid sirens announcing enemy planes approaching like she had during her stay in London. There she had felt as if they were constantly dashing to the nearest Anderson shelter or disappearing down someone's cellar steps while the bomber planes droned overhead. It had been a huge shock, just how fiercely the Germans were trying to destroy the country she loved. She had been relieved to come home even after a few days and wondered how she had ever lived in such a place as London. She knew that she wouldn't rest easily until Claire was back as well. The frequency of the bombing raids both at night and during the day had increased while she was there and the Londoners she spoke to had started to refer to it as the Blitz . There had been no let up so that she had never felt safe and she encouraged Claire whenever they spoke on the telephone to come back as soon as she could.

Sylvia had not been close to Hannah for many years, but she was her sister and Sylvia respected her memory. Thankfully, Hannah and her husband had several extremely close friends as well as distant cousins who instantly rallied round so that Sylvia was confident that even after she returned to Greenhill, her niece wouldn't be left on her own.

Now that the shop was finally empty Sylvia put up the closed sign. She was pleased to have some time alone so that she could sort out the stock that she kept behind the scenes and make up an order for replacement sewing cottons. She had gone to London with Claire on the train from Manchester's London Road station almost as soon as the police had informed them of the dreadful news and on Sylvia's insistence the shop had been shut up completely for several days so that she could be there to support her niece through the horrors of a joint funeral. Sylvia would have liked to have stayed after the ritual *shiva*, the seven days of Jewish mourning, had been observed but she had been persuaded to return home to re-open the shop, Claire insisting that she was well enough to be left in London for a short time at least in order to consider her future and arrange her parents' affairs.

Sylvia hadn't quite appreciated how much she relied on her niece. She was surprised how many other people in the village seemed to miss her, too, and she was touched by the number of customers who had dropped in to offer their condolences to Claire on the horrific and premature death of her parents. As the Golds' house in Cricklewood had been all but destroyed, Claire and Sylvia were grateful for the offers of hospitality from close friends and distant family members who also provided a venue for them to sit *shiva*. Many of the Greenhill residents wanted to know about the London bombings, too. They were all as shocked as she was to hear about what was happening and worried about the bombers heading north.

'You will let me know what else I can do for you,' Sylvia had said as she bade Claire a tearful farewell at Euston station. 'And you must come back very soon. I don't like the way this war is hotting up. That was why your mother wanted you to come to live with me in the first place and sadly she was right.' She'd hugged Claire closely. 'For as long as I'm there I want you to know that there'll always be a home for you in Greenhill.'

On her return Sylvia busied herself in the shop more

than she ever had before and she welcomed her days being filled even by the most routine of tasks. Not surprisingly, the tragedy in London had overshadowed everything else so that it was taking even longer than she might have expected for Sylvia to take on board the full impact of her visit to Derbyshire, which now seemed like a long time ago. She was finding it difficult to think calmly about the potential consequences of Archie's actions and whenever she was able to think about him, she still wasn't sure she actually believed what he'd done to her and their marriage.

She had been trying to remember when Archie's lies had started. They had begun when he had pretended to be renting digs in Matlock on the odd occasion when he had worked late and claimed to be too tired to come home. It had occasionally crossed her mind that there might be someone in Derbyshire that he was spending those evenings with, but she had quickly dismissed the idea and had never taken the thought of another woman too seriously. She had certainly never imagined him becoming so deeply involved with someone outside of his marriage to the extent that he would go as far as breaking the law. The idea of him going through a sham marriage ceremony with another woman, and forcing her to unwittingly commit an offense was beyond all she had come to expect from Archie. The nerve of the man!

He obviously had no regard whatever for anyone

else's feelings. Sylvia realised that she actually felt sorry for Leanne. Although her first reaction had been to consider reporting the bigamous marriage immediately to the police, as she had threatened, she had begun to wonder why, when the people it would hurt most would be the poor innocent children, victims of their father's wantonness. She pictured their forlorn faces as they'd scrambled upstairs at their mother's command. What would happen to them when the authorities found out?

Sylvia was still unsure about what she should do next for much as she hated to admit it, she had been duped as well as Leanne and while Archie was gaily living a double life he was damaging not only their marriage but the status the family enjoyed within the Greenhill community as well.

Sylvia was so wrapped up in her thoughts, that when the shop bell rang she was surprised, for she had already drawn the blinds to indicate she was about to close. But she automatically sprang into action coming through from the back and slipping in behind the counter ready to serve.

'Can I help . . . she started to say, but she didn't complete the question for when she looked up she realised that the solitary customer facing her was Leanne. Sylvia stiffened, not knowing how to react, and she grasped hold of the edge of the countertop to steady herself.

Leanne marched up to the counter and stared at her

openly. 'Glad to see I've got the right place then,' she said. 'It's a good job there's only one haberdashery shop in Greenhill.'

'Yes, you've got the right place,' Sylvia said stiffly. 'I take it you were looking for me?'

'Is there anywhere we can talk?' Leanne asked, briskly.

Sylvia checked the time, then she crossed the floor to flip the sign, slide the latch on the door and turn the key in the lock. 'You'd better come with me,' she said and she led the way through to the living quarters.

'I . . . I was wondering what you'd done about . . . Have you been to the . . .?' Now it was Leanne who looked awkward and sounded unsure. She had sat down stiffly on one of the upright kitchen chairs and Sylvia made no move to relieve her discomfort. 'I've had another cheque since . . .' Leanne tried again. 'Since I saw you last and I wasn't sure what you wanted . . .'

'No, neither was I at the time,' Sylvia said, looking down at her hands in her lap, 'though I've had time to think about things since then.'

'It was just that you said—'

'I know what I said,' Sylvia interrupted. 'And I hope that you realise that if I had told the authorities you would already be facing not only a huge fine but you'd probably be in prison by now.'

Leanne gave a heaving sob. Her shoulders shook and tears began to flow freely.

'I've been thinking about your two little kiddies, that's what,' Sylvia said. 'That's why I haven't taken any action yet, because they're the innocents in all this and yet they're the ones who are going to get hurt. You're going to have to do something to protect them.'

Leanne looked at her in surprise. She stopped crying as suddenly as she'd started. 'What can I do?' she said, frowning.

'I don't suppose you've got any other income coming in, so you could try to get a job for a start, because you won't be able to rely solely on my husband's money for much longer.'

Leanne shook her head as she blotted the tears with a scruffy handkerchief. 'No, of course I've no other income. I've got two kids!' she said sharply. Then her voice softened as she said, 'I used to work in the cotton mills but since we were wed, I've only ever had what Archie gave me when he was still working, and since then . . . well, you know.'

Sylvia gave an exasperated sigh as she thought back to the arguments she and Archie had had about money, and about the number of times he'd taken cash from the shop without so much as a 'by your leave' and never even thought to replace it. What would she have said then if she had realised he was using her hard-earned shop money to support a second family?

'The longer you stick around Archie the more likely you are to end up in jail,' Sylvia said. 'Your best bet would be to get well away from where you are living now. Go and rent a room, start again somewhere new completely, though I know that's easier said than done.'

Leanne looked startled. 'But where would I go?' There was a catch in her voice now.

'Well, I can't be worrying about that, I'm afraid,' Sylvia said crossly. 'It's really Archie you should be asking about that. He got us both into this mess so he should be the one to find a way out of it. He needs to take some responsibility, as it's all down to him at the end of the day.' Sylvia sighed. 'Sadly we both know he is hardly in a position to do anything right now. But I'm just warning you, that's all, that you will need to get away from him somehow if you value your kids and want to save them from shame for the rest of their lives.'

Leanne seemed to sink lower into the chair, her face clouding over as tears threatened once more.

'Do you have any friends or family that could help?' Sylvia asked more gently. 'Anyone to leave the children with if you could get a job?'

'The elderly lady next door. She looks out for them if I'm not there when they come home from school.' Leanne shrugged her shoulders. 'But I don't know where we could move to.'

'Anywhere to make a clean break, would be my suggestion,' Sylvia said, 'so that you can forget about Archie.'

Leanne looked at her in horror. 'I can't just walk out on him . . .' she protested. She seemed to wake up to what Sylvia was saying. 'I still love him.' She lowered her voice and then she burst into tears.

Sylvia looked shocked. 'But you've been living a lie. He's been totally dishonest!' she countered. 'And what's more, he's knowingly dragged you into breaking the law.' Sylvia broke off in frustration. She could tell from Leanne's face that she was getting nowhere. 'Yes, I can see that he can still be quite the charmer, can't he?' Sylvia said with heavy sarcasm. 'And I'll admit, I thought I loved him once. But do you see this . . .?' Sylvia leaned towards Leanne and scraped her hair back from the side of her face to reveal a nasty-looking scar.

Leanne gasped and her hand flew to her mouth but then she sneered. 'Are you going to pretend Archie did that?' She turned away, refusing to look.

'I'm saying you're lucky that you don't have one to match . . . yet,' Sylvia said quietly.

'Now you're just being nasty,' Leanne said, 'because he's been more dishonest with you than he has ever been with me and you're trying to get your own back. You said last time that you wouldn't divorce him, so you're obviously determined to hang onto him out of spite. But you don't fool me. You still love him. That's the real problem. And that's why you won't let him go.' Leanne's voice ended on a triumphant note as if she had caught Sylvia in a lie.

Sylvia stared at her. 'Oh, I meant what I said about not giving him a divorce,' she said, gravely. 'And it's not because I still love him, I can assure you of that. It's because I don't intend to let him make a fool of me and to ruin my life entirely. You may not care about it because it will mean little to you, but we have our own place within the community here,' Sylvia said. 'The Barker family have good standing in this town and I'm not about to let Archie Barker spoil that. I've worked hard to get where I am, and I intend to hang onto my position.'

She folded her arms firmly across her chest, her face determined. 'And there's another thing,' she said. 'I want him to know what it's like to be afraid of someone, not knowing when they might turn on him. He's broken the law and I have no intention of making life easy for him, not after the way he's treated us. Hanging onto something that gives me a hold over him for the rest of his life is the very least I can do for me and my daughter, Rosie.'

Sylvia leaned forward, looking directly into Leanne's eyes. 'I can assure you that I do not intend to be pitied or looked down on as some poor discarded divorcee who couldn't hang onto her husband. Nor will I have my daughter branded with the stigma of coming from a broken home. I'm sorry for you, cos I realise that your children will probably always have some kind of stigma attached to them, but that, I'm afraid, is something for Archie to have on his conscience, not me.'

Sylvia gained a certain satisfaction from saying those words; each time she said them it reminded her that for once in her life she had the upper hand, knowing that she could continue to hold over Archie the threat of breaking her silence if he ever came after her or tried to steal from her again. Sylvia had already questioned whether she was prepared to live with a man who had betrayed her and hurt her so deeply, and she'd queried the wisdom of locking herself forever into a loveless marriage in order to salvage what was left of her pride but, whichever way she considered it, it seemed the lesser of the evils.

What she hadn't settled on however, was what she would say to Archie when she was finally ready to tell him that his dirty little secret had been revealed.

After a long silence, Sylvia decided it was time to speak out. She looked directly at Leanne and said, 'I want you to know I've given a lot of thought and consideration to your predicament, to our predicament actually, and there is one thing that I'm prepared to do. I have a suggestion to make.'

That caught Leanne's attention and the two locked their gaze once more.

'What if I don't inform the authorities?' Sylvia said slowly, and she saw a spark of interest in Leanne's eyes. 'Well, not right now, at any rate,' Sylvia said. 'And I won't tell Archie just yet what I know. That way you can then keep on receiving his naval pay for a bit longer at least until Archie comes home or until you can get yourself set up with a job. '

For a moment, Leanne looked as if she was about to argue but then her shoulders dropped with a huge sigh of relief and she mopped up the tears that were still streaking down her cheeks. Sylvia set her lips in a thin determined line. 'I suppose I should say thank you,' Leanne said eventually and sat back, seeming to think better of saying anything further.

Sylvia stood up and opened the door leading into the shop, indicating that the discussion was over. Leanne gave a brief nod but neither woman said anything further. As Sylvia watched Leanne walk slowly down the street, head bowed, towards the stop for the bus back into Manchester she felt a fleeting moment of satisfaction and of power. But she was trembling once Leanne was out of sight and when she felt her legs give way, she clung to the door for support. She locked the shop door quickly and adjusted the blind before she went back into the living quarters where she sat down heavily on the couch and with her head in her hands, began to sob.

Chapter 30

CLAIRE

Claire sat in the empty compartment, numb. There was pandemonium at Euston station and she only hoped the train would be able to pull out soon. Ever since the Germans had invaded the Channel Isles and occupied Guernsey over the summer, people were concerned about how far Hitler might come and what might happen next.

The Phoney War was well and truly over. Bombing raids were increasing, in daylight hours as well as at night and people were in despair, wondering if the droning of the planes was ever going to stop. More and more people in the capital were trying to evacuate the city, though luckily many children had been evacuated when war was declared.

It was no wonder Sylvia was anxious for her to leave London as soon as possible. Claire had been lucky to find a train that was going directly through to Manchester without having to change at Crewe and she considered herself fortunate to get a seat. Once she had tipped the porter who had hoisted her luggage onto the overhead rack and departed, she pulled together the doors of the compartment and rolled down the blinds. She sat back thankfully and closed her eyes. Her thoughts were spinning and, each time she cautiously opened her eyes and stared ahead for a moment or two, she felt as if the whole carriage was rotating. Quickly, she would drop her eyelids again, her thoughts tumbling about as she wondered if there would ever be a time when she would be able to think of her family without crying.

Suddenly, she was jolted out of her misery by a child's shrill cry – 'Mummy, Mummy, there's plenty of room in here!' – and the doors slid open as the compartment was invaded by a boisterous family of four. By the time they had settled and the children had stopped jumping about, Claire realised that the piercing whistle she had just heard had set the whole train in motion and it was actually making its way out of the station. As she peered out of the murky window, she could see that the carriages were curving around the first bend in the tracks and the train was ploughing its way through the billowing steam and smoke that had enveloped the farthest end of the platform.

'We're moving!' 'Let me see!' 'No, I want to sit by the window, it's not fair!' The children's cries didn't let up for a moment as the train slowly pulled out of the station and chugged its way into the grey dullness of the afternoon, but by this time their shrieks and shouts no longer bothered Claire. She barely heard them for she was wrapped up in her own thoughts.

The hooter sounded one more time as the train picked up speed and Claire found it hard to believe that she was leaving behind her old life, and that things would never be the same again. But she had to accept that there was nothing left for her in London, certainly not her future, and she wondered if she would ever feel able to go back there again.

With her parents gone and their home – her home – destroyed, she no longer felt the same ties to the city like she had before and she was grateful for her aunt Sylvia's offer of a permanent home with her and her uncle in Greenhill. She had alerted Sylvia, who had left several days previously, when she would be returning and she wondered how it would feel to be stepping across the threshold of Knit and Sew knowing that that was the place she would now have to call home.

She wished she could say she was looking forward to being reunited with Violet. It would have cheered her to know that she was coming back to pick up their friendship once more, but the sad reality was that Violet didn't want to know her and Claire wondered how she would feel if they should encounter one another again.

Claire hadn't expected to be met at the station so she was thrilled to see Sylvia waving at her from the other side of the ticket barrier. 'I thought it best not to get a platform ticket in case I missed you in the crowds. The guard said the train was very busy,' Sylvia said as they hugged and linked arms as they walked down the station approach.

'That case looks awfully heavy, would you like me to carry it for a bit?' Sylvia offered and Claire laughed. 'I don't think you're any stronger than I am,' she said, 'but honestly, I didn't expect to have anyone meet me,' she said, her eyes misting.

'Well, it wasn't as if I had to shut the shop or anything, this is a good time for you to have travelled.' Sylvia dismissed her thanks. 'Now let's get down to the bus station; we should be in good time for the next Greenhill bus.'

Claire was surprised and delighted that the shop front and their familiar living quarters felt so warm and welcoming, even cosier than she'd remembered, and she was grateful that her aunt had changed nothing while she had been away.

'Oh, but there has been quite a bit of post for you,'

Sylvia said, producing a small tray covered with a pile of letters. 'There have been an awful lot of well-wishers dropping in notes and their good wishes, you know what it's like around here.'

Having heaved her suitcase up the stairs with some difficulty, for Claire was convinced that she had lost a lot of weight and strength, she filled both sides of the wardrobe and drawers with her clothes, wondering which ones would still fit. When she came downstairs again Claire sat down in the kitchen where Sylvia presented her with a warming cup of coffee followed by a plate of chunky vegetable soup that Sylvia admitted to having made specially.

'I didn't think you'd appreciate a heavy meal at this time of night,' she said when Claire, touched by her thoughtfulness couldn't stop thanking her, 'but I knew you were bound to be hungry.' And Claire was. Sylvia's face was wreathed in kindness as she welcomed Claire back and fleetingly the newly orphaned young girl caught a glimpse of her mother's features in Sylvia's fond look. The likeness was more than she had ever noticed before and each time it flashed in front of her eyes her throat tightened; but she was determined not to get maudlin or let it overwhelm her.

'You were right about there being a pile of letters,' Claire said, forcing an almost cheerful tone into her voice. 'I've never had so many all at once before, not even on my birthday. They're mostly from Greenhill folk with a few from old friends in London who didn't manage to come and see us during the week we sat *shiva*.' She hesitated, not sure whether to say anything further, but Sylvia anticipated her query.

'And before you ask, No, there's nothing from Violet,' Sylvia said, 'and I'm afraid she hasn't been one of the visitors since I've come home, either.'

Claire shrugged. 'I had hoped . . . but never mind. There is one more letter left,' she said. 'I've no idea who it's from, but somehow I don't think it's from Violet.' She picked up a large brown envelope that filled the bottom of the tray and inspected it carefully on both sides. 'There! What do you think?' she said, putting it on top of the placemat on the table. 'I've saved the biggest till last so let's hope it's the best as well, even though I don't recognise the writing.' Claire gave a nervous laugh but she quickly slit open the top of the envelope. Inside was a small sheet of paper wrapped around another sealed envelope and on it was written in an unknown hand, *Letter forwarded as promised, I think it is time,* and the flourish of a signature at the bottom that she didn't know said, *Squadron Leader Georges Duval*, and she felt her heart almost missing a beat as she held it in her hand. She squeezed it gently and it felt quite thick as she sat down to cautiously lift the top flap to reveal a letter that looked infinitely longer than a single page.

My dear Claire, the inner letter began and as her

stomach lurched she hastily turned to the last page to confirm that the signature at the bottom said *Daniel*.

Claire had written several times to Daniel as she had promised, and had not been surprised when he had not replied, but she was certainly surprised now for he was the last person she had expected to hear from today.

My dear Claire, Claire read the words again wanting to say them out loud and roll them on her tongue. She was grateful that Sylvia, having peered briefly over her shoulder, had now left her alone and disappeared upstairs. *If you are reading this then I may no longer be with you – or then again, I could be a POW or even more frustratingly 'missing in action'*. Claire gasped and for a moment thought she was going to faint. *No longer with* . . . What did he mean? She wasn't sure that she dared to continue reading. But she had to know . . .

It has occurred to me that as you are not family, next of kin, or yet my wife (!), in the event of anything happening to me you wouldn't officially be informed. So, I have decided to write to you myself in order to inform you or at least lay out the possibilities and I have asked my squadron leader and best buddy Duval to post this letter to you in the event that I don't come back from one of our ops. Claire's palms felt clammy and her hands were shaking so badly that she had to spread the sheets out on the table, not sitting too close to them so that her tears would not splash onto the page and smudge the ink.

If I am not coming back then I ask that you don't mourn for me, I've not had a bad life, but please know that I loved you, albeit briefly. Claire caught her breath and she did feel a few tears plop directly onto the table. *My only regret is not meeting you sooner and not being able to take you back to Canada with me to show you off to all the family.* She paused as she was unable to read the next lines through her tears.

On the other hand, I may be a POW and I'll be back when it's over!

Or I could really be 'missing in action' and I'll find my way home.

Claire wasn't sure whether to take his words seriously for she could hear Daniel's voice on the night they had managed to have a drink in the pub together when he had been determined to spell things out for her.

'If anyone ever tells you one of the pilots is missing in action,' he had said jokingly, 'comforting as it may sound, I'm afraid you mustn't believe them because what they really mean is that the plane has been shot down, lost and it's curtains for the crew.' He had then made the chilling gesture of a throat-cutting action with his hand slicing across his neck though he had laughed as he'd spoken. Claire remembered staring at him in horror. 'I don't find that a bit amusing, Daniel.' She had shivered as she'd admonished him. Daniel had tried to chivvy her out of what he called her uncalled for strop but Claire had refused to let up. 'I really don't know how you can make jokes about such things,' she'd said. 'It's your friends and family you're talking to, and I'm sure they'd be horrified to hear you talk in such a flippant way when it doesn't have to mean that at all.'

Daniel had shrugged. 'But we all talk like that at our base, I'm afraid. I guess it's our way of coping,' he'd said. 'Ask any of the lads in the squadron.'

'Well, if that's your way of dealing with it I would rather you kept your thoughts to yourself, thank you very much,' she'd said. 'It's real people you're talking about who have real feelings for the people they love. It's not just something . . .' She'd had to stop then, her voice choked.

'I'm sorry,' Daniel had said, holding his hands up in a gesture of surrender, 'but I'm afraid that we are dealing with the cold hard realities of life and death and most of us would rather not deal with it.'

Now, Claire wanted to cry as she thought back to that day, for she knew that she would never be able to accept his interpretation of missing in action. She put the letter to her lips and kissed it, then held it to her nose, inhaling deeply, trying to believe that a part of him had been imprinted on the paper. She would never give up hope that one day he would return.

Chapter 31

RUBY

Despite Ruby's optimism it took another couple of visits before Geoff could be persuaded to get up and move about the room but Ruby was delighted on the day she finally found him no longer spread-eagled on the couch.

'I have a surprise for you today,' the vicar said when Ruby arrived and he stood back after pushing open the sitting room door. It was indeed a surprise for not only was Geoff standing by the open French windows letting the breeze gently brush by his face and ruffle the hair that was not bounded by the bandage, but for once the room itself was flooded with fresh air and light even though Geoff couldn't see it, an irony that was not lost on Ruby. Pepe was standing guard by his young master as he always did although he turned his attention to Ruby as soon as she entered the room. He bounded over to her, then jumped up at her and Geoff alternately, swishing his tail back and forth with excitement and uttering a deep-throated gurgle by way of a welcome. He looked almost as if he might try to fly out of the window like Peter Pan's Nana and Ruby was glad to see that his leash had been fastened to the collar at his neck while the other end was looped securely around Geoff's hand.

'Pepe seems to think that we're going out for a walk,' Geoff said. 'He brought me his lead first thing this morning. It's a miracle he's not tried to drag me off anywhere yet, he was obviously waiting for you.' Geoff turned in Ruby's direction and she was delighted to see he had a smile on his face. 'What do you think to that, Ruby?' he asked. 'I thought it might be a good idea for us to go out as it's not raining. It doesn't seem fair to Pepe to keep him cooped up so much of the time and there's only so much Dad can do. Do you fancy a walk today?'

'I think that sounds like a great idea, Pepe knows what's good for all of us,' Ruby said, ruffling the dog's long fur. 'Vicky won't be expecting me back for at least half an hour, and I doubt any of us will last much longer than that.'

'The garden's not that big,' Geoff said, and reaching out he managed to push the French window open wider.

'Here, let me go first,' Ruby said, and stepping outside onto the path she grasped Geoff's hand and guided him to do the same. Pepe followed and subtly nudged Ruby out of his path as he led the way into the garden. Ruby laughed. 'He may not have had any kind of special training,' she said 'but he's not half protective of you, Geoff.'

And it was true for the dog did seem to know instinctively which way to guide his master as Geoff took his first tentative steps out into the garden. 'I was only worried that you could get entangled in his leash but having watched him I'm sure he won't let that happen. He knows what he's doing.'

'I don't think it's that surprising,' Geoff said, 'he's been with me for a long time, you can get very close to an animal. What I can't get over is how quickly he's taken to you.'

Ruby was glad that he couldn't see her face redden. 'Have you got a dog?' he asked her.

'No, Mum and Dad won't let me. They don't think I could handle one, though I'm working on them.'

'I'll give you a reference if it would help,' Geoff said, 'and I bet Pepe would, too, if he could talk. You've certainly got a way with dogs.' Ruby was delighted to see he was smiling as he said it.

*   *   *

241

Ruby went down to the vicarage more frequently after that and so long as it wasn't raining, she and Geoff took Pepe for a walk each time. She could see from Geoff's eager greetings that he looked forward to her visits as much as she did and they always seemed to have so much to talk about. The more they talked the more relaxed Ruby became in his company and when she realised that he could no longer see her ungainly calliper she even stopped worrying about the awkwardness of her gait and how clumsy she might look when she walked. She had to remember to answer him when he was speaking rather than just nod as she was used to doing with other people and it started to give her confidence whenever she came to visit. One morning however, Ruby was surprised to find Geoff stretched out on the couch and the room once more plunged into semi darkness. Only Pepe looked pleased to see her and he bounded over as usual, barking eagerly as he went in search of his lead.

Geoff sat up slowly as Ruby gingerly crossed the room. 'I'm sorry but I'm not feeling very well. I didn't sleep much last night and I'm too tired to go for a walk today,' he said, stopping Ruby in her tracks before she reached the foot of the bed. 'Perhaps you wouldn't mind taking Pepe?'

'I will if you tell me what's going on.' Ruby felt bold enough to say. 'It's only a couple of days since I've seen you, has something happened in between?'

Geoff shrugged. 'I suppose you could say that.' He sounded depressed. 'I got a letter from the hospital this morning. They've given me an appointment for my operation. I have to go back next week.'

Ruby realised she didn't have to hide the sadness from her face as she pulled up a chair and sat down. 'Well!' she said, being careful to keep her voice sounding cheerful. 'That should be a cause for celebration, shouldn't it?'

'Who knows?' Geoff said. 'All I know is that this is the big one. The critical one that might or might not restore my sight, as they've always been at pains to point out.

'Then we must be optimistic,' Ruby said. 'That always helps at such times, believe me,' she said, looking down at her leg. 'I know from bitter experience. And you must have complete faith in the doctor,' she added with a confidence that even she didn't quite feel. 'I thought you told me that you have?'

'Only up to a point,' Geoff said. 'And I know my dad will be praying.'

'So will I,' Ruby whispered.

'But the thing is,' Geoff continued as if she hadn't spoken, 'I can't forget what he said to me just before I was leaving the last time.' Ruby looked at him in surprise. She thought they had already talked about the operation. Was there something specific he hadn't told her? 'The doctor also said he didn't want me to build up my hopes only to have them dashed.'

Ruby frowned. 'Why should they be dashed . . .?' She almost felt too afraid to ask.

Geoff didn't move as he said, 'He didn't want me to be too optimistic about my chances and wanted to be sure I understood the dangers of the surgery. The chances of the operation being successful are only fifty-fifty.'

Chapter 32

VICKY

It seemed that a few kind words was what Tilly had needed most, and after promising to consider their situation Vicky was pleased to see that Tilly was already looking more relaxed; she was smiling more and not constantly snapping at Eddie. Even her father noticed.

'Has she come into some money or summat?' Arthur asked, and Vicky laughed.

'Not yet, but you never know, stranger things have happened.' She wasn't yet ready to talk through the plan that she had been formulating; she would save that until she had tried it out on Tilly, something she was eager to do as quickly as possible.

Vicky waited until there were only the two of them left after tea before she said, 'Don't go upstairs just yet, Tilly, I'd like you and me to have a little chat. In fact, I'd like you to sit back and listen to what I have to say before you wade in.' She met Tilly's gaze and refused to look away.

Tilly looked surprised but she remained seated. 'All right, I'm listening.'

'I've been thinking a lot about your situation and I've a suggestion to make,' Vicky said.

Tilly eyed her cautiously.

'Why don't you leave Eddie with someone else during the day while you go out and seriously look for a job?'

'But I can't do that! Your poor dad would end up having to look after him all day and I couldn't possibly expect him to do that.'

'No, you couldn't,' Vicky agreed with a laugh, 'but that's not what I'm suggesting, any more than I'm saying I could look after him all the time either.' She held up her hand, when Tilly looked as if she was about to interrupt. 'What I thought was that it might be possible for my mother-in-law, Mrs Buckley senior, to do that.

Tilly opened her mouth to interject.

'Now before you say anything,' Vicky spoke quickly, 'you need to know that this is not something I've conjured up on the spur of the moment. I've already talked it over with her and she is very willing to help. She seems to think it's a good idea.

'But I don't want to give Eddie up.' Tilly sounded unsure again.

'Of course you don't, and you don't have to. He's your son and I know how much you love him. But you will be free to get a job knowing that he is safe. Then you could begin to have a life of your own, start planning for the kind of future I know that you're longing to have.

'You'd really do that for me?' Tilly sounded astonished.

'I'd do it for Eddie.' Vicky sidestepped the question. 'He is my nephew, after all.'

Tilly frowned, deep in thought, then suddenly her face lit up. 'Do you know what I'd really like to do?' she said, her eyes brightening. 'I want to go into the forces. Army, navy, air force, I don't mind which, they've all got lovely smart uniforms. I've seen the posters and they're always begging for women to sign up. I'd be able to do that, wouldn't I?' Her voice had changed and now sounded full of enthusiasm. 'Just imagine, me in a tight skirt and cap, saluting and marching up and down.' She swung her arms by her side like she was on parade and touched her hair as if she was teasing it into place in front of a mirror.

Vicky had been relieved at first that she had hit the right button with her suggestion but Tilly was getting carried away and she needed to calm her down. Vicky could see that there were flaws in the plan and Tilly was not thinking through all the implications, but Vicky was not about to point them out now.

'Don't get too carried away, we might need to think a bit more about how to make it work and you don't have to make your mind up about which particular job you could go for right this minute. Let the idea sit for a few days then you can see how you feel, and we can talk about it again.'

'No, you're right, but it's a smashing idea, Vicky, I never would have dreamed . . .' Tilly began and she wrapped her arms about herself with a grin before giving Vicky a cursory hug.

Chapter 33

CLAIRE

Claire felt badly adrift after she returned from London to Greenhill; she had so much on her mind that most days she didn't know what to concentrate on first and no matter how much her aunt tried to help her to settle, she found it almost impossible to pick up the strands of her old life. She had been devastated by what they had found in London and although she was grateful to her aunt for her help in sorting out her parents' affairs, there were still some significant matters outstanding. The bombings in London had also been a nasty surprise, but the fortitude and the bravery of the Londoners who carried out their daily business as usual made Claire feel stronger than she might have felt ordinarily. On a couple of occasions, Claire had been caught outdoors after dark and had been forced to take shelter in one of the busy underground stations. Another surprise for her was the jolly atmosphere with singsongs and lots of good-natured banter among those taking shelter. When she had emerged one morning, it took her breath away to see what had happened above ground during the night and to find the smouldering ashes of the streets around the station.

She was glad to return to Greenhill. Claire prayed that the war wouldn't escalate further, for the sake of the people in London and also so that she would be able to go back to complete what still needed to be done such as the ordering the double gravestone and arranging for a consecration service in around ten months' time which would be an important final rite of passage that was part of the Jewish bereavement process.

She forced herself to share with her aunt the fact that Daniel might be missing in action, or worse, although in her heart she was only able to hear Daniel's own interpretation of the words and she refused to accept that he could possibly be dead.

The other major stumbling block to picking up life again in Greenhill revolved about Violet and although she didn't like to admit it, Claire was upset that throughout her recent trials she'd heard no word from her old friend. She realised now that if she was to continue to live in Greenhill it would be of critical importance for her and Violet to make peace. She needed a friend, someone of her own age who might be able to understand what she had been going through, someone who could offer the kind of friendship that she had truly believed she and Violet had once had.

She had thought about Violet even when she had been in London and she couldn't prevent a blush coming to her cheeks as she recalled the embarrassing incident in Manchester that had forced them apart. In the light of all that had happened since, their feud seemed so trivial that Claire had made her mind up then to end it as soon as possible once she and Sylvia returned from London. However, that was easier to say than to do and as she had carefully sifted through all the correspondence that awaited her homecoming, it was obvious that while she had been away the schoolmistress had made no attempt to communicate and seemed to have no intention of being the first to apologise.

Chapter 34

SYLVIA

Sylvia was relieved to have Claire back in the shop even though she could see at times how much she was struggling, but the younger girl seemed to be adept at putting on a smiling face to greet the customers regardless of how she felt. Sylvia commended Claire that she always spoke brightly to people even when she was feeling down, for it was something Sylvia didn't always manage to do.

'Well, thank you, I will take that as a compliment,' Claire said, though she looked embarrassed when Sylvia broached the subject. 'I'm glad because I do have to make a conscious effort sometimes. But I reckon it's good for me. If I force myself to look cheerful I find it will often lift my own mood.'

Sylvia smiled. 'Good!' she said. 'I'll remind you of that the next time you grumble when we have to go down to the Anderson shelter if those wretched sirens begin to scream.' The bombings weren't just confined to London anymore and the rest of the country was now starting to experience some of what London had. A bomb had yet to fall on Greenhill, but no one was taking anything for granted.

Claire shuddered and Sylvia apologised with a wry smile.

'All I can say is that you're like a breath of fresh air as far as I'm concerned,' Sylvia said. 'You're really a good companion to me as well as an able helper and when you're cheery and pleasant to the customers that cheers me up no end.'

They had been standing together in front of the counter in the empty shop and Sylvia gently squeezed Claire's shoulder. Claire patted her aunt's hand and moved away to sort some of the spare balls of wool that had been tossed into the 'remainders' basket. When the bell tinkled and the front door was pushed open Claire looked up, clearly surprised to see a man on crutches, a kitbag on his back, filling the doorway. His hair was unkempt, his naval uniform looked dishevelled and there was several days' hair growth on his chin. He stood awkwardly for several moments trying to stop his right leg from making contact with the ground. She stared at him for it wasn't someone she immediately recognised.

Sylvia had no such trouble and her jaw dropped open. 'Archie?' she said, although her voice was almost reduced to a whisper. 'What are you doing here?'

'Now there's a warm welcome!' the man said mockingly. 'I do happen to live here you know, or maybe it's been so long that you've forgotten?'

Sylvia drew in breath sharply. 'There's no need to be sarcastic when you've been gone for months with hardly a word to anyone.'

Archie shrugged. 'I've sent you postcards.'

Sylvia looked over to Claire, grateful to see her niece had turned away. Claire kept her eyes hidden as she always did when Archie was about and Sylvia checked herself from saying more.

'Where have you come from to look like that?' Sylvia said. 'Though no doubt you're not supposed to tell me anything about where you've been, what you've done or where you might be going.'

'No, you're right. I'm not.' Archie looked relieved as he carefully put down his kit bag. 'But one thing I can tell you is that I could murder a cuppa tea.'

'Then why don't we go through to the kitchen.' Sylvia responded more quickly than she had intended and hoped she hadn't sounded too eager. 'I'm sure Claire can manage perfectly well on her own out here.'

As Archie moved away from the door and came closer to the counter, he seemed to exaggerate his limping. 'How bad is it? What happened to you, then?' Sylvia thought she'd better ask, pointing to his leg. 'Are you allowed to tell me that much at least?'

'It's nothing too serious, thankfully,' Archie said, 'though it is the reason why I'm here, so you could at least try to sound sympathetic.'

Sylvia frowned, quickly getting over the surprise, her anger now resurfacing. 'You must have come back for something. That's the only reason you're here, isn't it?' Sylvia said and she let him lead the way into their living area behind the store. He was walking so slowly and deliberately that Sylvia quickly pushed her way past him, almost bundling him into the back room. She made sure the door was shut behind her before she turned to face him. Archie looked as if he was intending to sit down on the couch, but he somehow swivelled more quickly than his good leg would allow and he fell clumsily into the nearest chair in obvious pain. He took several deep breaths and glared at Sylvia without speaking.

'If it was sympathy you were after, I'd have thought you'd have gone to Matlock.' Sylvia did her best to maintain a deadpan stare, deliberately meeting his gaze until he had to look away.

'What do you mean?' he said gruffly. 'What's Matlock got to do with anything except that it's where I work?'

Sylvia laughed. 'Don't try to pretend to me, it doesn't suit you. Surprising though it may seem, you're not a good enough liar,' she said. There was a pause before she added, 'What's happened to Leanne? Did she throw you out?' This time she was gratified to see the shock register on Archie s face. 'What? Did you think I didn't know about her?' Sylvia laughed again. 'You're not as clever as you think, Archibald Barker!' she said. 'Did you honestly think I wouldn't try to find out where your salary was disappearing to? Because it certainly wasn't coming here.'

Archie shifted awkwardly in his chair in obvious pain, but Sylvia chose to ignore his grunts and grimaces. 'I'm surprised she hasn't told you that we've been in touch,' Sylvia said. 'I felt sure she'd have written to you by now. Oh yes, the lovely Leanne and I have had several conversations, so I know all about your "situation". I've even seen where she lived and poor girl, she was not pleased to meet me any more than I was to see her. Neither was she happy to find out that with one word from me, and you and she could both go to jail.'

What little colour was left in Archie's face underneath the thick stubble drained away and his eyes grew large.

'Where did you get that piece of rubbish from?' He tried to sound dismissive but the words caught in his throat.

'I can assure you it isn't rubbish.' Sylvia said. 'You don't doubt it, do you?'

'It hardly matters, cos I know you wouldn't act on it.' He looked at her defiantly.

'You think so? Ready to put that to the test, are you?'

Archie looked startled. He was breathing hard and from the look on his face she could see he was trying to think quickly. 'Well!' he said eventually, with a sneer, 'as you seem to know all about what goes on in Matlock, perhaps you can tell me what's happened to Leanne?'

'What do you mean?' If she was honest Sylvia had been enjoying watching him squirm and she was determined not to show any signs of weakness now even though she wasn't sure what his question was referring to. But Archie's smile was not pleasant, reminding her of other occasions when he had glowered at her like that, and Sylvia felt an icy trickle down her spine like a warning.

'If you must know,' he said with an almost triumphant note in his voice, 'I've already been to Matlock.' He let the words hang and much as she tried not to, Sylvia looked at him in surprise.

'And?' she said.

'And nothing. She wasn't there. No one was there. The place is deserted, all shut up and according to the neighbours, awaiting a new tenant.'

A smile sat on Sylvia's lips as she settled back into her chair. 'Sensible girl. As a matter of fact, I was the one that told her to get out while she still could, before I put the law onto you and got you both put away for a long time. But I must admit I didn't actually think she'd do it.'

Sylvia was so gratified to see the horrified look on Archie's face that she was able to enjoy a few moments observing him while he stared at her in shocked silence. 'You're serious, aren't you?' Archie whispered.

'Never more so,' Sylvia said, praying that she could hold her nerve. 'So, what is wrong with your leg? How badly are you hurt?' she asked, more out of curiosity than concern.

'No details but if you must know there was a bad fire in the engine room on the frigate I was on, and me and a few of the other lads caught the raw edge of it,' he mumbled. 'I was lucky it wasn't worse though I've already had several operations and I'm not really supposed to walk on it, even now.' He stared at Sylvia but she didn't react. 'I'm supposed to be at home resting up, before I get my new orders.' He tried again. 'But what do I bloody get instead?'

Sylvia was alerted that he was suddenly breathing hard and there was a dangerous rise in pitch of his voice. 'The both of you conspiring so that I've nowhere I can even call home.' He was almost shouting by this time, but Sylvia was wise to his outbursts now and forced herself to stay calm. She sensed he was whipping up his anger, much as he had in the past, though for once she didn't feel afraid.

'People get no more than they deserve, and you certainly don't deserve a decent home,' she said with contempt. 'Leanne has already shown you what she thinks of you, oh and you can forget about getting a divorce from me. But if you think you can come crawling back here and expect me to offer to look after you for nothing then you've got another think coming.' Sylvia spat out the words. 'For a start you'd have to pay for your keep.'

Archie looked startled. 'What are you talking about, woman?'

'I'm talking about you making sure I get some of that navy pay packet that you get so regularly; the monthly cheque that's been going to Leanne all this time. The cheque that I told her she could hang onto while you were away. But now that you're back, if you want to buy yourself any kind of nurse from this establishment then I'm afraid you'll have to redirect at least a chunk of that money to me, your legitimate wife, and find some other way to pay for your poor illegitimate kiddies.'

Archie looked at her in astonishment. But Sylvia smiled. 'I'm glad to see Leanne had some sense in the end and took off. I hope she finds someone far more deserving than you to make a home for.'

Archie's face looked thunderous. 'I might have known that it was you who put her up to it all.' He hissed out the words. 'She's not bright enough to have done anything like this on her own.' Archie tried to stand up but fell back into the chair when his leg gave way under him.

'What's your love life got to do with me?' Sylvia said, her eyes widening innocently.

'Very little it seems and all I want is at least part payment of what's rightfully mine.'

Archie glowered at her from the chair, but said no more. Sylvia wasn't finished, however.

'And if you want a cuppa, then you can take that look off your face and start behaving with a bit of respect.' With that, Sylvia left Archie with a frustrated look on his face, and having to suppress a smile, she went to put on the kettle.

Chapter 35

VIOLET

Violet didn't remember ever having been so ill except once as a very young child when a particularly virulent strain of influenza had swept through the Greenhill school, forcing half of her class to stay off for several weeks. Now, thank goodness, it was the summer holidays so at least she didn't have to worry about being off work. And that was just as well for she felt incapable of doing anything besides sleeping, and for days she slipped in and out of consciousness and sometimes delirium, her thoughts scrambled, her memory confused, much to her mother's consternation. Violet was extremely grateful that her mother was there to look after her, for her entire body ached and she could barely lift her head from the pillow.

When her temperature finally began to drop down towards normal and her hacking cough was no longer so painful on her chest, she still felt too weak to be able to get out of bed. But each time she surfaced from a confusion of dreams, odd thoughts remained at the back of her mind; she was left with ideas hovering that for some reason she must get out of bed and go away, out of the house. She was left with the feeling that there was somewhere she needed to be even though she couldn't be sure where that was. Then, images of her old friend Claire popped into her head, the two of them arguing and turning their backs on each other and the idea that they needed somehow to patch up an old quarrel was hovering near the surface each time she came back to consciousness. But her thoughts were so jumbled and disjointed that she did her best to repress them and however hard she tried she could barely remember what the quarrel had been about.

Was it something to do with Daniel? Yes, that was it, though she couldn't recall the details. She tried her best to sift through her memories, but nothing specific came to mind. She only knew that she felt a sharp pain whenever she thought about Daniel and that she preferred not to think about him right now. She knew she needed to shut off her mind from some tragic events connected with him that were lurking somewhere just below the surface, but she found that was impossible to do.

It was several days before she was able to tolerate the bright sunlight of the summer's day and she gingerly opened her eyes when her mother drew back the chintz curtains. 'I've got to get up or I'll be stuck here forever,' Violet said croakily, folding back the sheet and blanket.

'Well, it is dinnertime.' Eileen said gaily and I agree it's high time you made a move.' She helped Violet as she tried to sit up before she flopped back onto the pillow with an exasperated groan.

'I don't know why you're so surprised you've no energy when you've hardly eaten a thing for at least a week,' Mrs Pegg chided when Violet looked with disdain at the spoonful of homemade soup she was trying to offer her from the bowl. 'You really shouldn't turn your nose up at it when folk round here would give their eye teeth to have something as wholesome to eat at this,' she said crossly. 'I can't afford to throw it out. Do you know how hard it is to get any decent scraps of meat or veg to make soup like this these days? When I've made it especially for you so the least you can do is to taste it.'

'I'm sorry, Mum, I don't mean to be ungrateful, I just don't feel hungry,' Violet said pushing the spoon away and she tried not to pull a face as her mother forced her to take a couple of sips.

'Until you eat something you won't be getting out of this bed, I can tell you that for nothing. You've got to build up your strength,' Eileen said.

'Oh, but I must! I've remembered now that one of the things I've got to do is to go and see Claire,' Violet said, frowning, 'though I can't for the life of me think why.'

Eileen stared at her daughter, her forehead furrowing in concern. 'Do you mean you don't remember what's happened to her parents?' she said.

Violet gasped as if a light had suddenly been switched on. '*Oh, yes!* Of course I do,' she said. 'It's coming back to me. All those dreadful images that have been going round in my head that I couldn't get rid of, they were all to do with Claire?'

Eileen nodded. 'Most likely.'

'They weren't only bad dreams? I didn't imagine them?' Violet asked. 'That stuff really happened? To . . . her parents? It's all true?' A lump rose in Violet's throat.

'I'm afraid so.' Eileen's mouth set. 'Claire had to go to London for a while, though she may be back by now. It's been the talk of Greenhill as you can imagine and of course you will have to go and visit her, but not until you're a good bit stronger yourself, young lady. If you want to go out, then you'd better start eating again cos you're not fit to go anywhere as you are.' She held the bowl out once more and Violet reluctantly took hold of the spoon and began to sip small mouthfuls.

'But I am getting better,' Violet insisted.

'Hmm.' Eileen's tone was sceptical. 'That remains to be seen. Anyway, are you really sure that Claire will want to talk to you just yet? What about the business with Daniel? Did you ever sort out your differences? Do you think she knows what's happened to him or were you planning to tell her about it?'

Violet started at the mention of his name. Daniel . . . Of course . . . The memories of the details of her quarrel with Claire came flooding back into focus. She had to close her eyes to stop the images from overwhelming her.

'If she doesn't know then you might end up only adding to her misery,' Eileen said.

'How could she know?' Violet managed to whisper. 'His family don't know about her like they knew about me.'

'No, I don't suppose they do. Any road, you've got time to think about that one 'cos, as I say, you're not going out anywhere yet.'

Violet looked as if she was about to object but then she sank her head back on the pillow and a sob escaped her lips.

Eileen put her hand firmly on Violet's arm. 'I know what's happened to Daniel has been a dreadful thing for you when you were just getting to know one another,' Eileen said, 'and it will be terrible for poor Claire, too . . . Another tragedy on top of her parents. But you can't be thinking about rushing off to see her just yet, not at the expense of jeopardising your own health.'

'No, I suppose you're right,' Violet said scrubbing the tears from her cheeks. 'Not that we know exactly what's happened to him. I'll postpone any visits until I'm feeling a bit stronger.'

Eileen raised her eyebrows and gave her a sideways look. 'That's the first sensible thing you've said. It's not as though Claire's on her own. She at least has got her aunt here in Greenhill in the meanwhile, though I'm sure she'll be very glad to hear from you when things have begun to settle down.'

Violet nodded and sniffed.

'Now come on, lass,' Eileen pointed to the bowl of soup.' Hurry up and finish it before it goes cold!'

Chapter 36

RUBY

Ruby limped along nervously, stopping to peer into all the shop windows and cafés in the town square behind the high street without really seeing anything. She was wondering if it was too soon to go back to the hospital where she had left Geoff waiting to see the doctor on the ward. He'd had his operation the previous week and while she was taking Pepe for a walk, which she had got into the habit of doing and which the vicar was grateful for, she had dropped in to see him as he waited for the doctor to come and remove the bandages.

Her leg was aching, and she was ready to sit down and rest, so she was glad when Pepe obediently paused and sat down beside her as soon as she stopped. She smiled when she realised that she had stopped outside the shop that before strict rationing had been imposed was her favourite sweet shop; it still sold sweets, but much less choice than previously and they now mostly took the form of liquorice twist and barley sugar, which you could get on the ration, rather than the toffees and wrapped chocolates that she loved so much.

Pepe was panting as he looked up at her with his soulful eyes and when she patted his head, he gave a plaintive whine. 'You feeling the heat, too, eh, Pepe?' she said softly. 'Or is it that, like me, you're scared of what's going to happen with Geoff?' She sighed. 'We've got a lot in common, you and me. It isn't easy, is it, all this waiting?' The animal's ears twitched and Ruby entertained the idea for a moment that he might be listening.

'There's no point in going back too soon, they'll only throw me out; so long as I'm there before the end of visiting time,' she explained and the dog again looked as if he understood. 'Of course they're not going to let you in, I'll have to leave you outside in the garden again so be grateful that it isn't raining.'

It hadn't been a particularly good day for Ruby for she'd been worrying about Geoff from the moment she woke up, but as ever she relied on her own special way of turning things into a positive, which had always helped to see her through such days in the past. Wasn't that why Geoff had asked her to come and be with him on such an auspicious day? Didn't he say that she would be the only one who'd be able to keep his spirits up while he was waiting? *Things can only get better* was her unfailing mantra and she had said it over and over to him, ever since they knew that today was to be the day that he would find out the results of his operation.

She had assumed at first that so long as he survived the surgery itself then things would be fairly straight-forward and that the removal of the bandages would be a routine matter. She knew he would have to get used to seeing bright lights again and his brain would have to learn once more how to interpret what it was that he saw but so long as the mechanics worked well then there would be every chance that given time his vision would be more or less back to normal.

Thankfully, he had survived the operation and made a good recovery but it was only then that she realised that even after the bandages were removed there was still a long way to go. It wasn't until Geoff had suggested that she might like to come and visit today, that she realised that he was scared that there could be problems, too, and she considered what other scenarios could possibly occur. It was then that the notion of, 'What if . . .?' began to plague her thoughts. She relived her own hospital experiences and she recalled the amount of discussion that had gone on until it had finally been decided that she was capable of breathing on her own outside of the iron lung that had encased her for so many months. She thought of Geoff with the heavy bandaging wrapped around his head sheltering him from the world, and the world from him, and it was only then that she began to worry about all the things that could go wrong. That was when she began to doubt whether she was the right person for the job of keeping Geoff cheerful and positive. She had been wondering how to tell Geoff of her misgivings, when she realised that to desert him now would be to let him down completely and she certainly didn't want to do that.

Ruby found the gardens that had a small seating area, at the back of the hospital, where visitors and occasionally more able patients could enjoy the sunshine and where she knew no one would object to her leaving the dog. She talked to Pepe as she tied his leash, hoping to persuade him to sit quietly and wait without barking while she went back to the ward. It was as if the dog sensed the seriousness of the situation for as she wrapped his lead around the leg of the bench and crouched down to his level to remind him not to make any further noise, Pepe promptly sat down obediently without so much as a squeak.

She saw Geoff through the window as she walked down the corridor and her heart began to beat faster to see him sitting up in bed with not a bandage in sight. He was staring ahead and she waved to alert him to her presence. There were no lights on in the ward and thinking she must be in shadow, she wasn't surprised that he didn't wave back as she strode confidently towards the bed. As Geoff turned his head in the direction of her footsteps, she slowed down and was aware almost at once that he couldn't see her.

'Geoff?' she said, tentatively, watching his face carefully, and she was aware that there were tears in his eyes and that his whole head had switched direction as he tried to locate the sound. He slowly shook his head then rubbed his eyes with his fingers before swiping across them with the back of his hand. Ruby gasped audibly and her hand flew to her mouth. 'Are you really supposed to do that?' she asked. 'You might . . .'

Geoff shrugged. 'Might nothing,' he said. 'What difference would it make what I do? My sight has gone for good anyway.'

Ruby felt that she should say something, offer words of comfort, but she didn't know what words to use.

'It's all right.' It was Geoff who filled the silence but his voice was a flat monotone. 'Why don't you go home for now? I don't really feel like talking. Perhaps come again on another day.'

Chapter 37

CLAIRE

Claire had read Daniel's letter at least a dozen times but found that with each reading she came to a different conclusion. She desperately wanted to believe that 'missing in action' meant just that and that he really was still a free man – or at worst a prisoner of war – perhaps somewhere in France. But a part of her mind couldn't block out the whispering in her head that he was dead and that the sooner she accepted that and began the process of grieving for him the better off she would be. She conjured up once more the spark she had felt that she had seen reflected in his eyes the moment they met outside the department store in

Manchester. She remembered in accurate detail the sequence of events on that day. It had all been so new and exciting, the thoughts, the sensations; she couldn't bear to think of him as no longer alive.

They had had precious little time to get to know each other after that, although she treasured the memories of the time they had managed to step out together. She had no history of courting to look back on, or experience of serious boyfriends to compare him with, but she felt confident in her belief that what they had shared was what she'd heard her friends describe as 'being in love'; it felt to her like 'the real thing'.

She thought that both her aunt and her mother would have approved of him. Daniel wasn't orthodox or religious or anything, but Sylvia understood from her own experience of 'marrying out of the faith' that it did make a difference that Daniel was Jewish, and Claire knew that her mother would have been delighted by that fact alone. It made Claire smile when she thought about the irony of it all. It seemed such a trivial thing to grasp onto, but she knew that in the house she had grown up in it was an important factor when viewing someone as prospective husband material, and was something that would have pleased both of her parents.

Of course, Claire couldn't think about Daniel and the day they met in Manchester, without thinking of Violet. Suddenly, choked with emotion, she decided that she should wait no longer. Without saying anything to anyone, even her aunt, Claire determined that as soon as she closed up the shop that evening, she would make the first move towards making up with her friend.

It was a warm bright evening as she walked down to the Peggs' house. They lived close to the school, and she was surprised to see a figure she assumed was Violet standing on the doorstep. She looked a lot thinner than Claire remembered. She seemed to be waving to Mrs Pegg who was walking away on the arm of a young man Claire recognised as Martin, from the refugee committee. Claire waited until the pair had turned the corner and Violet had gone back inside before she approached the house. Violet answered her knock promptly and swung open the door as if she was expecting her mother to return.

'What have you forgotten? Violet said, with a sigh; then she gasped, her hand flying to her mouth when she saw Claire.

'I hope I've not forgotten anything,' Claire joked, and she watched Violet's cheeks redden. 'Have I caught you at an inconvenient time?'

'No, no, not at all,' Violet said. 'That is, if it's me you're looking for?'

Claire laughed. 'Who else would I come to see here?'

'Martin was just here, you might remember him from the refugee committee. He and Mum have just gone out for a walk. She's been stuck in the house since I've been ill,' Violet explained. 'But do come in,' she added almost shyly, and opened the door wide to let her in. Claire stepped inside and followed Violet down the familiar hallway and into the sitting room where the early evening sun was still streaming through the streaked windows.

'I fully intended . . .' Violet said, indicating the comfortable armchair for Claire to sit in.

'I've been meaning to come but . . .' Claire said as they both began speaking at the same time.

Then Violet laughed with a sound more like a scratchy cough and they both paused. Violet completed her sentence first. 'I really was most dreadfully sorry to hear about your parents,' she said sincerely. 'I understand you had to go back to London.'

Claire could immediately feel her eyes welling as they usually did when the tragedy was referred to and she didn't attempt to reply but just nodded her head in acknowledgement.

'I was going to come and see you when I heard you were back,' Violet said, 'but unfortunately I've been ill. I had a nasty bout of flu that laid me flat for a few weeks.'

Claire felt Violet didn't need to tell her. Anyone could see that she was not making excuses.

'Sorry to hear that, hope you get fully fit soon.' Claire smiled. She was doing her best to relax.

They were both hesitant, their conversation polite and a little stiff but after a stuttering start it eventually flowed more naturally. That is, until Daniel's name was mentioned and it was Violet who first brought it into the conversation.

'Actually, there was another reason why I wanted to see you,' Violet said after a particularly awkward pause. Claire stiffened. She guessed what might be coming next and struggled with her emotions. 'I received a letter from Toronto.'

Claire looked at her questioningly; that wasn't what she had expected, but Violet refused to meet her gaze as she spilled out the upsetting details of Louis Gabinsky's letter. 'I don't imagine they would have known to write to you because . . .' Violet said eventually, although she never finished the thought.

'It's all right, Violet,' Claire said. 'You don't have to apologise. I understand that I'm the incomer here. They most likely don't even know about me in Canada so they wouldn't think to write to anyone else but you.' She smiled at Violet, not wanting to say anything that might cause either of them more pain than was necessary. 'I don't know if you were aware that Daniel and I did step out together a few times before the flying operations began,' Claire said. She felt the blood rise to her cheeks as she remembered and tried to blink away the tears, not daring to look at Violet now. 'But nothing happened that was worthy of him telling his family about me when they were so many thousands of miles away.' Claire looked down into her lap. She was aware of Violet scrutinising her face while she was struggling to decide how much she should tell her about her own letter and that it had come directly from Daniel himself.

'I was naturally upset when I heard from Louis,' Violet said, 'and I have to say I felt bad knowing Daniel was missing and thinking that you didn't know. I was going to tell you and I would have if I hadn't been so poorly but . . .' Her voice tailed off.

'Don't feel too badly,' Claire said, feeling huge relief that the official word was that Daniel was missing and not something worse. 'It was awkward for both of us when we hadn't spoken for so long. It seems like there has been a lot of misunderstanding that we both have to take some responsibility for; it wasn't all your fault.' Claire paused as Violet now looked to be on the verge of tears but then she added softly, 'If it makes you feel any better, it wouldn't have made any difference, because I already knew something had happened.' She went on to tell Violet about the letter she had received from Daniel. Claire could see that Violet still had feelings for Daniel and she was doing her best not to make her romance sound like the wonderfully passionate whirlwind it had been. 'So, it's true, he is only listed as missing,' Claire said finally, 'and there is always the chance that he could still . . .' Her voice faltered as she avoided saying out loud that he might still be alive. Claire wondered if she should share her hope, however unrealistic it was, but she decided to keep it to herself.

'I think I'd better go,' she said. 'It looks as if I'm tiring you out. I don't want your mother coming after me.' She tried to smile but the word mother unexpectedly stuck in her throat almost cutting off her breath and Claire stood up abruptly.

'Don't go yet. I haven't even offered you a drink.' Violet said, standing up slowly.

'You've been poorly,' Claire said with genuine sympathy, 'and I'm sorry if I exhausted you.'

'I suppose we don't have to catch up with everything in one night,' Violet tried to make a joke. 'Hopefully, there will be other times now that we've broken the ice.'

'Of course,' Claire said. 'It's good to be able to talk to you again.' And she reached out to squeeze Violet's hand.

'I'm glad we're friends again,' Violet said, 'and I know my mum will be pleased, too, when I tell her.'

'So will my aunt,' Claire agreed. 'Isn't it amazing how anxious they both get about other people's lives?'

'I suppose we should be grateful for their concern,' Violet said. 'No doubt we'll be the same when we're their age.'

They both laughed as they made their way to the front door and they promised to meet up again very soon.

Chapter 38

VIOLET

Violet wondered if she had underestimated Claire. She seemed to have misjudged her. Claire did seem to have been closer to Daniel than she had realised, for him to have sent her a letter like the one Claire had described. Daniel must have thought a lot of her to have prepared such a letter in advance. She wondered if there might have been something she had missed in any of the letters he had sent to her.

When Claire had gone, she went up to her bedroom and took out a large box with the letters she had received from Daniel. There were so many of them she knew it would be an impossible task to try to re-read them all. She wasn't sure what she was looking for but she selected two recent ones that he had written since he had been in England and decided to read those in case there might be something in them that could be significant. She laid them out beside her as she sat on the bed. Violet thought again of the last letter Claire had described that Daniel had written to her and she was shocked to think that he had written far more intimately to the person he had known for the least amount of time, more intimately than he ever had to Violet herself. It was strange to think that Claire knew more about him than she did.

Violet put down the last letter she had received from him and had to brush away the tears that had begun to spill down her cheeks. Compared to Claire's letter, her own seemed formal and stiff, though she hadn't been aware of that at the time. She looked at the dozens of letters in the box. If she had the time and energy to go through them all, would she find that that was true of all the letters she had received from him? Had she had read things into their correspondence over the years that didn't really exist? The more she thought about it, the clearer she was that he had never actually declared his love for her even when she was foolish enough to think she loved him. Had she made a mistake thinking of him as her boyfriend? Maybe she had been unfair to Claire and if she had thought about it properly, she might have predicted what had happened that day in

Manchester. The romance was all in her head. Had he only ever seen her as a friend? If that was so, when he had met Claire he wouldn't have seen it as a betrayal that he fell in love with her. Violet couldn't prevent the sob that caught in her throat.

She felt confused. Pleased for Claire but sorry for herself. She thought back to the earlier part of the evening when Claire had been talking about Daniel and how she had thought then that Claire's love for him had shone through. Maybe Violet didn't love him as much as she had thought.

Her thoughts were interrupted when she heard the sound of a key in the lock and she hastily stuffed the letters back into the box. She heard the front door bang shut and she listened carefully to see if she could detect the footsteps of one person or two. Martin must have brought her mother back, but had he come in? She rubbed her eyes gently trying not to make them red in case and then cautiously she went downstairs.

Chapter 39

VICKY

Vicky was pleased that things seemed to be working out well regarding her move to the Buckleys'. Tilly had moved into her old room at the post office, giving her and Eddie more space. Tilly seemed to be adapting well and had got herself a part-time job at the Carpenter's Arms, and between herself and Mrs Buckley, they'd been able to cover her shifts in the evening.

However, things didn't always feel quite right, and sometimes when Tilly got home very late after her evening shift, Vicky suspected that she was more than a bit tipsy.

Fortunately, Vicky adored Eddie, and even though

he was having overnight stays at Mrs Buckley's more than she'd originally intended, no one seemed to mind in the slightest as he was a jolly, happy bundle of fun.

Vicky had always been pleasantly surprised at how well she got on with her in-laws and now that Roger had been shipped overseas, his parents welcomed her even more warmly into their home. It seemed to have worked out for everyone as the old doctor still enjoyed the occasional card game with Arthur of an evening and Vicky was able to see more of young Julie, too.

She particularly looked forward to Wednesday afternoons when it was half-day closing at the post office and she was free to take over baby-sitting duties from her mother-in-law, giving her the time to get to know her nephew Eddie more. She would never have believed how much she would enjoy looking after the children. She was starting to feel as if both of them were her own and she wrote to Roger knowing it would amuse him to hear anecdotes about her young charges.

Some Wednesdays she would take the baby to visit her father, and if the weather was nice she would prepare Eddie's bottle and gather whatever scraps were left in the kitchen cupboard to make a picnic for the two of them to take to the park. Arthur would even push the pram proudly, showing off his young grandson to anyone he met.

'You know, I must admit I wasn't sure at first how you'd get on with your move to the Buckleys',' Arthur

Parrott said one particular afternoon as they settled into their favourite spot, 'though I know Roger were always keen.'

The sun was shining and the wind had dropped so that the air was still and pleasantly warm. The whole park area was so quiet Vicky could hear the bees buzzing on their nectar search, and the air smelled richly of new-mown grass. They had found their usual bench to sit on where they could enjoy their sandwiches, shaded from any overbright rays of the sun by a large ancient sycamore. Vicky had taken the baby blanket from the pram and spread it out on the grass. From their vantage point on the bench, she and her father were able to watch Eddie laughing and making gurgling noises as he played happily with his best loved toys: a well-washed cuddly giraffe and an almost threadbare plush elephant that had once been among his father's much-loved favourites and now went everywhere with Eddie. He was sitting up sturdily although he was not yet crawling efficiently but as soon as he was settled on the grass, he did his best to roll over on the blanket and somehow shuffle across from one side to the other on his nappy-padded bottom.

'And now?' Vicky said, looking at her father intently. 'Have you decided I've done the right thing?'

'Aye, I do think that for once in your life you have made a sensible decision,' Arthur said.

Vicky shot him a startled response not sure what to

make of his answer, but to her relief she actually saw laughter in his eyes.

'Go on,' he teased her, 'you can tell me it was all Roger's idea.'

'No, I won't!' Vicky said, laughing now, too. 'Though it was something we thought we might do if and when he was shipped overseas.

'And how does Tilly feel about it, I wonder?' Arthur asked. Do you think she's pleased with the arrangements? I hope she's not living to regret moving into the post office.'

'I don't see how she can, at least she's got a roof over her and Eddie's head. I don't think she'd dare to complain.'

'She were late back again the other night.' Arthur said, his mood shifting a little.

'Perhaps they take a long time to bottle up, it can get quite busy at the weekends.' Vicky tried to sound reassuring. 'Anyway, she told me she was looking for a better job.'

'That lass will never be happy one way or t'other.' Arthur said darkly.

'Come on, Dad, give her a chance.'

It seemed that Arthur was about to say something else when, at that moment, there was a loud cry and Vicky looked up to see Eddie grabbing at her father's walking stick, but only managing to hit himself in the eye. '*Oh, my goodness!*' she cried. '*Dad! Watch out!*

Honestly, kids . . . you can't take your eyes off them for a minute.' She removed the stick before Eddie could do any more damage, and before her worries about Tilly could take hold in her thoughts.

Tilly wasn't back yet when they got home to the post office, but Vicky didn't think anything of it as she set about making up a fresh bottle of milk for Eddie, and preparing her father's tea. But as evening turned to night time and Tilly still hadn't appeared, Vicky began to get worried.

'Her night shift at the pub finished ages ago,' Vicky said. 'I know she's entitled to some time with her friends after work, but we've never known her stay out as late as this before. She usually likes to kiss Eddie goodnight.'

Arthur's head was buried in the evening's newspaper and he merely grunted, 'you know what I think about that one.'

'I'll have to be going home myself soon,' she said, tidying away the dishes. 'Will you be all right if I leave you now? Eddie's fast asleep and Tilly's bound to be home soon.' At that moment, the telephone rang in the front post office and Vicky and Arthur both jumped. 'Who can that be at this time of night?' Vicky said.

'Answer it and you'll know.' Arthur's temper was short.

Vicky ran to the telephone behind the counter, her

heart beating quickly as she answered it. It could only be an emergency at this time of night she thought.

'Hello, Greenhill Post Office.' Vicky could hear the tell-tale pips that meant someone was calling from a telephone box.

'Is that you Vicky, can you hear me?'

Vicky immediately recognised Tilly's voice. 'Where are you Tilly, has there been an accident? What's going on?'

Tilly let out a peal of laughter, followed by a hiccup. 'No! Don't be daft, I'm perfectly fine. Listen, I don't have much change and can't talk for long, but I've got some good news.'

Vicky thought she could hear laughter and the voice of a man in the background. 'Tilly, are you in the Carpenter's Arms?'

More laughter again. 'Of course not, I don't know quite where I am but I'm on the way to Portsmouth! I've signed on to the Wrens today in Manchester and they've sent me off straight away to the naval base there. Isn't that exciting!'

'Tilly, what on earth has got into you? What about Eddie?' Vicky's voice was cold now, feeling a wave of anger wash over her at Tilly's irresponsibility.

'Let's face it, you know I'm not a very good mother, Vicky, and the country can make better use of me. Eddie will be fine, I know you and Mrs Buckley will look after him.'

'A child needs his mother, Tilly. How could you do this?'

'Don't take on so, the country needs me and I'm doing my bit. Tell Eddie I love him, and I'll write to you as soon as I can. Bye!'

Vicky was stunned, and stood for a full two minutes with the phone to her ear once Tilly had rung off.

'What's going on out there?' Arthur's voice drifted in from the living room

'Well!' she said, as she came back to sit next to her father in a daze. She flopped down heavily in her chair.

'Who was it?' he asked. 'You look like you've seen a ghost.'

'That was Tilly,' Vicky said, not knowing quite how to break the news to her father.

'But where was she? Why isn't she here yet? What did she have to say?' Now Arthur put down his paper.

'She wasn't sure where she was but she's somewhere on the way to Portsmouth, she said.'

Arthur stared at her in disbelief. 'Portsmouth? What the devil is she doing down there?'

'She says she's heading for the naval base. It was hard to tell, she was slurring her words like she was very drunk. But if I heard her right, it seems she went into Manchester this morning and joined the Wrens.'

Arthur raised his brows in astonishment.

'Maybe we shouldn't be so surprised,' Vicky said,

though shock registered on her face, too. 'You know she's always talking about joining one of the services.'

'I know she loved the idea of dressing up in uniform, and being somewhere where there were lots of young men, but I never thought she meant it seriously. What else did she say? When's she planning on coming home?' Arthur said, looking as if the truth was slowly dawning.

'That's the point, Dad. She's not. At least not for some while,' Vicky said as the implications of Tilly's actions began to sink in.

'But this is madness. What about Eddie? What's supposed to happen to the poor mite?

'She sent him her love, though much use that will do him, and I suppose she's assuming we'll take care of him.'

'Is that what she said?' Arthur asked.

'Pretty much.'

'What was she thinking of?' Arthur was dumbfounded.

'She wasn't thinking, that's the problem. She's always made it sound as if joining up was like having a holiday. You'd have thought the war was almost over to hear her nonsense and you'd have no doubt that she was going to play a critical role in winning it. You know what she sounds like when she gets over enthusiastic about something. I told you she was drunk out of her mind.'

Arthur scratched his head and looked towards the stairs where fortunately all was still quiet.

Vicky followed his gaze. 'I could take him back with me to the Buckleys, just for tonight, but I don't want to disturb him now he's settled.'

'I suppose you'll have to stop here for the night and we'll see what we can sort out tomorrow,' Arthur said.

'She said she's going to write to us, but I don't see how she's going to explain this. We can't let the little chap suffer. We'll have to come up with our own plan.'

'I suppose this is the way she deals with all her problems, dumps them in someone else's lap.' Arthur shrugged. 'It's probably served her well through some of the tough times in her life,' he said, and Vicky was surprised to hear a note of compassion in his voice.

Vicky decided not to tell Arthur about the laughter she'd heard in the background. Compassion was the last thing she felt for Tilly right now. She was a selfish young woman, who cared little for her son, and Vicky's heart hardened. Tilly would have to come home sometime and then she'd really let her know what she thought of her shocking behaviour. Until then, they'd have to put their own feelings aside and do their best for Eddie.

Vicky sighed as she heard a cry from the little boy upstairs calling for his mother. It was going to be a long night.

Chapter 40

VICKY

They had all agreed that it would be best in the short term at least for Vicky to take Eddie with her to stay at the Buckleys'.

'We have plenty of room,' Freda Buckley assured her, 'and you could always go and stop over at the post office any time you were worried about your father being on his own.'

Vicky was enjoying being a part of the Buckley household for it had brought its own rewards. But when Tilly left so abruptly and Eddie automatically moved in with her, this had a greater effect on Julie than anyone realised and it wasn't until it was almost too late that

Vicky understood that she may have taken too much for granted As she might have expected, Dr and Mrs Buckley had no difficulty accepting Eddie as a new member of the household but it had not proved so easy explaining to Julie why the baby had suddenly invaded her home.

Julie had never known her own mother except from old photographs, several of which she kept by her bed and Vicky had worked hard establishing a good relationship with her stepdaughter. Julie had been an only child for her entire life and although Vicky and Roger had talked light-heartedly in front of her about the possibility of the eventual appearance of a sibling or two one day, neither of them had dreamt that a new baby might become a reality so soon. Tilly's departure from Greenhill had occurred so swiftly that Vicky had been forced to take Eddie with her before she had had time to prepare the ground for Julie.

'Isn't he adorable!' Vicky had said gaily when she saw Julie peering at him over the side of the pram that had been temporarily set up in the sitting room at the Buckleys' on the day of his official move. 'Aren't we lucky?'

Julie seemed surprised. 'Why?' she wanted to know, her face not looking as if she felt particularly lucky.

'Because he's a very jolly baby who will fit right into the family. I'm sure he'll be no bother to anyone.' Vicky gave Eddie an indulgent smile. 'Your daddy and I did tell you that you might be lucky enough to have a brother or sister one day, didn't we? Well, Eddie's like your step-brother. He may have come a little sooner than we thought but he's one of us now.' She laughed. 'I know lots of people who would love to have such a gorgeous little boy arrive on their doorstep.'

Julie frowned. 'But I hadn't told you what I wanted yet,' Julie said.

'How do you mean?' Vicky was genuinely puzzled.

'I hadn't made my mind up yet whether I wanted a brother or a sister, or a step-anything,' Julie said.

Her tone was serious and her face so solemn that Vicky couldn't help laughing. 'Well, I'm very sorry to tell you that we don't actually have any choice in the matter.'

Julie's eyes widened. 'You mean we can't send him back?'

'No, we can't. His mother has had to go away and he's staying with us until she comes back.' Vicky was surprised by the look on Julie's face, which seemed determined not to crack a smile. 'I'm sure once you get to know him you won't want to send him back, though,' she said, trying her best to sound reassuring. 'You'll have no reason to. He's already a part of our family.'

'No he's not!' Julie stamped her foot and glared up at Vicky. 'I don't want him!' she shouted. 'I can't even play with him.'

Now Vicky smiled. 'Yes, you can, look!' And she

demonstrated a nursery game drawing circles with her fingers in the palm of his hand then tickling him up the length of his arm as she recited the well-known rhyme, 'Round and round the garden . . .' Eddie gurgled with delight and held out his hand for more. 'See!' Vicky said. 'He likes that. You do it.'

Julie folded her arms across her chest with a look of disgust. 'That's not playing, that's only for babies. I bet he won't like my dolls. Boys don't like dolls, do they?' And she glared up at Vicky. 'They only like cars and soldiers. *Yuk!* I hate cars and soldiers.'

She spat out the words so vehemently that Vicky was taken aback.

'When's Daddy coming home?' Julie wanted to know before Vicky had quite recovered. 'He won't like having a little boy here so you'll have to send him back, then.' Julie gave a triumphant smile.

Vicky was horrified but she tried to keep her voice calm as she said, 'I'm sure he will like him. He's already told me how much he was looking forward to meeting Eddie. And he hopes that you might have another brother or sister to play with one day after he comes home.'

'You mean there could be more *brothers*?' Julie's eyes opened wide, her lip curled contemptuously.

'Most definitely there could be more, but not before Daddy comes home,' she thought she had better add as Julie seemed to be on the verge of tears.

'Do I have to share my toys with . . . him?' She jerked her thumb in Eddie's direction without actually looking at him.

'Of course, eventually, that's what brothers and sisters do,' Vicky said, feeling on slightly safer ground, 'But not until he's older. For now, why don't you help me feed him? Perhaps you could go and fetch his bottle from the kitchen, and I'll show you how to test it to see that it's not too hot.' She smiled at Julie in what she hoped was a reassuring manner but to her surprise Julie merely stamped her foot and shouted, 'No I will not!'

She said the words so emphatically that Vicky gasped and she could only watch speechless when Julie started to cry as she ran from the room.

Tears welled in Vicky's own eyes as she stared after her although she remained rooted to the spot, horrified by the temptation to slap Julie's legs and tell her not to be so silly. Vicky grasped hold of the side of the pram to steady herself and to stop her hands trembling when she heard Mrs Buckley's soft voice saying, 'Oh dear! I am sorry! I suppose it has all happened rather quickly. But don't worry, she'll come round.' She put a consoling hand on Vickie's arm.

'I suppose being a stepmother is not going to be quite as straightforward as I'd thought,' Vicky said with a sigh. And Freda Buckley merely smiled.

Chapter 41

VIOLET

Violet had been glad of the warm evenings that had filled the remainder of the summer holidays. They'd brought a certain calm into her life amid the chaos that otherwise prevailed. She knew she was on the mend when she finally began to think of picking up on her charity work and to once more attend the refugee committee meetings. But she hadn't yet recovered fully from her illness and it still took some time before she felt well enough to go out regularly in the evening.

'I hate having to keep missing them, but there's a meeting tonight that I don't feel I can go to, not after a day's work. I'm too exhausted to think of going out again,' she said one night to her mother and there was a wistful note to her voice as she felt overwhelmed by feelings of helplessness. 'Why don't you go instead of me? Then you can tell me what's happening. I'm sure Martin would be delighted to see you. You know they appreciate any help they can get and you said you enjoyed meeting so many of the other workers when you came with me last time.'

Eileen gave her a startled look as if actually getting involved at a meeting wasn't something she had ever considered. 'They do seem to be doing invaluable work, I must admit,' Eileen conceded. 'But I'm not sure working with all those . . . foreign people is for me.'

Violet never ceased to be amazed by her mother's attitude towards people who came from overseas even when she could see most of them were refugees desperately looking for a place to settle.

'There are people all over Europe right now who are being displaced from their homes and who are looking to Britain for help. People of all ages coming from many different countries. Imagine if that had happened to one of us.' Violet was choosing her words carefully hoping she might stimulate her mother's interest. 'It's not only the Jewish children from the Kindertransport like Eva and Jacob who need help, although they are an important part of our work, of course, but there's lots of ways we can make a difference.'

'So I gathered from the meeting that you took me to before you were ill,' Eileen said. 'We did hear some heart-breaking stories that night including the one from your Martin. I must admit I hadn't realised there were so many people in need or so many people on the move.'

'If you listen to the BBC news on the radio you'll realise that there's been many forced migrations from lots of different places. Not just "my Martin" and his family as you put it,' Violet said, 'and please don't let him hear you call him that!' She laughed at the thought of what she felt sure would be his predictable response to such a name tag. 'There are thousands of people, from small communities in particular who have been displaced and forced to flee for their lives in the last year or so alone, from places where they'd settled and had once thought of as their homeland.' She shook her head. 'Sadly, the Nazis have other ideas and are doing their best not only to move them on but in many cases to destroy them entirely.'

'That's not right,' Eileen agreed. 'I can understand why you want to help.'

'At least thanks to our group and several other similar ones, countless lives have been saved, and people have been able to find new homes.' Violet got up and went over to the large wooden cased radio that stood in one corner of the room and she switched it on adjusting the knob to reduce the humming and crackling that were in danger of drowning out the crystal cut tones of the BBC announcer.

'The committee do indeed do good work,' Violet said, 'and it's important not only that it continues but that other people get to hear about it, too, and are willing to join us.' She was pleased that she at least had engaged her mother's attention.

'So, how about it then? Will you go to the meeting instead of me? I do feel rather tired tonight and it doesn't have to mean you're committed forever.'

'I'll think about it,' Eileen said. 'I wouldn't have to leave this minute . . .'

'No, of course not,' Violet said. At that moment, there was a loud knock on the front door.

'Who can that be?' Eileen frowned.

'We won't know until we answer it.' Violet gave her stock response to what was her mother's trademark question and couldn't keep the irritation out of her voice as she got up to turn the radio off before she went to answer the door.

'Why, fancy that!' she said. 'We were just talking about you. Come in, Martin, it's only Mum and me. We're on our own.'

Martin took off his cap and clutched it to his chest as he bobbed his head respectfully in Eileen's direction. 'Good evening, Mrs Pegg,' he said.

'What can we do for you?' Violet said. 'Or is this merely a social call?'

Martin's cheeks reddened. 'I hope it will prove to be both,' he said in his precise clipped tones. 'I don't know if you are aware that there is to be a committee meeting tonight?'

'Yes, indeed, we were just talking about it in fact because I'm afraid I'm not really fit enough to go. Not after I've been on my feet at work all day.'

'I understand and forgive me for not asking about your health first. I had hoped you would be fully better by now.'

'You can blame me for not wanting her to go out at night,' Eileen said. 'She likes to pretend that she is better, but her chest is still not a hundred per cent, I'm afraid.'

Violet was overtaken by a spasm of coughing as if to prove her mother's point.

'I'm sorry to hear that. I was hoping to persuade you. There are some sticky problems we need to sort out. But I quite understand,' Martin said . . . but his anguished look said otherwise.

'And you think Violet could help?' Eileen asked.

The redness in Martin's cheeks deepened.

'Is it something we can talk about here before you go?' Violet asked. 'I was halfway to persuading Mum to go tonight in my place so maybe she could say something on my behalf if it's important.'

'That would be a very good idea,' Martin said, turning his rather bashful smile towards Eileen. 'We can perhaps consider the matter here first.' He looked at the large old-fashioned wristwatch on his arm. I have a little time before I need to go.

The precision of his language always made Violet smile. It was how she imagined the white rabbit might speak in *Alice in Wonderland.*

'The thing is this,' Martin said as he looked rapidly from mother to daughter, 'we are desperate to find more accommodations.

Violet raised her brows. 'We can't help you there, you know that?' she said quickly without looking at her mother.

'I know of course that you offered a home to Eva and her brother Jacob and that they were assigned to stay here when they first arrived,' Martin said, 'until you realised about the TB they were carrying. They went to another place then where the couple had no children and thought that they might wish to adopt them.'

Violet was surprised when Martin got up and paced about the room. Then she understood what was coming next and looked anxiously at her mother.

'I'm afraid nothing has changed in our situation,' Violet said softly, but if Martin heard her he showed no sign.

'There has been for Eva and Jacob, a bit of a disaster,' Martin said. 'I went to check last week that everything was well but . . . I found that the wife she is now expecting a baby. Not only one baby, but twins. They feel they can no longer keep Eva and Jacob.'

Violet felt her stomach lurch as she thought of the poor children, being posted about like parcels from one destination to another. What felt like minutes ticked by before Martin said, 'At this moment, we have nowhere for them to go.'

Violet deliberately avoided his gaze. She longed to reach out and say that they would take the children, who after all were not complete strangers, but she wasn't sure what it would take to convince her mother.

'I ask because you know them and they know you already. We know they are healthy. We have a certificate to say this. ' Martin directed his comments to Eileen and Violet closed her eyes, aware only of the clock ticking on the mantelpiece.

'How long a stay are you looking for?' Eileen asked eventually and Violet's eyes opened wide.

Martin shrugged. 'I believe you have a saying, how long is a piece of string? Well, I am afraid that is my answer. They are growing up. They will wish to leave school soon to go to work. They will leave the house when they are older but when?' He shrugged his shoulders and spread his palms.

'If we offered them a home it would have to be forever. We couldn't suddenly whip it away from them again.' Violet recognised her teacher's voice taking over even though she was addressing her mother. 'That's what we did last time and that's what has just happened to them again. In their situation I can only begin to imagine how unsettling, not to say heart-breaking that must be.' She paused and took a deep breath. 'But it works both ways. What if they don't want to come back here, have you thought of that?'

A look of disbelief flashed momentarily across Eileen's face then her expression softened. 'Yes, I can see what you mean.'

Violet was caught unawares by the sudden gentleness of her mother's tone. 'When do we need to let you know by?' Eileen asked.

'As soon as possible,' Martin said. 'They are in an emergency hostel.' He shook his head. 'Never very nice.'

There was a moment of silence then Violet said, 'Mum, why don't you go with Martin as we were talking about before? See in a bit more depth some of the work the committee is doing, hear what they have to say about this particular situation, see how you feel about it and then we can talk about it again when you get back.'

Chapter 42

SYLVIA

It felt strange to Sylvia having Archie in the house getting under her feet. It was not something she had had to put up with for a long time. Much against her wishes, she did end up cooking for him and cleaning up after him; that was not easy to avoid. She even dressed his wound occasionally as she didn't want it on her conscience that she had neglected his injury, allowing his bad leg to get worse. But she made it clear from the start that she would only let him to move back into the house, if he was prepared to accept her terms and she was relieved to find that for once he knew better than to argue.

She refused to entertain the idea of him sharing her bed, offering an extra pillow and blanket for the couch downstairs instead in the hope that it might encourage him to return to his ship as quickly as possible. For once, Sylvia felt very much in charge and she gave him no opportunity to exploit her good will as he had done in the past. She kept their communications to a minimum, refusing to engage, in the hope that it would make things easier for both herself and Claire. Sylvia didn't expound about the situation to her niece and was grateful that Claire busied herself with the shop whenever possible.

It seemed ironic, Sylvia thought, that she had Leanne to thank for this turnaround in her position, for she now held sufficient evidence to threaten Archie. She had made it quite plain to him, as she had to Leanne, that if he overstepped the mark in any way she wouldn't hesitate to report his bigamous marriage to the authorities.

Sylvia did wonder what had happened to Leanne and the children and she hoped that the sad little family had got well away from Matlock and from Archie. Every time she heard an air raid siren wailing or the steady drone in the sky of a bomber plane approaching, she prayed that they were alive and well and safely hidden in a shelter somewhere. She wondered if he had tried to look for them since his first abortive attempt and when she caught him riffling through the post one morning, she wondered briefly if they might have been corresponding. But that would hardly have been Archie's style.

'Expecting something?' Sylvia surprised him as he collected together all the envelopes from the floor and she tapped her foot impatiently as she stretched out her hand.

'A letter from naval headquarters, for starters,' Archie muttered, looking decidedly uncomfortable. 'They're supposed to send me a date for a medical before I go back.'

'Do you really think you're ready for that?' Sylvia looked at him hopefully.

'As ready as I'll ever be.' He shrugged. 'Don't tell me you won't be glad to see the back of me.'

Sylvia didn't respond. 'Will you be going back to the same ship?' she asked.

'Dunno, 'Archie said. 'If not, then no doubt they'll send a whole new set of orders. They're bound to want me back as fast as possible, they need every able body they can get. Either way I'll be out of your hair soon enough.' He stopped scanning the envelopes and picking out a large white one, made a great show of deciphering the name and address. With a surprised look he turned it over to examine the official-looking stamp on the back before grudgingly handing it to Sylvia.

'This seems to be addressed to you.' He scratched his head as Sylvia pointedly held out her hand. Then she turned her back as she slit the envelope open and couldn't help a little smile tugging at the corners of her lips as she pulled out a cheque. It was not as much as she'd hoped for, but she wouldn't complain. She would see it as a part payment, replacing some of the money he had unashamedly taken from the shop till over the years. She thought of Leanne and the children who she thought of as the sad losers in all this, but there was nothing she could do. She had laid down the boundaries from the start and Archie had soon realised that he had no grounds for complaint. She had made it quite clear that as far as she was concerned, divorce was not an option that she would ever be willing to consider. She would never allow Archie Barker to take what she had worked so hard to earn, a respected place in Greenhill. It might not mean much to her daughter who had chosen to follow a different path but maybe her niece would be able to take over that place in the future.

Chapter 43

CLAIRE

Claire was pleased that she and Violet had taken the first step towards retrieving their friendship but she still felt restless at home and was finding it difficult to settle. One disturbing factor was that things all around her seemed to be constantly changing and she was finding it difficult to change with them. In some strange way people were adjusting to the war so that it was no longer unusual to hear planes flying overhead, to hear of fresh bombings or to see long queues and empty shelves in all the shops, but whenever any of these things came to mind Claire would remember London and be reminded of the devastation of her family and home and would refuse to think about them at all.

One of the hardest things for her to get used to in Greenhill was having her uncle Archie at home all the time. He had never seemed to be more than an inconsistent visitor in the past and nothing had ever been said about any difficulties her aunt and uncle might have been having in their marriage. Once he had joined the navy they had hardly heard from him at all. But now he was a permanent fixture in the house. Since he had returned on leave no actual physical arguments had taken place between her aunt and uncle in front of her but Claire was often aware of the sharp tone of their exchanges whenever they thought she was out of earshot and the underlying tension that so often filled the air when they were together. She tried to discreetly enquire how long he might be staying.

Sylvia smiled. 'Don't worry, he won't be in Greenhill for too much longer. Thank goodness, his leg does seem to be healing,' Sylvia said, 'but I've been wanting to talk to you, Claire, because whether he's here or not, I think some changes need to be made.'

Claire looked at her, alarmed, but to her relief Sylvia laughed.

'Maybe it's me who needs to make changes and I've been blaming it on you.' Sylvia said.

'What kind of changes have you in mind? Is it that the shop can't properly support us both?' Claire asked cautiously for that was one thing she had been thinking about but hadn't liked to say.

They were sitting in the kitchen and Sylvia pulled her chair closer to the table.

'From my point of view, I think I need to keep myself busier than I have been of late,' Sylvia began. 'I think things would work better for us both if I took back the running of the shop and threw myself into it full-time.' Sylvia was still smiling but Claire's stomach plummeted and her eyes began to mist.

'That would be enough for me although it might be possible to think about expanding the range of what we sell.'

'I've always enjoyed working in the shop and I like being busy,' Claire said.

'I know but in many ways that's meant that I've not been paying you your full worth,' Sylvia said.

'You gave me a home and a job, you fed me and clothed me,' Claire interrupted. 'Isn't that enough?'

'But did I give you a chance to really shine at the one thing you're extremely good at?' Sylvia seemed determined to go on. 'Let me tell you about my idea,' she said, her face becoming animated. 'I know you like dealing with the customers, making up outfits from commercial ready-cut patterns and you could still do that, but I honestly think your real skills are being wasted just serving in the shop.'

'Oh, but I don't mind that,' Claire said.

'It's not about minding,' Sylvia said, 'it's about getting excited and enthused about something.' She paused. 'Which is what you do when you're talking about designing your own patterns. I honestly believe that your true skills lie in developing those patterns, the ones that you actually design yourself and make up specially for individual customers. I've seen your notebooks filled with little sketches and new ideas. You really are very creative and you need to do something with them,' she went on. 'We've all heard the talk about clothes being rationed. It's all about make do and mend, people will be pulling old things out of their wardrobes and needing someone to make something new out of them, you mark my words. Just think how creative you could be and how satisfying that would feel,' she said.

Claire sat back and looked at her aunt in surprise, for that had been her dream. She had no idea Sylvia had ever seen the scribbles that she herself had always dismissed as a bit of fun. But she was really interested to hear the way Sylvia talked about them. Maybe her aunt had hit on something and she should give it some serious thought.

'That's where proper use of your skills will come in,' Sylvia said. 'A nip and tuck here, a few extra ruffles there and you could easily make things that are exclusive without being expensive.' Sylvia sounded as if she had already given the matter much thought and she had ideas of how to make both aspects of the new venture succeed.

'You could still help me out with the ordering, and serving in the shop from time to time as I know you do enjoy that side of things,' Sylvia jumped in before Claire could speak. 'and you could help me think about what lines we should expand into.'

Claire's jaw dropped open and at first, she didn't know what to say. 'But you've already let me make up customers' special orders from patterns,' she managed at last when Sylvia finally stopped talking.

'Yes,' Sylvia conceded. 'You've shown me that that side of the business has the potential to do well. You've already found new ways of dealing with the shortages of basic raw materials. I think you could go far.'

'Yes, I suppose that's true that's what I enjoy the most,' Claire said, 'although I don't have as much time as I would like to try new things.'

'My point exactly,' Sylvia said with a satisfied smile. 'Unfortunately I don't have any extra space here that you could work in but I have been thinking if it might be possible to maybe rent a room nearby,'

Now Claire's eyes opened wide and she was about to protest about the cost, but Sylvia hadn't finished. 'You could take the old sewing machine that you use at the back of the shop. I know you said it may need a bit of work to get it sewing smoothly but you could ask your uncle Archie to take a look at it before he goes. He can be quite good with mechanical things like that if he puts a mind to it.'

'Phew! Stop!' Claire managed to say eventually when Sylvia paused for a moment. 'That's one heck of a lot to take in, Aunty Sylv. You've really been busy letting your imagination run wild.'

'I've gone one step further than mere imagination,' Sylvia said triumphantly. 'I think I may have found you a suitable room, not very far from here.'

'What! Where?' Claire felt as if her aunt's enthusiasm was rubbing off on her.

'I don't know if you know that Vicky has moved out of the living quarters behind the post office?' Sylvia said. 'She's vacated her room and gone to live with the Buckleys.'

'I knew she was intending to move, and I suppose she had to after her sister-in-law and nephew arrived,' Claire said.

'Her father is still there and her one concern was that she would be leaving him alone for long periods, particularly at night. Well, I had a quiet word with Vicky when I heard about her plans and it seems she would be willing to let someone use what used to be her old bedroom free of charge if they would be willing to sleep over and be there for her father if necessary.' Sylvia paused for a moment before she added,' I know you were doing that hospital visiting stuff that you passed onto Ruby when we had to go to London. I thought maybe you wouldn't mind looking out for Arthur Parrott. You could turn Vicky's room into a bedroom-cum-workshop. And before you ask you would still have your room here of course to keep all your things and to use anytime you want if you aren't needed over there.' Claire sat back as Sylvia paused for breath and closed her eyes. She was picturing her own special place and trying to take it all in.

Chapter 44

RUBY

It was at Geoff's request that Ruby called in to the vicarage after he had finally been allowed home so she was startled when the housekeeper Mrs James greeted her at the door and expressed surprise.

'I'm delighted to hear that he's changed his mind,' Mrs James said, 'As he keeps saying he doesn't want to see no one. You're the only one but you do seem to have a way of keeping him cheerful. Do come in and I'll make you a cup of coffee.

'I understand why he might not want to be bothered with visitors,' Ruby said. 'I know how hard it is to get your mind around things when your body has taken such a bashing.' She was thinking back to the time when she had been in the grip of polio and the last thing she had wanted was to listen to someone prattling away, trying to sound cheerful.

'Pepe keeps him company most of the time as I'm sure you can imagine and for the moment that seems to be enough,' Mrs James said. 'But why don't you go through to the sitting room. You know where it is.'

As Ruby entered the dimly lit room Pepe sprang up from his basket beside the day bed where Geoff was resting. The dog gave what sounded like a welcoming throaty whine as he bounded over towards her and rubbed his body against her leg. Having met only the metal rods of her calliper, he proceeded to nuzzle his nose into Ruby's outstretched hand. 'Hello, Pepe,' she said as she bent down to stroke the top of the dog's head reassuringly. 'It's good to see you again, boy. It's been a while.'

'Ruby? I presume that's you?' Geoff called out.

'Yes, it's me,' she replied, 'I hope I'm not disturbing you but . . . I wanted to say hello.'

Geoff pushed himself into a semi sitting position and turned his face in her direction. 'I was hoping you'd come, though I'm warning you, I've not the energy to talk much.'

'You don't have to worry I won't stay long,' Ruby said, keeping her voice light, 'but it's great to see you even if it's only for a minute or two.' Ruby quickly covered her mouth with her hand as she spoke without thinking.

Geoff gave an ironic laugh, though his expression remained dour. 'It's all right,' he said as if reading her thoughts. 'I've given up trying to monitor people's language, even my own. I wish I had a penny for every time I've used the word see. We don't even think about it.' There was a crack in his voice as he added, 'It's amazing what we take for granted.' He gave a prolonged heavy sigh. 'Who would have thought I'd need help finding my way around my own house? Thank goodness for Pepe, is all I can say. Isn't that right, old boy?' At the sound of his nickname Pepe padded back to sniff around the day bed and he licked the hand that Geoff extended in his direction before curling up once more in his basket.

Ruby cleared her throat, unsure how best to steer the conversation when, thankfully, Geoff spoke again. 'I don't know if there's a chair for you to sit on, Ruby?' he asked. 'Forgive my manners for not clearing a space for you but I can't always remember where I've dumped things. Dad's always telling me about leaving stuff on every available surface. And even sometimes on surfaces that aren't available. I have to rely on Pepe to stop me tripping over everything. He sort of nudges my feet out of the way.'

'You're forgiven.' Ruby gave a laugh in an attempt to lighten the gloom that had descended on the room.

'And you don't have to worry about me. I know exactly what it's like trying to recover from major surgery,' she said. 'It takes time and it can be pretty frustrating. Hopeless and helpless, I always used to say.' She thought for a brief moment that Geoff had smiled as she was talking and she drew her chair closer to his bedside. Pepe promptly stood up, his eyes appealing for a show of affection as he projected his face into Ruby's lap. She hoped she hadn't spoken out of turn and she looked at Geoff anxiously but she wasn't able to read his expression.

'Yes, of course.' Geoff's cheeks had reddened. 'I sometimes forget I'm not the only person in Greenhill whose life has been turned on its head by some major catastrophe.' He coughed to cover the break in his voice. 'It's just so bloody hard being treated like a baby and having to learn things from scratch.'

Ruby's first reaction was to draw her lips into a resigned smile and to nod her head in agreement, but instead she spoke to Pepe. 'You know I always wanted a dog,' she said. 'I would have loved to have one like you. But my mum and dad were overprotective when I came out of hospital. They were convinced that I would trip over everything and wouldn't let me have any kind of a pet.'

'That was exactly my dad's argument against Pepe,' Geoff said, his voice suddenly animated. 'I had him before I went into the army and Dad wanted to get rid of him as soon as I was called up, but I refused to let him go. It would have hurt his feelings. I always say that dogs are far more sensitive than we give them credit for.'

'I'm glad you kept him, Ruby said. 'Maybe the next time I come we could take him out for a walk?' She tried to make the thought sound casual, not as if she had been pondering for ages about how she would introduce the idea, but she was disappointed when Geoff stiffened and balled his hands into fists.

'Maybe,' he said. 'But right now I'm too tired,' and without further comment he pulled the blanket up to his chin and slid down under its cover.

'Yes, of course, and it's time for me to be going, in any case,' Ruby said, trying not to be phased by the suddenness of his mood swing. 'I can come back another time.' She stood up hastily and tidied the chair away to the farthest corner of the room out of harm's way. She tried to say goodbye, but Geoff had turned on his side and pulled the blanket over his head before she had even reached the door.

Chapter 45

CLAIRE

Claire was delighted to find that Vicky's bedroom was significantly bigger than the one she had been using at Knit and Sew, and with the spare bed removed there was plenty of space for the renovated sewing machine her uncle Archie had restored and her cousin Rosie's chest of drawers Sylvia had given her to keep all her knitting and sewing paraphernalia and equipment.

'Don't you think it's just perfect?' Claire couldn't help gushing with excitement the first time Sylvia came to visit. 'Thank you so much for letting me have all this, I can't wait to see my first customer here. I hope the posters we've put up in the shop will do the trick.'

'You have to thank Vicky for all this.' Sylvia laughed. 'And she has a bunch of leaflets at the post office that she's been handing out to the local shops to display as well. A lot of people already knew about your work so I'm sure the word about the move will soon spread. You're beginning to get a very good reputation locally.'

'Special thanks must go to Uncle Archie,' Claire felt she had to say even though at times she had found him extremely difficult to deal with and wished she had never asked him for his help.

'I must say the sewing machine looks a treat. It's come up like new,' Sylvia said.

'And it works properly, too.' Claire laughed. 'And he very kindly offered to put that up as well so that I could display some of my personal things to make it feel more like home.'

'Oh, goodness!' Sylvia said, looking at the veneered wood shelf and its contents approvingly. 'Is that what I think it is on there? Has it come all the way from London?' She reached across to pick up a ceramic teapot shaped like a cottage, 'It's remarkable that you've managed to find something in one piece from home. It was my mother's, you know. I'd always wondered what had happened to it.'

'I'm sorry, I didn't realise,' Claire started to apologise, 'Do you want it back? My mum had it for as long as I can remember. She loved it and she kept it in pride of place in the display cabinet in the living room.'

'No! It's as much yours as it is mine,' Sylvia assured her. 'You enjoy it, it's just good to see it again,'

'It's the only memento that I have from home.' Claire's voice changed. 'I found it when we were in London and I could hardly believe it was still intact. It was one of the few things I managed to salvage from the rubble.'

'Your mum and I used to vie with one another as to whose turn it was to make tea in it when we were kids,' Sylvia said, her voice wavering, and she picked up the old tea pot that now stood proudly propping up Claire's pattern books on the new shelf. It was made of painted ceramic pot styled like a country cottage with flowers painted around the leaded windows. It had a thatch coloured roof for a lid and a brown handle and spout that had been moulded to look like chunky twisted tree trunks.

They both stood for a moment staring at it each with their own memories and Claire was grateful that her aunt said nothing more as she put the pot back on the shelf and gave her a huge hug.

Claire had been happy enough living with her aunt and uncle even though she had no young companion of her own age now that her cousin was no longer there. It wasn't until she moved and was spending more time on her own in the quiet of the workshop that she realised how much tension there had been in the house. In the short while since he had been on sick leave from the navy Archie had become very restless, often pacing about like a caged animal. Fortunately, he went out a lot although he never said where he was going and Sylvia would look anxious especially when he came back the worse for drink. Sylvia didn't completely relax until she heard that Archie had passed his Navy medical and had been called back to return to his ship which had now been pronounced sea worthy. The first high tea Claire and her aunt shared together after he had gone had an air of celebration about it as they indulged in shop talk and Archie's name was barely mentioned again.

'As this is a new adventure, I think you should start things off with a treat – like a special buying trip into Manchester,' Sylvia said gaily.

'And what would I be buying that I haven't already got?' Claire asked.

Sylvia thought for a moment. 'The stuff we've got in the shop right now is pretty much run of the mill. My advice would be for you to look for some bright and new materials as well as some fancy trimmings, the type of things that would help you to impress your customers that their garments are unique.'

Claire looked at her in surprise. 'But wouldn't that be expensive?'

'It doesn't have to be. If you choose carefully and find something different you'll more than make your money back in good time. Folks round here may not have a lot but they know how to spend wisely and make their money go a long way.'

'I've never thought about that,' Claire said.

'Well, it would be worth your while to think about it now because believe me, it's those kinds of little extras that are going to make all the difference between an ordinary outfit and something that you can call a Claire Gold Exclusive. You could have some little name tapes made up to sew into each item you make, and you'll be able to charge just that little bit more.'

Claire's eyes opened wide.

'You need to go and scour the shops to see what they have to offer,' Sylvia said. 'I bet you could get lots of ideas if you look. Places like Lewis's will probably have quite a range of things, though not as many varieties as they used to, and I'm sure there are other shops in Piccadilly or on Deansgate that sell that sort of thing, too. I don't know how well you know the centre of town but you should go and have what my mother used to call in Yiddish a *shmy* — a good look about, window shopping without necessarily buying – and the look on your face already tells me you like the idea,' Sylvia said with a satisfied smile.

Claire grinned back at her. 'My only problem would be trying to rein in the cost,' she said.

'Oh, you don't have to buy much, maybe a few samples. But you'll need paper and pencil to draw all the things that you like and the thoughts that they might spark by the time you get home that will help you to develop your own ideas. But you must let the shops carry the stock until you have firm orders – that's one of the first lessons I learned in business.'

Claire nodded. 'Why don't you come with me?' she said. 'Don't they always say two heads are better than one? We could go on a Wednesday afternoon when the shop will be shut,' Claire said brightly. 'When was the last time you had a day out?' She said this light-heartedly but to her surprise Sylvia blushed, her eyes misted over and she didn't answer.

She shook her head. 'No, why don't you ask Violet instead, I'm sure she must be feeling better by now.'

But would Violet want to come with her, even if she was, Claire wondered.

Chapter 46

VICKY

It took longer than Vicky might have hoped to get her stepdaughter's forgiveness. Julie didn't speak to her more than she had to for several days, but by the time she had received a letter from Roger the situation finally began to resolve itself and to her relief the mood in the house noticeably brightened. This was in marked contrast to the mood in the country. London had been hit hard but other cities were starting to suffer, too.

Even though winter was approaching, the weather was bright and clear, the sun still shedding some warmth, and as there had been only a handful of recent air raids, when she came home from work Vicky took advantage of the lovely garden that surrounded the Buckley's house. She sat on the bench absorbing the gentle perfume of the pale pink tea roses and thought she would enjoy reading Roger's letter with no one to disturb her. But she had barely completed the first page when she became aware of a shadow falling across the lawn. Looking up, she saw Julie staggering up the path struggling under the weight of what looked like two large tomes. She made it as far as the bench, where she dropped them thankfully beside Vicky. She waved a letter at Vicky.

'Daddy's written a letter specially to *me*,' she cried out happily clutching it to her chest.

Vicky smiled. 'Then you will have to write back to him, won't you?'

'Of course,' Julie said. 'And then can we go to have it weighed at the post office?' she said importantly.

'Definitely.' Vicky leaned across to look at one of the tomes that she could now see were photograph albums and she pushed them away to make room for Julie to sit next to her on the bench.

'Daddy said that he's got some photos that he keeps with him all the time, one of the three of us all dressed up at the wedding that he keeps in his shirt pocket and one beside his bed of me on my own that he looks at every night before he goes to sleep. He said that if I look at some of the ones in the album then maybe we'll be looking at the same ones at the same time.'

Vicky's throat constricted, and she felt as if she couldn't speak. Trust Roger to say something so sentimental.

'Do you think that's a good idea?' Julie gently enquired, but Vicky could only nod her head and smile. Julie began to leaf through the album, stopping only to tell Vicky who each picture was. 'That one is me,' she announced stopping at a baby picture that could have been anyone. 'Daddy took it. And is that you holding me?'

'No,' Vicky said, looking at the picture of the pretty smiling woman in the photograph. 'That's your mother.'

Julie grinned. I know that really,' she said, 'but I don't remember her, except that Daddy said she had lovely hair. I used to wear mine like that, you know?'

Vicky nodded. 'I do know. You told me that the first time I met you. It's a very pretty style.'

'But you're my mummy now and you're Eddie's mummy, too.'

'No, I'm just looking after him till his mummy comes back,' Vicky said, not sure where this was leading. 'We are all part of one big family now,' she said, suddenly feeling hot under the collar. She had not come prepared for this type of conversation although maybe it would help to clear the air. 'As you know, things can get a bit complicated about who is related to whom, but all you need to know is that me and Daddy, Granny and Gramps and Granddad Arthur are all your family. And

Eddie's,' she added, hopefully. 'We all love you, and each other and we're here to look after you, even if sometimes we can have a little argument and maybe fall out about little things.'

'And I call you Mummy, don't I?' Julie didn't want to let go. 'Will Eddie call you Mummy when he's old enough to talk?'

'He's got a mummy, and she'll be back one day, so we'll have to see.' Vicky smiled.

'Well, I hope so,' Julie said, 'because that's what I've been telling everyone at school. Although I know not everyone believes me, they say you don't get new brothers and sisters that fast and that I'm just making it up.'

Vicky laughed when Julie said that. 'When Daddy comes home maybe he'll have to go to your school and have a word with them,' she laughed, 'and you can show them that we're all one big happy family.'

Julie grinned as she picked out two photographs that matched the ones her father had described and without another word, she snuggled up towards Vicky and planted a large wet kiss on her cheek.

Chapter 47

VIOLET

Violet was relieved when she was finally fit enough to attend the refugee committee meetings once more for she didn't feel she could ask her mother to go in her place again after what had happened the last time. She was grateful that Martin had accompanied Eileen that night for her mother had been quite distressed when she had returned home and she was adamant that she never wanted to go back. It took some time for Violet to coax out of her at first exactly what had happened. Eileen had refused to talk about it and it was Martin who eventually revealed the full story.

'It was my fault, Violet. I didn't fully understand

the situation. I have apologised to your mother and will do so again if she will give me the chance,' he said.

'How could it have been your fault?' Violet looked puzzled.

'You have a saying about jumping over the rifle?' Martin asked.

'Jumping the gun, I think you mean.' Violet tried to keep a straight face.

'Well, whatever it is, that is what I did. I understood that they were desperate to find somewhere for the children to stay,' Martin said.

'You mean Eva and Jacob?'

'Yes, yes, and I had thought what better place than here where they already knew you?' Martin was clearly upset.

'You came here and persuaded us. But that wasn't what the committee had in mind?' Violet guessed.

'No, they didn't want that, because . . . because of what happened the first time they came. The committee were concerned you might change your minds again. But nobody told me. '

'I understand and I did apologise for that first error of judgement,' Eileen said.

'Your mother was brave. She stood up and said why she had changed her mind, but they still refused her offer.

'Is there somewhere else for them to go?' Violet asked.

'What will happen to them if they don't come here? I thought the committee were desperate.'

'They were, they still are,' Martin replied, 'but they didn't want to even consider them coming here. '

'I see.' Violet could picture the scene as the group had no doubt discussed the issues openly in front of her mother and she could understand why Eileen was not keen to go back when they had turned down her well-meant offer.

'They were nice about it,' Martin said, obviously trying to soften the blow, 'but they were clear they didn't want Eva and Jacob to come here. I felt they were blaming me.' He looked crestfallen. 'It was humiliating for us both.'

'They are a wonderful group and I can see that they have valuable work to do,' Eileen spoke up at last, 'and they don't really need the likes of me gumming up the works.'

Violet shrugged. 'But I'm as much to blame as you two. I could have insisted that the children didn't leave here the first time.' She didn't know what else to say for her mother was right, and she wasn't surprised that the committee were now divided in their opinions as to what should happen to the children despite Martin's desperate plea before the meeting had taken place. 'But what's going to happen to them in the end?' she asked.

'I don't know. All I know is that I feel guilty about them,' Martin said.

'You shouldn't,' Violet said. 'It was our fault that they were sent away from Greenhill, Mum's and mine. You did your best.'

Martin shook his head but didn't say anything.

'And we all agreed that they need to have something as stable as possible from now on,' Violet said. 'I suppose it's understandable that they might be concerned we would change our minds again.'

'I can see that,' Eileen agreed with a sigh. 'I would have liked an opportunity to make it up to them if I could, but there may be other ways.'

Violet felt sorry for her mother who was obviously distressed that the committee had not allowed her to make amends and to take back the children now.

'Will it still be up to you, Martin, to find somewhere else for them to go or are you in the bad books, too?' Eileen asked.

To Violet's surprise, Martin smiled. 'No. I think they cannot afford to put a black mark against my name. I am too valuable,' he said. 'In the end they need people like you, and I know you will not make the same mistake again. I can understand why you are upset, Mrs Pegg, but I hope it will not stop you coming to the meetings, Violet?'

'No, probably not,' Violet said. 'I know there is still so much work to be done, but maybe I'll keep well away from any discussions about the housing list and instead start offering those extra English classes to the newly arrived children like I've been promising.'

'Maybe you help me with my English,' Martin said with a laugh. 'I know that I could . . . umm—' He broke off abruptly, blushing, and didn't finish the thought as he stood up to leave.

Violet was surprised he looked so bashful but she saw him to the door and when she returned found her mother was grinning. 'What a charming young man he is,' Eileen said. 'I'm surprised you treat him in such an off-handed manner.' She shook her head. 'You do know he's really sweet on you, don't you?' she said.

'Don't be so ridiculous! Or so old-fashioned!' Violet dismissed her mother's comments. 'If he really liked me that way then he would have asked me to step out with him. He knows where I live.'

'He certainly does,' Eileen said with a chuckle. 'He comes round here often enough on the pretext of so-called committee business.'

Violet raised her eyebrows and that made Eileen laugh. 'Don't look at me like that,' she said. 'He's here at least as often as he's at home.'

Chapter 48

RUBY

Ruby had never seen Geoff's exposed wounds at close quarters before and as soon as she walked into the sitting room at the vicarage, she was instantly aware of his vulnerability. The dark tinted sunglasses he insisted on wearing only covered up the worst of the scars and it was easy to see how those that remained criss-crossed large areas of his face as a constant reminder of the accident. *It's no wonder he doesn't want to see people*, she thought. *Nobody does when they've been so badly damaged*. She automatically reached down and ran her hand over her calliper. She wondered what kind of reception she would get today as she announced herself diffidently, though she had not expected anger.

'What are you doing here?' he snapped. 'I thought I'd told Dad I don't want to see anyone.'

'*Ah!* But I'm not just anyone,' Ruby quipped, knowing that she probably sounded more confident than she felt. What she really wanted to do was to turn and run but she thought she saw his mouth relax for a second with the hint of a smile.

'I thought I would come to cheer you up because I think the problem is that you're bored.' Ruby didn't give him much space to reply. 'You must be by now, I know I was when I came out of hospital. That's how it gets when you've had nothing to do for ages and don't seem to have much to look forward to.'

'What can there be to look forward to now, for the likes of me?' Geoff sneered. 'You may as well take me out and shoot me.'

'I think that's a bit dramatic.' Ruby was shocked by the strength of the emotion behind his sad words. 'I'm sure if we tried we could think of lots of things for you to do, a whole new world to explore.'

'Oh, yes, and how do you work that out?' he said scornfully.

'Well . . .' Ruby hesitated. 'I believe you've already started going out.'

'Into the garden!' he scoffed.

'I know you must feel you want your old life back,

but I'm afraid that isn't going to happen. Things are going to be different and you've got to work out how to deal with them.' Ruby was scared that she might be on dangerous ground as she could see instantly that she had hit a nerve.

'What would you know about how I feel?' he yelled angrily.

Ruby took a deep breath, determined to hold her ground. 'A heck of a lot more than you realise,' she snapped back. 'I can assure you that when I lost the use of my leg, I thought my world had ended and in a way it had. For ages I felt as if I had nothing more to live for. So I know exactly how you feel.'

There was an awkward silence. Ruby thought she could see tears running down Geoff's cheeks.

'At least you learned to walk again,' he said. His voice was softer though he sounded extremely bitter. 'I'll never be able to see.' His voice cracked and Ruby couldn't respond immediately, she was finding it too difficult to see him in such distress. At that moment, the door was pushed open, and Pepe bounded into the room, a leash trailing from his mouth. It fell to the floor as the dog gave a loud bark and he pushed his face into Geoff's hands. Then he almost bounced across the room to where Ruby was sitting. He lifted his front paws into her lap and she had to laugh as he balanced precariously. Fortunately, Geoff laughed, too, and the tension of the moment was broken.

'So sorry, but I've brought you both a drink.' Mrs James bustled in with a tray. 'Shall I leave Pepe here? He always seems to know when Ruby's here and he had to come in and check.'

'Hello, old boy, and I'm pleased to see you.' Ruby turned her attention to Pepe and ruffled the fur on his head. 'I saw your empty basket and I was wondering where you'd got to.' She greeted the dog fondly and let him lick her face in delight. 'And you couldn't have timed your entrance better,' she said, 'because I was just going to suggest to Geoff that we might take you out for a walk.'

'I hardly think this is a good time,' Geoff said gruffly.

'On the contrary!' Ruby was insistent. 'It's teatime for most honest folk so there'll be no one else about. We only need go for a short spin. How about going across to the memorial garden?' she said. 'Pepe can guide us. I'm sure he knows his way around there like I know the back of my hand.'

'I . . . I'm not sure I'm ready to go that far.' Geoff sounded nervous.

'*Nonsense!*' Ruby took hold of his hand. 'You can think of it as your first adventure.'

It took a little more persuasion but to Ruby's delight when they had finished their drinks, Geoff did agree to set off down the path and across into the old grave-yard. At first Pepe walked by Geoff's side almost as if he was a guide dog but Ruby realised too late that he hadn't been trained and when he took it into his head to run about in circles, he virtually tied Geoff's feet up in his leather lead. Ruby called out immediately for Geoff to stop but she wasn't quick enough and he clipped the corner of one of the flagstones with his heavy duty boots. He went down like a sack of potatoes, tumbling across several of the older lichen-covered gravestones that had been hidden by the long grass and landed on top of the dog. Pepe barked loudly and managed to roll out from underneath seconds before Geoff landed with his full weight. Fortunately neither Geoff nor the dog was hurt, but Geoff looked extremely shaken and it took several minutes for him to stand up steadily while Ruby untangled the leash.

'It's hopeless. I knew I shouldn't have come.' Geoff sounded more angry than upset but Ruby could see that behind the glasses, tears were beginning to accumulate. 'How can I ever hope to do anything useful when I can't even see what's in front of me?' he said, brushing down his jacket and trousers.

'Well, you have to look on this as trial and error,' Ruby said as brightly as she dared, not wanting to acknowledge how frustrated and humiliated Geoff must be feeling.

'I'm a bloody invalid, that's what I am and no one can change that. I hate the thought of people staring at me and pitying me!' Geoff shouted.

Ruby took hold of his arm, relieved that he didn't

try to shake her off. 'That's one thing you don't have to worry about tonight,' she said softly. 'There was nobody about to see us.' She guided Geoff to the wooden bench and shortened Pepe's leash so that she could pull the dog closely towards them both.

'If it helps, I don't like people staring at my leg either, even after all this time.'

'Your leg?' Geoff said vaguely.

'Yes, my leg with the calliper.' For once Ruby couldn't help snapping.

'*Oh, gosh!* Of course, Sorry. I keep forgetting because I don't think of you like . . . that.' Geoffrey looked ashamed. 'Now that I don't see it.'

'No, you don't, that's what I'm trying to say. Nobody who matters to me sees it after a while and it will be the same for you, believe me,' she said more softly. 'The more you go out the more people who matter will get used to seeing Geoff the man and nothing else.'

Geoff looked mollified for a moment, but he still wanted to argue. 'You manage to do normal things, how on earth do you do that?'

'What do you mean *normal* things?' Ruby asked. 'I'll never be able to walk properly like other folk, no matter how hard I try.'

Geoff shrugged and was silent for a moment, then he said, 'You always sound to me as though you're doing regular things. Are there still things that you can't do?'

'Lots, but that doesn't stop me from trying,' Ruby said. 'Some people still stare at me, and say unkind things. But they're mostly strangers so that doesn't stop me. There's not much you can't do if you really put your mind to it.'

They sat in silence, the sun beginning to drop and the air suddenly chilling. 'But seriously, what could I do?' Geoff still sounded sceptical. 'Weave mats? Plait cane chairs?' His voice was mocking.

'The first thing you could do is to put together a list of what you'd like to try. You might be surprised.'

Pepe had spotted a butterfly, but this time Ruby was alert when he made a sudden movement towards it and she pulled hard on his leash to anchor the dog at her feet. 'Maybe getting a properly trained guide dog could be one thing to think about,' she said, tickling Pepe's head.

'I won't get rid of Pepe.' Geoff was immediately defensive.

'Maybe you won't have to, but that's something you could at least find out. Maybe we could both try to think of all the things that you might have a go at, then we could go through them one by one.'

'What good will that do?' Geoff said crossly.

'When we've eliminated all the crazy sounding things maybe we'll come up with something that you really could do.'

'Such as what?' he said scornfully.

'I don't know. That's the whole point of the exercise. I'd have to put my thinking cap on. And so would you but I'm sure there must be loads of things.'

'What, like learning Braille?' His tone was disparaging.

'Why not? It could prove to be extremely useful. Or what about a spot of gardening?' Ruby's face suddenly lit up. 'You could easily make your own Victory garden and grow your own vegetables and things. My mother has started to grow some herbs and vegetables not just for us but to sell in our shop. I bet there would be any number of people happy to work with you and help you to sell what you grow.'

'You sound serious.' Geoff still sounded dubious.

'I am serious. I think you should talk to my mum and dad they would know how to get going.'

Geoff shivered. 'Has the sun gone down? I'm beginning to feel cold,' he said.

'Yes, you're right, it has,' Ruby said, pleased that Geoff hadn't dismissed her idea totally. She released some of Pepe's leash and linked her arm through Geoff's. 'Come on both of you, it's time to go home. It is getting cool,' and she gave a little smile happy that she had been able to give Geoff something positive to think about. Now all she had to do was to help him recognise that the future might hold something for him after all.

Chapter 49

CLAIRE

Claire sat alone on the bus back to Greenhill from Manchester, sorry that she hadn't been able to persuade Sylvia to go with her or to follow up on Sylvia's suggestion that she should ask Violet.

'It might be a good way for you two to really get back together,' Sylvia had said, and Claire knew that she was right but she could only think about their last trip together into the city when they had gone to meet Daniel for the first time and tears sprang so readily to her eyes even now, that she wasn't sorry that she hadn't asked Violet. The trouble was, she realised, she didn't have anyone else that she could ask. She vowed that once the new workshop was up and running she would apply herself and get involved with one of the charity committees again and make some new friends. But that was for another day. It would have been nice to be able to share the fun but today she was grateful that she had enjoyed herself. Even though she had been alone she had had a wonderful day out not only exploring the city but looking for exciting ways in which she could woo new customers.

She was exhausted when she finally got back home and she was touched to find that Sylvia had laid out a high tea for them both in readiness. It looked like she had scrimped and saved from her rations and as they ate together, Claire showed her gratitude by talking excitedly to her aunt about all the things she had seen.

The arrangement with Vicky was working out well as far as Claire was concerned. Arthur had been keeping in reasonable health, not requiring much help, and this evening was the first time since she had moved into the workroom at the post office that Vicky had asked her to stay over. After the delicious supper, Claire went back to her room, where she had promised Vicky she would spend the night whenever necessary to keep an eye on Arthur.

'He's been amazing ever since you took over my room,' Vicky had said when Claire had dropped in to the post office before she'd set off for Manchester, 'but his chest has been playing up this week, so I wondered if you would mind stopping over tonight as I'd rather he wasn't on his own . . .'

'It will be no trouble at all,' Claire said, 'that was our agreement after all,' never thinking to ask how she would get the old man down to the basement if the air raid siren sounded during the night.

Claire sat on the divan bed in her new room re-reading her favourite Agatha Christie. She skipped through several pages before she realised that she hadn't read any of them properly and she put the book aside aware that her thoughts were drifting and her mind was only filled with thoughts about where she might go to make new friends. She had thought about going back to the hospital committee but was concerned that her presence might make it awkward for Ruby, who she'd heard was well in favour with the vicar now that she had taken over visiting Geoff Laycock.

She heard a bell ringing softly in the distance and looked at the alarm clock beside the bed. It wasn't late though she realised that she must have dozed off for a few minutes. Now she felt wide awake and the bell seemed to have stopped. She climbed down from the bed and opening the bag of samples she had bought that afternoon. began stacking them in tidy piles on her new shelf. As she did so, her hand somehow caught the edge of a pattern book that had been propped up against one of the book ends and it slid across the shiny veneer and knocked over her beloved cottage teapot.

Claire gasped as it smashed on the wooden floor and she stood staring down at the jagged pieces in horror. The last vestige of home to survive, now only fit for the bin. Cold shivers ran down her spine and she started to cry as she opened the door to go downstairs in search of a dustpan and brush.

'Vicky! Is that you?' Mr Parrott's raspy voice called out as soon as the door creaked and she stepped out onto the tiny landing.

'It's not Vicky, it's me, Claire, Mr Parrott,' Claire responded immediately, concerned that she had woken him up.

'Someone's been ringing the bell for ages at the back door, haven't you heard it!' he shouted angrily. 'No idea who on earth it could be at this hour.'

Claire shivered though not with cold. 'I'm going downstairs to check,' she called back, her voice sounding stronger than she felt. One of the lamps was still on in the sitting room behind the post office as she crept down the stairs and she checked round the room tentatively, hoping that it was merely Arthur being forgetful. She jumped when the bell rang again, for it sounded quite loud this time. She was armed only with the dustpan and brush in one hand, while she desperately flicked away the tears that were clouding her vision with the other.

'All right, I'm coming,' she called out to the impatient caller as the bell sounded again and, taking a deep breath, she pulled open the door so violently that she slammed her forehead against it. For a moment she thought that she might be concussed, for she didn't believe the vision she saw filling the doorway. *I must be hallucinating*, she thought, letting go of the dustpan and this time she used the knuckles of both hands to rub her eyes.

Chapter 50

VIOLET

Violet had finished her after-school 'English for beginners' session in the school hall and was ready to go in search of the caretaker to lock up after her. She gathered her small pile of books and teaching aids and tucked the stack of homework exercise books under her arm that her pupils had eagerly handed in for her to mark.

This was one class where she willingly gave up her own time and was never in a rush to finish. It gave her a lot of pleasure to teach the young refugees out of hours and neither she, nor they, viewed it as work; they were like little sponges, soaking up the grammar and vocabulary of the English language and were never afraid to speak out for themselves. They were well motivated; they came from all over Europe and unless they had siblings in the school, had no common language other than English which Violet thought was probably why they all continued to make such amazing progress.

'Please Miss, I went to the greengrocer's to buy some vegetables,' one of the brightest girls in the class couldn't wait to tell her in an almost flawless accent before the class had even started, and all of them had giggled and had given her a clap. Violet, also, had been quick to praise her attempt to pronounce the difficult words so clearly.

They had worked diligently as usual, and Violet was reviewing the session and thinking proudly about what they achieved when she heard a knock and saw the outline of a tall man on the glass panel in the door that led into the corridor. She looked up as the door swung open and was surprised when Martin stepped inside.

'I . . . I . . . hope I'm not intruding,' he said, his initial bubble of confidence seeming to burst as he came further into the room. 'I was told you were finished for the day, but I can come back if . . .'

'I am finished,' Violet said. 'Do come in Martin. Is everything all right?' She never could understand his diffidence.

'Yes, all is fine, thanks. I am sorry to come to your

school like this; I know I shouldn't.' He looked down at the floor. 'But I wish to talk to you, on your own.

Violet wanted to laugh and make a flippant reply, but he looked so earnest she didn't want to upset him. She could see that he was so agitated and unsure of himself that she hadn't the heart to make a joke.

'Why don't you walk me home?' she suggested. 'Then we could talk on the way.'

He brightened at this suggestion. 'If you're sure you're ready to go. I'd be happy to carry your books.'

'Thank you,' Violet said, touched by his old-fashioned chivalry . 'I'm ready to leave right now,' she said. 'I can pick up my bag from the staff room on the way out.'

'Perhaps we can go into the park,' Martin said as they cleared the school gates. 'There's a bench there, we could sit down. It might be easier.'

Easier for what? Violet looked at him keenly, but he was staring at the ground once more.

Violet sat on the park bench unnerved now by Martin's demeanour but not wanting to ask him what was on his mind.

'You must think it strange me suddenly appearing at your school ,' he said, 'but you haven't been to any of the committee meetings recently and . . .' He turned towards her and she saw him take a deep breath. 'I miss you. I am not going to beat the bush,' he said clumsily. 'I don't know whether you know how much I like you.' He was clasping and unclasping his fingers.

Violet was taken aback, not knowing how to respond. This was not what she was expecting.

'And I respect you, too,' he said.

He looked away 'Do you think you could ever love me?'

Violet gasped. She knew that her face must have registered shock but his outburst was so unexpected she didn't know what to say,

'I know that I love you.' He said, as he sat back and closed his eyes. 'But I realise it might be a shock for you to hear the words. I do not expect you to reply immediately. Maybe you cannot love me . I only know how I feel, and if I do not tell you –' he gestured with his hands – 'I think I will explode.'

He turned to look at her now, his eyes searching her face. Violet was aware that she was staring at him open-mouthed.

'I think you may already have a boyfriend?' Martin asked. Then he shrugged his shoulders. 'Perhaps it is not my business. '

Violet was silent as her mind immediately turned to Daniel. Did she really love him? Was he alive and safe somewhere? She realised that she hadn't thought about him for some time. Even though she wanted him to be safe, had she in her heart conceded that he belonged to Claire?

'There's no one at the moment,' Violet heard herself say and as she said the words she knew that her dream of marrying Daniel, was in the past. 'But what about you? I thought you had a girlfriend?' Violet said.

Martin hesitated before he said softly, 'Had, yes, but sadly that was in another life.' She noticed unshed tears shining in his eyes and his shoulders sagged.

'I'm so sorry. I didn't know,' Violet said.

'I understand why you do not answer.' Martin said, his face anxiously scrutinising hers. 'But I will hope . . .' He put out his hand and grasped hers, more confidently now. 'Why don't we meet on this bench in one week? If your answer is no then we stay as friends.

'And if the answer is yes?' Violet challenged, trying to keep her voice light.

'Then we dance a little and go to tell your mother.'

'You're serious, aren't you? Violet looked at him steadily.

'Yes,' Martin nodded. returning her gaze.

'Then it's a deal,' Violet said gaily.

She put out her hand to shake his and they both laughed.

Chapter 51

CLAIRE

Claire had always believed that Daniel would turn up one day alive and well, but she found it hard to accept that he was here now standing in front of her; when she opened her mouth to speak the shock was such that at first no words came out.

'Daniel?' she whispered eventually.

'Flying Officer Daniel Gabinsky reporting for duty,' he said with a mock salute. 'I apologise for the lateness of the hour, and if I've woken anyone else in the household please tell them I'm sorry, but it was the only time I could get a ride. 'I wanted to come in person to let you know that I'm still very much alive, but I can't

365

stay long. I know Georges sent you my letter, so I had to come and talk to you.'

'But . . . is it really . . .? I can't believe it.' Claire cupped her chin and smoothed her hands over her cheeks.

He reached out and clasping hold of one of her hands covered it with his own. 'It's a bit chilly out here at this time of night,' he said, rubbing his hand over hers. 'Aren't you going to invite me in?'

Claire shook her head vigorously as though to clear it. 'No . . . yes . . . of course. Come in,' she said, not taking her eyes off him for a second, 'although, I need to touch you first to make sure you're real. Can I touch you? Are you real?'

He laughed at that. 'I'm real enough, for now,' he said. 'Here, want to make sure?' He held out his arms.

Claire caught her breath as she took a step towards him, holding out her own arms. The next moment she was breathing in the wonderfully vital smell of him. Even the odour of recently smoked cigarettes seemed sweet. She could feel the warmth of his body underneath his fleece-lined pilot's bomber jacket and she reached up and ran her fingers over the dark spiky stubble that covered his face.

'Oh, Daniel!' she moaned. 'Is it really you?' And she pulled away to scrutinise him once more.

'It's me. You better believe it.' He nuzzled his face close to hers as he drew her to him again.

'Where have you been?' she asked.

'It's a long story,' he said, 'and not one for now. I'm here, and I'm just so pleased to see you and that's it.'

'But how did you know to find me here and not at Knit and Sew?' was all Claire could think of to ask and Daniel laughed again.

'I think that having found my way across France in enemy territory, then over the English channel, and travelled from the south to the north of England, you shouldn't be questioning my navigational skills,' he said with a twinkle in his eyes.

'Is all that true or are you just trying to impress me?' She smiled up at him, her heart racing. She was standing so close she was sure she could feel his own heart throbbing next to hers.

'Both,' he said. 'And one day, I'll tell you the whole story. But for now, I wanted you to know I'm alive.'

'Thank you,' Claire said. 'You might not believe me, but do you know something, I never really doubted it. I always believed that you were alive.'

She let Daniel into the kitchen and sat down in one of the chairs by the table. He tried to pull Claire onto his knee, but she took a step back, suddenly diffident.

'Do you need anything? A drink or something? I take it you've not just arrived?'

'No, I've been back a few days, been debriefing. You know what the authorities are like when someone's been missing, or maybe you don't, but they want to know every last detail of what happened to me since the moment I disappeared off their radar. They wouldn't let me out before this. They've not strictly speaking let me out now, I sneaked a ride with one of my buddies. In fact, he's waiting to take me back we . . . er . . . borrowed a motorbike that didn't seem to be doing anything.'

She examined his face but without touching him this time 'You look very tired. We can talk again as you said. Surely they won't send you away again so soon?'

Daniel shrugged. 'Who knows what they'll do? There is a war on and there aren't enough of us pilots.'

'But will I get to see you before you go? Properly I mean. Somewhere we can really talk.'

Before he had time to answer a sharp voice yelled out, 'Claire! Is everything all right? The bell's stopped.'

Claire gasped and put her hand to her mouth. 'Oh, goodness, I forgot!' She ran to the foot of the stairs. 'Everything is fine!' she called up. 'You did hear the bell ring, I'm sorry if it disturbed you but it was someone for me.' She hesitated before going back to the kitchen and waited until she heard Arthur's door firmly close.

'Oh, Daniel,' she sighed, as she sat down again and stretched her hand across the table. 'Promise me you'll never disappear like that again.'

'I wish I could but I'm afraid I can't. The only thing I can say is that I'll do my very best to pop back up again *if* you'll promise to wait. And when all this is over, you and me are going to book a special suite on a great big ocean liner and go on a long, slow, calm cruise across the Atlantic and up the St Lawrence Seaway right into the heart of Montreal.' He took her hand in his and squeezed it gently as he gazed into her eyes and smiled. 'Then we'll have all the time in the world to talk.'

'That sounds wonderful,' she said, squeezing back. Her heart was pounding so hard she thought it would pop out of her chest.

'It might take a while. Will you promise me that you'll wait?' he asked. 'No matter how long this war takes?'

Claire made sure not to lose eye contact as she said, softly, 'Forever, if necessary.' They sat like that, holding hands in silence for several minutes, then Claire cleared her throat and said, 'What about Violet?' She tried to keep her voice matter-of-fact.

'What about her?' Daniel sounded surprised.

'Have you been to see her?'

'No.' He sounded puzzled.

'But I thought you loved *her* and, more to the point, she once thought that you did, too.'

'We go back a long way, Violet and I, as you may know. We corresponded for years and I like her enormously,' he said. 'But I don't think that's the same thing as being in love, do you?'

Claire nodded in agreement.

'Does she think she's in love with me?' he asked.

'I don't know, we haven't seen too much of each other while you've been away, but I do know she cares so it might be best if you try to see her for yourself and then we won't get into a tangle like last time.'

'You're a good friend to her, Claire,' he said.

'And I'm going to be a better one from now on,' she answered with determination.

Daniel stood up and gathered her into his arms once more and she realised in that moment that she had never loved anyone as she loved Daniel.

'I think everything is going to turn out OK,' he whispered to her as he held her tight. And Claire believed him with every beat of her heart.

Acknowledgements

No book can be written completely in isolation even during a Covid crisis. Well, perhaps it could but I believe that most books benefit from the input of others in however small or large a way, and *The Schoolmistress* is no exception. Even though for most of us life has begun to return to some form of normality, Covid is ever-present and is still rife. However, thanks to modern technology, it is not difficult these days for an author to research, verify, corroborate and confirm any facts that may be relevant to their book. They can research whatever aspects they need regarding the setting, developing the plot, the characters and the story without having to leave their desk. But there is still room for a book to be enhanced by an anecdote, or a bite-sized piece of specialist knowledge that can be slotted into the overall jigsaw of the story providing that little bit of extra something, possibly adding some extra depth.

Thanks in this regard for contributing in this way go to Katka Stanclova, Susan Bulmer and Gillian Maude who provided such nuggets for *The Schoolmistress*. Thanks must also go to those whose input took the form of support, preventing the book's development from becoming a lonely and isolating process. There were those who were there with an ear, a shoulder, or even a suggestion or two. Stand up Ann Parker and Jannet Wright, and best-selling authors and fellow Romantic Novelists Association members, Sue Moorcroft and Pia Fenton (Christina Courtney)!

And a special thank you goes to those who were part of the bigger picture, the members of the teams that have supported and encouraged me throughout my fiction writing career: my editor, HarperFiction editorial director Kate Bradley, my agent Kate Nash and publishing director Charlotte Ledger from One More Chapter. Their encouragement and belief is without equal.

Finally, no book could be produced without the belief and support of family and close friends; Miriam Feldman, Rita Kersner, Mary Hughes, The Finlay family take a bow, and others too numerous to mention, including the remainder of my family even though they are a long way away.

If you enjoyed *The Schoolmistress*, read Maggie Sullivan's compelling and heart-warming Coronation Street series . . .

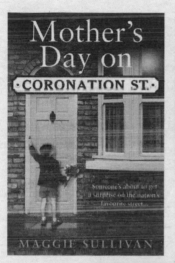